NIGHT SIREN

David Tanager

I

"I remember there was a postcard from Odessa," Josie said. "It was tacked above an ash tray and a stack of immigration papers in a checkpoint on the East German border."

As he spoke, Josie's stare was distant, to a place far away from Bosnia and to a time that had passed long ago. A man with a briefcase stood next to him in silence, his gaze much closer, towards the Neretva Valley on the edge of the horizon.

"It was so curious for me at the time," Josie continued, "that little card and the way it was displayed. You know, at first I thought maybe it was sent from one of his relatives when they went for a holiday by the Black Sea. Then I began to reason that maybe one of his old Army comrades sent it to him. But the longer I stood in that line, and the more I thought about it, I realized that the poor bastard probably sent it to himself. I bet he did it just to prove that he had actually been somewhere in life other than the little concrete box he was sitting in." Josie took a breath. "Even Odessa is somewhere."

"Yes it is, Lieutenant." The Man with the Briefcase answered nervously.

"It had taken me four hours in that passport queue to get to where I was standing." Josie shook his head. "Four hours is a long time to think about the hell of a mess you're about to get yourself into."

The Man with the Briefcase stared straight ahead and nodded in agreement.

"I remember he held the entry stamp over my passport in such a way that it was only an inch or two above the paper, and if he had hesitated much longer, my temptation to strike his hand down to ink the page may have proven irresistible."

Crowds passed by without taking notice of the two men standing next to each other on the Old Bridge in Mostar. Tourists fresh from the Croatian beaches of Dubrovnik and Cavtat could care less about Josie or the Man with the Briefcase as they were all too eager to get a snapshot of a bullet riddled house or bombed out ruin left over from the war.

"He glared at me with those eyes, those sunken desperate eyes that were longing and dangerous and all of the things that eyes can be when you have spent the last twenty years surviving on potatoes and borsch," Josie said. "I could respect those eyes, and the passport I held allowed me freedom on both sides of The Wall. While I was entering the Bloc he knew I could just as easily turn around and leave, yet he would be there forever."

Summer rolled down from the limestone cliffs above the Bosnian city where they stood, radiating heat without relief or mercy. The Man with the Briefcase was now sweating profusely as he loosened his collar. He was by nature a nervous and suspicious man. These traits alone had gotten him to his present position within the Agency and his rapid advancement was a source of frustration to his jealous colleagues, but now these very qualities threatened to unravel his composure when it was most needed: Which one of them set me up? Am I about to die? *Relax...god damnit! Relax*!

The Man with the Briefcase could not relax, because the man standing next to him was a ghost, someone believed to have died over four years ago, and someone the Man with the Briefcase thought he had killed.

"He waited so long to give me my entry stamp that my nerves fired out warnings that he recognized my passport for the forgery that it was. In the end, the longer he waited the more I could see that he was only causing delay in hopes of securing a bribe. My rucksack contained a leather jacket, Adidas tennis shoes and a pair of jeans. I am certain that even just one of those items would have been sufficient, but I was not willing to part with any of them unless it was absolutely necessary." Josie confided these details with a hint of a smile etched across his tanned face.

The Man with the Briefcase looked down nervously at the waters of the majestic Neretva River moving beneath his feet. He had never before noticed how striking its colors were as they mixed with the silt on the banks, greens and blues lazily emulsified in a constant train of color carving its way between the rocks. Truthfully, he didn't give a damn about the colors, the river or this city, and wished in that moment that he could be anywhere else in the world but where he was standing.

"Finally," Josie resumed. "The impression of the stamp sounded in my ears and after another few minutes of organizing papers and signing documents, I took my first steps into East Germany. I remember the guard looking at me as I passed. I'm sure he was asking himself all sorts of questions. Where was I going? Where had I been? Why had he been cursed and born on the wrong side of The Wall? All of these, of course, were the wrong questions for a border guard to ask himself: what he should have asked was what was I going to do with that five-inch, stainless steel forty-five tucked underneath my jacket."

Americans, Brits, and countless Japanese tourists paused to take photos in the mid-day heat before they crossed the bridge and made a hasty retreat for the shade of the bars and marketplaces. Couples talked, children laughed, and the Man with the Briefcase wondered whether Josie still had that forty-five and if so, just how desperate he was to use it.

"That was twenty years ago." The Man with the Briefcase spoke after a long silence.

"We were Rangers then," Josie said, fixing his stare on the man next to him.

"Yes, yes we were, Lieutenant."

"I know why the Agency is in Bosnia," Josie said. "I know what you're looking for."

"The Agency!" The Man with the Briefcase acted as if the accusation were without merit. "I would venture to say that years in hiding have made you paranoid."

"Paranoid?" Josie scoffed. "It's about paying attention to all the little details. It's about observation."

"Maybe it's best we go to Sarajevo?" The Man with the Briefcase suggested, referring to the US Embassy where Josie would surely be imprisoned.

"I've been to Sarajevo." Josie declined the invitation with a wave of his hand. "You know, it was nearly a month ago. I was passing Zagrabacka Street and it was there that I saw someone familiar walking, someone who had been searching for me for years, someone who tried to kill me. That someone was you."

The Man with the Briefcase fingered the old mortar between the stones on the walls of the bridge as he continued to look at the water below.

"That night when I went back to my apartment, I sat down and pulled out a bottle of Shljivovitza and told myself that it couldn't have been you, not here, not now. I retraced every single move I've ever made since I left Yemen, searching for some mistake that would have given away my location."

"You didn't make any," the Man with the Briefcase admitted.

"I know I didn't, and for the past three weeks I've been following you and very quickly I realized you're not here to find me. You're searching for something else." Josie paused. "The Agency is searching for something."

"After what happened to you in Yugoslavia years ago, the last place I would have expected to find you was back in the Balkans."

"Bosnia suddenly became convenient after a Hellfire made my home in Africa quite uninhabitable." Josie spoke with a sense of loss in his voice.

"Everyone at the Agency thought you died during that drone strike. At first so did I, but deep down I knew you were still out there." For the first time, the Man with the Briefcase had the courage to turn and look at Josie to see whether he actually existed.

"None of that matters anymore," Josie said. "What matters now is you, old friend – and the consequences when you discover the reason why the Agency sent you here."

"As if you have any idea," the Man with the Briefcase began.

"Of right and wrong?" Josie interrupted. "Of power? Of truth? I know exactly what you're searching for, but what I don't know is what you will do when you find it."

"I find it hard to believe that you risk everything after all these years to warn me about..." The Man with the Briefcase began before being interrupted once again.

"You are an honest man, Gibbs." Josie smiled. "Couldn't tell a lie if your life depended on it. The truth was always in your eyes."

"A weakness," Gibbs admitted and slowly eased his grip on the briefcase. "So this is about more than my current assignment?"

"Of course," Josie said. "It's about a name."

"A name?" Gibbs echoed, gaining confidence since absorbing the fact that Josie wasn't a ghost or a figment of his imagination. He had half expected to look at Josie and see a skeleton smiling back at him. "I don't give a damn what you want to know! Jesus Christ, Lieutenant, I will shoot you where you stand if I must!"

"Your apartment by the train station on Hamida Vuka Street," Josie smiled casually. "At least you could have asked the Agency for a room with a better view. I used to do it with a pencil. A bit of tape over the eraser and then I would put it down the barrel and pull the trigger."

Gibbs stood rigid with a defeated look in his eyes, a surplus of sweat traced its way down his overheated forehead.

"It leaves a nice little indentation where the firing pin struck." Josie nodded modestly, holding up a small, angular piece of steel in his hand. "Lets you know that no bastard has taken it out of your gun."

He flicked the firing pin into the river far below like a used cigarette and his right hand reached down to casually finger the indentation of the pistol in his waistband.

"A name?" Gibbs repeated.

"It took me years to find him. Years of risking everything, sometimes just for a bit of intelligence as insignificant as a laundry receipt or medical record. With a new identity, a bit of plastic surgery, and an arsenal of forged credentials from the top universities stateside, he must have thought he was safe. They say that at times, the best place to hide someone is right out in the open." Josie tapped the pistol playfully. "Right out in the open."

Gibbs was incredulous. The fact that Josie had avoided capture by the Agency for all these years after he had escaped from prison was impressive enough, but to discover the true identity of the man who put him there was unbelievable.

"You must understand that my sources are not infallible. I still can't be certain. Gibbs, you're one of the few people in the world who knows the truth about the man I'm after." Josie paused. "He is an Ambassador now, isn't he?"

Gibbs looked at Josie. He held his breath. He tried not to blink.

"The eyes," Josie said, as a feeling of certainty possessed him. "Those wonderful blue eyes of yours, Gibbs. They always tell the truth."

"That's what this is about?" Gibbs hissed. "After over a decade of hiding, you reveal yourself just to confirm a suspicion?"

"Oh, I'm going to do much more than that," Josie said calmly.

Gibbs took a quick breath, his eyes widened, and he stood up arrow-straight. "You're going to kill the Ambassador?"

Josie didn't say a word. He didn't have to.

"You'll never even make it out of Bosnia alive!" Gibbs spat with contempt. "It's over, Lieutenant!"

Josie turned and leaned his back on the railing of the bridge as if posing for a photograph. "When I was a child, there was a story my mother used to tell me."

Gibbs wondered why Josie was being so casual. Why wasn't he afraid? Was he that confident? Or merely crazy? What Gibbs didn't know was that Josie knew the risks well, but it had been over ten years since he had talked to anyone who knew his true identity; it was a nostalgic feeling that led him now, and he had convinced himself that a few more moments of indulgence wouldn't hurt.

"Once upon a time, there was a jackal walking on a beach." Josie placed his left hand into his pocket. "There was a shark swimming next to him. The shark politely asked the jackal to come a bit closer and hop onto his back so that he could show him the wonders of the ocean."

"The ocean?" Gibbs whispered.

"Being naïve and innocent, the jackal agreed and soon they were racing out into the deep. After a wonderful little tour, the shark invited the jackal to dinner." Josie adjusted his hand and removed it from his pocket. "Only then did the jackal realize the shark's true intentions and knew that his tour was just a ploy."

"I don't understand." Gibbs grew restless.

"The jackal thought quickly for a moment and said that dinner would be an honor, but he asked if he could be returned to the shore to meet his friends and bring them along. It would be improper, of course, for the jackal to enjoy such a dinner while his friends were starving back on the beach." Josie looked down in his hand at the object he had retrieved from his pocket. "So the shark agreed and returned the jackal to the shore. In a few moments, three more jackals appeared on the beach. They called to the shark and asked if he could venture a bit closer so that they might all reach him."

"This was a bedtime story?" Gibbs inserted.

"In his anticipation for such a feast, the shark pushed closer and closer until he was horrified to find himself stuck on the sands – and the tide retreating. In vain the shark cried out for help, but the jackals turned back to the forest and left the shark to the gulls and crabs that follow the ebb tide." Josie concluded with a grim smile.

"What does this have to do with the Ambassador?"

"It doesn't." Josie's reply was blunt. "It's about greed, it's about not getting out when you should have, about staying in so long that you don't even have a soul anymore. It's about what you're searching for, what you will find. It's about right and wrong."

Josie shot his arm out and wrapped it in a faux embrace around Gibbs's shoulder, which instinctively hunched forward. Josie's left hand was outstretched and holding the camera that he had retrieved from his pocket.

"Smile," Josie directed, and a metallic click followed. "I'll be sure to send a copy to the Agency."

"You son-of-a-bitch." Gibbs struggled but Josie wouldn't release his grip. Instead, he tightened his embrace and whispered in his ear.

"I'm sure within a day or two you'll find the right Bosnian to bribe and learn all about my time here in the Balkans. They are good people, the Bosnians, but for the price you will pay for that kind of information, I can't blame them." Josie shrugged.

Gibbs was still resisting.

"But Serbs are even cheaper." Josie smiled now, his grip tightening as the crowds continued to take little notice of the two men. "Remember what I was telling you about details? About observation? Look out at the apartment to the right of Mehmed Pasha's Mosque. Do you see it?"

"Yes." Gibbs struggled to breathe under Josie's hold.

"Do you see the pigeons?"

"Flying?"

"Yes," Josie said. "Watch them as they approach the building looking for a place to land, but once they get to the roof they scatter and fly away."

Josie asked again, "Do you see it?"

"Yes."

"That's because there is something there that frightens them as they descend. The sunlight reflects off of it and into their eyes. It's a piece of glass, a lens actually. That lens is inside a scope, and that scope is mounted on a silenced Dragunov rifle." Josie paused. "That discount Serbian is behind the scope, and if you move, if you try to follow me, if you so much as even blink in a way that makes him uncomfortable, then this photo will be the last one taken of you alive."

Josie released his grip and returned the camera to where it had been in his pocket. "Remember...when you find what you're looking for...right and wrong...the shark and the jackal..."

"Lieutenant, wait!" Gibbs spoke after taking a few deep breaths. "Killing him now won't change anything."

"I'm not trying to change the past," Josie said. "No matter how much I wish I could."

Still not moving for fear of the sniper, Gibbs viewed Josie with dissatisfaction. "Why?"

"I've spent every day of my life preparing for this, and you ask me why? Because I'm the only one willing to go the distance, to do what it takes at all costs to make it right. If you see him Gibbs, if you see him before I get to him, tell him I'm coming - and I won't stop until it's all over."

In an instant the crowd absorbed Josie and he was gone, vanished into a mix of cargo pants, sports t-shirts and big sunglasses shaded under holiday hats. Gibbs stood in the most unnatural position, rigid and soaked from head to toe as his eyes scanned upon the distant apartment building. The pigeons rolled over the rooftops and circled behind the mosque; minutes passed, and they continued to seek their roost.

"There is something you should know, Lieutenant." Gibbs mumbled to himself as he watched the pigeons fly. *There is something that you need to know...*

II

Alija stood behind the bar. His mighty hand gripped a clouded glass as he polished it coarsely with a blue and white towel. Two men separated by an empty stool sat across the counter from him, and both stared forward, their watery, drunken eyes looking off lazily at the cracks in the bar's plaster wall. Bosnian music played from a large tape deck in the corner. The music was far too loud.

There were four doors in Alija's bar. All of them were opened in hopes that some passing tourist visiting Mostar would enter, yet none ever did. The bar was dirty and dark; its unkempt shadows crept menacingly to where the sidewalk began until their advance was halted by the midday sun. The next song played from the tape deck and Alija polished another glass.

Across the street, just out of reach, he could see the cafés and bistros full of tourists spending their euros, pounds or dollars. The delicate wrought-iron tables and chairs huddled underneath wide umbrellas that shaded the tourists from any discomfort the heat might cause. Some sipped from tiny cups placed on tiny saucers, a few sampled the local fare, and others smiled and laughed together in quiet conversations. Alija's stare at the scene across the street was not unlike the vacant ones of his customers; his eyes drifted without purpose from café to café. Suddenly, his focus narrowed. He cursed. He put down the glass.

It was her again.

Alija had seen her before, sitting alone across the street, accompanied only by a cup of coffee on the table and a cigarette between her fingers. Her legs were crossed in a relaxed manner and the top of her leather boots rubbed together in a way that aroused Alija. Tucked into those boots were a pair of jeans, tight and supportive in all the correct places. They added to her allure and mystery even from the distance where Alija stood.

Her hair was amber, the deeper strands colored with a black natural base that settled somewhere between her shoulders and lower back. Tinted wide-framed sunglasses rested above her delicate nose. Alija was certain that her eyes were brown. He had conducted many serious debates with himself on the matter. Her shirt was white – not pure, but of a hue that did not announce itself to the casual observer as anything but. She filled the shirt out nicely, but in a way that left his mind desperate to pursue the matter further. Alija thought that maybe her name was Olga - or possibly Suada - but he couldn't be certain on this point. What he did know was that while he had seen her across the street at the café often, he had never once seen her with a man.

One of Alija's customers stood, took a few moments to gain his balance, and then adjusted himself before reaching into his pocket. A few coins then dropped from his hand and arranged themselves on the bar as he lovingly cursed Alija and swore an elaborate oath that only a Yugoslavian could properly utter. The oath was to Alija, to the bar, to friendship and to Bosnia. After his words, he turned and walked out into the sunlight. Alija had another glass to polish.

"Dobro?" The woman across the street with the coffee and cigarette answered her phone.

"Cass?"

"Da." Cass calmly answered the frantic question, annoyed that Bombay was interrupting her coffee.

"Stop fooling around!" Bombay growled. "Someone got to Gibbs! Did you hear me? It's not safe!"

Cass felt her eyes widen in silent surprise and was happy that the sunglasses shielded her reaction from anyone who could be watching.

"It's not safe," Bombay repeated, nearly out of breath. "Don't go back to your apartment! Get to the safe house! *Now!*"

The phone disconnected. Cass continued speaking in Bosnian and smiling as if someone were on the other line. She extinguished her cigarette and then calmly removed the champagne-colored napkin from her lap, folding it neatly before releasing it from her fingers and onto the table. A few banknotes settled the charges and a coin or two was left for gratuity.

Despite the call's nature and how anxious Bombay seemed, Cass had worked hard on her cover and continued not to display a sense of urgency or alarm to any observer. From behind the protective lenses of her sunglasses, her gaze was free to search the masses to see if she was being watched, but Cass did not bother. Even momentary hesitation as she walked down the street would be enough to ruin her cover if a professional was somewhere out there.

Cass crossed the street.

The bartender had been watching her for months. She was well aware of this, but she also knew he was harmless and she was amused by the hopeless way he always tried to conceal his gaze when she would turn in his direction. As Cass passed the bar, she clenched her teeth and winced; the music was so obnoxiously loud, it too would have been comical if not for the pain the absurd volume caused.

In addition to those about the music, Cass had heard many complaints from the patrons of the cafés and bistros about Alija's bar. They said it was dirty and that the motley clientele was dangerous. The protests were always silenced by those who knew the truth: Alija had lost his entire family in the war, and he had survived numerous beatings, one gunshot wound, and countless hours of torture. The music was all that reminded him of the happier times when his wife and children had been alive. How could some highbrow on vacation from Piccadilly argue with that?

The safe house was only three blocks away, which did not give Cass much time to consider the seriousness of the situation. It did, however, give her enough time to send a regretful text message canceling dinner plans with her date while she turned off Buca Street and made her way down onto Kresina.

His name was Juka. Cass met him on a bus a few days after she had first arrived in Bosnia and had been seeing him quite often. There was no guilt in it for her, only pleasure. Her male colleagues pledged dedication to the mission, constant focus and resolve, but she knew quite well that all of them except for Gibbs visited the brothels across the border in Monte Negro as often as they could. Why should she be any different? At least she wasn't paying for it.

It had been over seven years since she graduated from Dartmouth, four more had passed serving in the Diplomatic Service, and it was one year to the day from when she had signed the contract for Virginia-based Herndon-Bradley International, Central Intelligence's primary defense contractor, which everyone simply referred to as the Agency. She was aware that the Ivy League diploma meant little in reality, as did her stint as a Foreign Service Officer. Her gift alone had gotten her into the Agency.

The gift in question was entirely accidental. Her brother gave it to her when he was nine and she was only four. On a cold New England day, her fate was sealed when a game of tag culminated in a push from behind on the dining room's slick wooden floor - and her subsequent contact with an exposed radiator. Wounds to the forehead always bleed like mad and Cass would never forget her mother's face when she entered the room. There was no trip to the hospital, stitches or even a lollipop to stop the tears. Her brother was scolded as the blood was cleaned and Cass was left with a permanent scar above her right eyebrow.

Nearly a decade later the gift was finally discovered in her Junior High Latin course. Within a few weeks she was at the top of her class, in a month's time she was fluent, and after two months she was correcting the teacher. There were countless medical examinations, and even a trip to Boston to meet a specialist, but a long list of theories could not explain her uncanny new gift with language.

Cass had once read that Pope John Paul II had suffered a similar injury to his head in his youth and had also possessed an amazing ability to learn languages. Unlike hers, his gift was not given to him by his older brother; instead, it was earned as he waited alongside a road and a German in a passing Nazi transport opened the door of the moving vehicle, striking the future Pope just above the hairline.

As a Foreign Service Officer in Istanbul, Cass had utilized her gift to its extreme. She translated briefings, worked with interrogators, and went on a few HUMINT field assignments. The U.S. Ambassador to Turkey was so impressed that he personally wrote her a letter of reference to Herndon-Bradley.

Cass had debated for months about remaining in the Foreign Service. The pay was great, and the prestige and nature of the work, rewarding. Everyone expected her to stay but she knew she needed a change – something different, exciting, and dangerous.

Turning off of Kresina and walking for only a minute more, Cass arrived at the safe house. The building appeared to be in ruins, surrounded by dense foliage and a few neighboring houses which were in an equal state of disrepair. Bricks and mortar lay about the vicinity, and large pockmarks resided on the walls where rounds from a heavy machine gun had snapped off of them a decade before. A large brick wall three meters high surrounded the property, obscuring the view of the safe house from anyone walking by.

Cass passed by a large iron gate, its paint faded and peeling under the intense assault of the Bosnian sun. Following the brick wall past the gate, she was soon around a corner and shielded by the foliage of the grape leaves growing wildly towards the sky. She produced and inserted a long skeleton key into the lock of a metal door that always opened with a distressed creak.

A few vehicles were parked under a canvas tent in the far corner of the courtyard. Two of the vehicles were unrecognizable to Cass, but she knew that the black Land Rover parked neatly beside them to belong to Gibbs. He was obsessed with order and to properly park a vehicle, he would need multiple attempts to place his Rover into a correct position that only he could understand.

Besides the order in which Gibbs parked his vehicle, the surrounding courtyard was a mess. Twisted sheets of metal rested against discarded plastic containers and rubber tires. The entire building was covered in vines and the parched soil was without life except for a black and tan stray dog named Sleepy, who always liked to slumber in the shade cast by the perfectly parked Rover.

He was not an exceptionally friendly stray but neither was he aggressive. Sleepy took his meals from whoever would offer one to him, but never showed the slightest hint of loyalty to those that did. No one knew when he had first arrived in the courtyard or how, but since the majority of his day was spent as his name implied, no one seemed to care.

Cass walked up a flight of concrete stairs and out to a wide balcony.

A sniper with a heavy-barreled and silenced M-16 took watch from behind the wall. Cass did not recognize him. He sat in a white plastic lawn chair next to a table, the top of which was occupied with a flak jacket, a few empty bottles of beer and a cellular phone. Another chair next to the sniper was arranged in such a way that it appeared as if someone had just gotten out of it. A sniper was missing.

Entering the building through a door and passing down a hallway, Cass walked over massive cords of electric, telephone, and cable lines taped together and stretching from room to room. The sounds of keystrokes and conversations could be heard so suddenly, it was as if they had waited in silence for her approach.

The missing sniper rounded the corner; a Hungarian AMD assault rifle fitted with a holographic sight was strapped tight across his chest. Unlike his equal outside, he was wearing his flak jacket along with a sidearm strapped on his right leg. Four bottles of beer were clutched between the fingers in his left hand while his right rested casually at his side above the pistol.

"Cerveza?" The sniper invited.

"We're not in Mexico," Cass answered directly.

"If you just close your eyes and pretend..." the sniper smiled in reply extending a bottle out to her.

Cass declined. She wanted to tell him that closing his eyes and pretending was as far as he was going to get with her tonight, but she held her tongue and kept walking down the hallway.

She turned left at its end and skirted an assorted lot of metal ammunition containers blocking the entry to a stairwell and continued down a long and narrow flight of stairs into the basement.

A large kitchen in the basement had been converted into a makeshift conference room. Gibbs paced nervously in ever tightening circles as he smoked a cigarette, while Bombay stood silently in the corner. Gibbs never smoked and Bombay was never silent. This was serious.

A man emerged from the shadows. His black slacks were far too short, showing his white socks tucked into his black polished loafers as he walked forward. His shirt was neatly pressed and tight against an oddly rounded belly while the rest of his frame was slim and wiry. Black Wayfarer glasses with a heavy prescription outlined his unremarkable face, and his graying hair was slicked back with a potent application of hair wax. Everything about him was dated.

He took no notice of Cass when she entered. He seemed unduly preoccupied with the pen in his hand, as if he were unfamiliar with its operation. After clicking it a few times, he put the pen to rest on a table before proceeding to unbutton and roll back his sleeves. While the man was of no imposing stature or presence, his energy was entirely unsettling and disconnected, robotic in a way that made Cass deeply uncomfortable.

He whispered quietly to Gibbs for a moment and calmly gestured to an empty chair next to the table, as if inviting him for dinner.

Gibbs hesitated for a moment before he grudgingly took a seat and snuffed out his cigarette beneath his heel.

"Mr. Gibbs," the man started to speak, but suddenly snapped his eyes directly to Cass as if she had just interrupted him.

Cass took a quick breath in surprise.

"Who's the paper shaker?" The man asked this of Bombay, nodding to Cass; his speech held a slight lisp but was otherwise entirely monotone and unremarkable.

"This is..." Bombay paused, noticing that the man's attention had already switched back to the pen on the table.

"Agent White." Bombay completed his introduction to Cass.

"Mr. Gibbs," Agent White said, rolling the pen around in his fingers, "Let's put it out there....right out in the open."

Gibbs's stare was as confused as Cass's.

"You're certain it was him?" Agent White asked, leaning up against the table. "You're certain it was Josiah Bircher?"

Gibbs nodded.

"Then why didn't you invite him to join us for our little conversation? Surely you were armed and could have captured him?"

"He had removed the firing pin from my gun," Gibbs admitted and began to tap his hard-soled shoe nervously on the linoleum floor.

Bombay bit his lip in frustration.

Agent White pushed free from the table and circled the chair that Gibbs occupied. "Did you follow him?"

"There was a sniper on the roof next to the mosque." A bead of sweat formed on Gibbs's nose. "The pigeons. I could see them flying, he told me not to move. He told me I would be shot."

"So there you stood for three hours until finally you found the nerve to move?" Agent White asked coldly.

Agent White stopped circling the chair and came to rest on the left side of Gibbs. In one sweeping motion he un-holstered the pistol and put his finger on the trigger. He held the barrel dangerously in line with Gibbs's temple as he studied the weapon. Then he suddenly dropped the magazine from the Sig Sauer, racked the slide, and field-stripped the pistol.

"Lighting up the tilt sign," Agent White remarked, holding up the stainless steel firing pin that he had removed from the slide. "It's called lying, Mr. Gibbs."

Gibbs was visibly shaken.

Cass looked at Gibbs. He was of average build but his shoulders were wide and his jaw squared; if he wasn't always so nervous, she would have been able to consider him handsome. Cass wondered what had happened to him, what had made him such a wreck and what it would take for him to be the man she was certain he once was. Cass was as guilty as all of the other employees in the Agency for having a few laughs at Gibbs's expense. She always felt badly after she threw him under the bus around the water cooler or mimicked the way he would turn his head from side to side rapidly as if under attack for no reason at all. It made her feel like a bitch. She knew she was too damned judgmental, and that Gibbs was a good man. One day she was going to tell him so.

"Mr. Gibbs, I can assure you that there was no sniper on the roof of the apartment building across the Neretva River by the Mosque." Agent White continued. "I can also assure you I wouldn't bet my life on what a terrorist asserts as the truth."

Bombay started to grow anxious in the corner.

"The meat and potatoes, shall we?" Leaning on the edge of the table, Agent White crossed his arms and left his legs spread out widely.

Gibbs stared down to the floor.

"Is it true that you were the man responsible for the death of Josiah Bircher ten years ago in Yemen?"

"Yes."

"Operation Midnight Justice," Agent White said, his lisp noticeable throughout the arrangement of syllables.

Cass narrowed her eyes. The operational names had always been foolish, patriotic, or overtly heroic. This one was no different.

"I was the team leader for that operation," Gibbs said. "And not by choice."

"Noted," Agent White said. "Were you aware that Bircher had escaped from Central Intelligence's prison facility in Poland?"

"I was briefed on everything." Gibbs continued to tap his feet. "Everything...including the Gradiska Incident."

"You were his best friend," Agent White stated casually. "Surely you must have had some sympathy?"

Gibbs remained silent but looked to Bombay in hopes of some relief. Bombay offered nothing as he sat on a chair in the corner with an angry sneer on his face. Cass's mind raced and her questions grew by the minute.

"Your team found Bircher in Yemen?"

"El-Hazm," Gibbs noted the location.

"Tell me, Mr. Gibbs, is it common for Rangers to leave the Army and move into one of the largest Al-Qaeda safe-havens outside of Pakistan?"

Gibbs had sweated so much that now, in the damp basement air, he began to shiver.

"At least he didn't join the Reds," Agent White observed while removing a plastic black comb from his pocket and adjusting his hair. Cass watched as small white bands of grease appeared through the fingers of the comb. "Do you know how Mr. Bircher found his way into Yemen?"

"Accidental," Gibbs guessed. "He told me once that he had befriended an Omani on a flight from Boston to Amsterdam. He said that the man had invited him to the Middle East. Something about climbing a mountain..."

Agent White returned the comb. "The Omani?"

"I never heard more about it from him," Gibbs said. "But it's the only way I believe that he could have disappeared so fast after his escape."

"What was the primary objective of Operation Midnight Justice?" Agent White questioned.

"Target elimination," Gibbs said, his reply laden with guilt. "Q-97 Reaper."

"Hellfires." Agent White's lisp overtook his robotic speech pattern again in his excitement. "Were there any boots on the ground?"

"None," Gibbs answered. "There was a quick reaction force on standby in Djibouti, but it was not required."

"My report of the operation details that there was a seven minute delay between the time when the weapons release command was given and when the target was engaged. Are you aware of what caused the delay?

"No," Gibbs answered truthfully. "I didn't even remember that there was one."

"The remains?" Agent White widened his stance even further.

"After the strike, I was released from the briefings and I was not involved in the recovery. I am aware though, that due to a diplomatic conflict concerning sanctions of certain Yemeni government officials, it took nearly five days to recover the remains."

"Dental?" Agent White queried, obviously having had studied the entire report of the operation very carefully.

"Dental," Gibbs nodded. "Dental only."

Agent White circled past Gibbs. He reached into a square brown briefcase that had been resting against the wall and pulled out a manila folder. Walking up to Gibbs, Agent White leaned close and whispered in his ear.

Gibbs shook his head to whatever question was posed.

Agent White asked it again.

Gibbs shook his head in affirmation.

Stepping back from their private conversation, Agent White asked Gibbs directly: "Do you believe in your country? Do you believe in the United States of America? Do you believe in freedom?"

Gibbs nodded.

"Well enough, son. Well enough."

Agent White turned to Bombay and handed him the manila folder. He then adjusted his hair once more before making his way towards the door. Halting suddenly, he spun on his heels and returned to the table. He picked up the pen, he rapidly clicked the button on its cap, ensured that the ballpoint was retracted, and placed the pen in his shirt pocket. He then exited the room and disappeared down the hallway.

Bombay opened the folder. Gibbs avoided eye contact with anyone. Silent minutes passed as the scent of sweat and mildew filled the air. Cass spoke first, motioning towards the door. "Is he one of us?"

Gibbs shook his head, his breathing shallow. "I don't even have the clearance to know who he works for."

"You're not serious?"

"He is serious." Bombay answered for Gibbs while rapidly pulling a small white box of dental floss out of his pocket. "Do you know what I'm serious about?"

Gibbs looked up.

Bombay threw the folder down in disgust on the table; a photograph slid out and landed a few inches in front of Gibbs.

"I'm serious about my career, my stock options, and my 401K." Bombay paused. "But above all, I'm serious about my god-damned life!"

Cass was used to Bombay's tendency to be irrational, but he was acting unlike anything she had ever seen before. He retrieved the dental string from the box and began to floss wildly. She had always felt uncomfortable when Bombay flossed near her and believed that every time he moved the string back and forth, small particles of food were landing all over her.

"Gibbs is correct," Bombay sneered. "Agent White does not work for Central Intelligence; in fact, Agent White doesn't even exist. For your own benefit, Cass, forget that you ever met him."

"I'm talking about some serious shit here, Gibbs!" Bombay was getting himself fired up again. "If they are involved in this, there is no telling what can happen!"

"They?" Cass questioned. "Who are they?"

Her questions went unanswered.

"I am talking about life and death, Gibbs! Life and death!" Bombay spat.

Gibbs had been through quite an ordeal in one day. His nerves were shot. He put his head down and held his temples.

"Serious shit, Gibbs! Yet here you are, having a goddamned Ranger class reunion on the Old Bridge!" Bombay yelled, pointing his finger at the photograph that was on the table.

Cass noted that the situation was deteriorating.

"The prison?" Cass interjected. "He was detained at one of our black sites?"

Bombay paced in disgust and continued to ignore Cass. Gibbs finally answered her: "Yes."

"Why was he there?"

Bombay stopped pacing. He raised an eyebrow to Gibbs. An unspoken conversation transpired between the two men: objections were raised, arguments made, and the debate was settled. Bombay had given Gibbs permission.

"In the early nineties, during the War in Yugoslavia..." Gibbs started.

Cass crossed her arms and listened intently.

"The Bosnians were getting it bad. Once the Croats sold their souls and joined the Serbs, the Bosnians were getting the hell shelled out of them from every angle. The Secretary General banned all imports of military hardware and made it criminal to try and smuggle any weapons into Bosnia." Gibbs paused. "Hell, it was so bad that the Bosnians in Sarajevo even begged Clinton to bomb them just to end their suffering."

"None of that matters," Bombay interrupted. "The truth was that Iran was training foreign fighters recruited from all over the Middle East and our intelligence reports suggested that thousands of these fighters were planning a major offensive with what was left of the Bosnian Army."

"There was a small village known as Gradiska," Gibbs said. "Satellite footage showed heavy troop-buildup in the area surrounding the village. Central Intelligence had agents on the ground. Their reports indicated that if allowed to start the offensive, the Bosnian Army, along with the well-trained foreign fighters, could have made a successful drive to liberate Sarajevo."

Bombay interrupted. "The President, along with the Secretary General, had spent the better part of the prior year brokering a cease-fire with the Serbs. Any new offensive by the Bosnians would have jeopardized everything."

Gibbs shot Cass a look which let her know that even in his nervous and broken state, it was clear that he believed that what Bombay had just said was bullshit.

"Due to the fact that the Croatians were shelling the Bosnians anyway and that their border was very close to Gradiska, it was decided that the Bosnians would be stopped from launching their offensive," Bombay said without the slightest empathy in his voice.

Gibbs picked up from where Bombay had left the matter. "The Croatian Army was supported in this operation by..."

Bombay finished the other man's sentence loudly. "Private security contractors with no affiliation to any government."

Cass knew this meant that they were Americans, possibly even Americans who worked for the same company that she did.

"The intelligence...." Bombay said, shaking his head. "The intelligence was less than reliable. The foreign fighters were far better armed than had been expected. A few of them even brought some old Stingers that we had given to them in the eighties when they fought the Russians."

"When one of the Little Bird helicopters was downed, it killed six private contractors and everything went south," Gibbs said. "The connection between our government and those men would have been revealed within hours and some believed it might have even brought the Iranians to arms."

"The Iranians had hopes of using Bosnia as a base from which to launch an offensive on Europe. If they could exploit the fact that the Americans were also killing Muslims, they could have whipped the Middle East into a furor." Bombay spoke as if defending his own pride. "It would have been a shit show."

"The incident at Gradiska needed to be covered up," Gibbs said quietly. "Immediately. The closest SEAL team was two hours away. We had to use the Rangers based in Trieste. We had no choice."

"Bircher." Cass understood.

"The fighting was so intense." Gibbs paused and rubbed his palms together for warmth. He still sat in the chair as if he were being interrogated; Agent White had clearly made an impression. "Even the Rangers almost didn't make it out alive."

Cass suspected that Gibbs was stalling. There was something he was not saying. Indeed, he looked to Bombay as if not certain how much to reveal.

"The entire village was massacred." Bombay got to the point. "Soldiers, women, children, everyone."

"Bircher was there," Gibbs said, as if defending him. "He saw what had happened. He knew the truth."

"It was going to be a nightmare," Bombay said, shrugging his shoulders. "He was going to go public. We didn't have a choice, so we locked him away in prison so that he would never be heard from again."

Gibbs shifted uncomfortably in his seat. His head was low and his eyes were focused on the floor.

Cass crossed the room to the table and looked through the debriefing papers that Agent White had left there. "The report here mentions something about an Ambassador?"

Gibbs again looked to Bombay, who shrugged.

"The Ambassador in question was a former Ranger." Gibbs was happy to be temporarily released from the assault of his superior. "When the fighting was over he was the one that ordered the executions. He ordered the massacre."

"I thought that you had served with Bircher," Cass said slowly. "Where were you?"

"Fort Stewart," Gibbs answered without hesitation. "I was on a jump training mission with the 82nd two weeks prior to the incident at Gradiska when one of those Airborne bastards got tangled up in my parachute during a drop. I was lucky to have survived it."

Cass shot a look at Bombay, who had seemed to momentarily lose interest in the conversation and was picking his teeth with the point of his tongue.

"Bircher is not your concern, Gibbs." Bombay's gaze was distant as if he were looking out of a non-existent window. "You know the Russians released Harkem so it's only a matter of time before he gets to Bircher anyway. The Ambassador is perfectly safe."

"I know." Gibbs nodded his head and thought back to when he had almost warned Josie about the release of the man named Harkem.

"The damned Pinkos must have known Bircher was alive this entire time." Bombay cursed.

"The Russians want Bircher as well?" Cass questioned. "Why?"

"Who the hell knows?" Bombay waved his hand as if it were nothing of importance.

"Wait," Cass said. "What about Harkem? Who is he?"

"Who, or what?" Gibbs finally stood and stretched his legs. Moving around a bit, he stopped shivering and the sweat on his shirt began to dry. "Some would say he is a person. Others would disagree entirely."

Bombay's cellular phone rang and he stepped out to the hall.

"I'm lost," Cass said, first looking to Bombay as he left the room, then back to Gibbs. "Harkem? Linguistically, the name sounds more Scottish than anything, certainly not Russian."

"Central Intelligence thinks he might be Scottish as well," Gibbs secretly admired Cass's gift with language. "But truthfully they don't know. What they do know is that he is one of the most dangerous men in the world."

Bombay could be heard in the hallway yes-siring someone on the other end of the phone.

"Who does he work for?" Cass asked the next logical question.

"Whoever will pay him most," Gibbs said. "The Vatican, Russia, the United..."

"It doesn't matter." Bombay returned to the room while placing the phone in his pocket. "The less you know about him, the better."

"I'm sure you know what happened in Saint-Dizier in Ninety-Two?" Gibbs ignored Bombay.

"Yes, yes I do." Cass thought for a moment. "There was a car bomb? Correct?"

"You are correct. The French press labeled it an act of terrorism by Black September on a group on Israeli agents. It was not Black September. There wasn't even a car bomb. It was Harkem."

"It's not the violence that makes him so dangerous," Gibbs said. "It's the list."

"The list?"

"In the late eighties, there was going to be a massive leak from the Vatican. A Bishop had accidentally discovered volumes of secrets that if released would have crushed the Holy See to the core. Harkem was paid to kill him."

Bombay again interrupted Gibbs and went directly to the point. "It's rumored that Harkem walked past a painting of a seventeenth-century king while awaiting payment from the Vatican. They say that Harkem was identical in appearance to that of the king."

"Reincarnation," Gibbs said in a hushed tone. "From that day forward, Harkem believed that he is the living blood and soul, the reincarnation of that king."

"How does that make him dangerous?" Cass asked, leaning up against the cold concrete wall near the door.

"The king was murdered. Harkem will not stop until those responsible for the death of the king, or essentially in his mind those responsible for his own death, are all six feet under."

"You mean the reincarnate of those people?" Cass offered hesitantly.

"Exactly," Gibbs said.

"How does he know who the reincarnate of..."

"It doesn't matter." Bombay dismissed her. "What matters is that we are certain Bircher is on the list."

"The entire notion is ridiculous." Cass stated. "It's crazy."

"Exactly," Bombay said. "Crazy doesn't play by the rules. That's why he is dangerous. Remember that, Cass."

Bombay passed by her and through the door, and then he called for Gibbs. Walking past Cass with his shoulders still arched forward and stress imprinted upon his face, Gibbs walked out the door. Cass had smiled to try to cheer him up. It didn't work.

Outside of the room, the two men were talking. The conversation was rapid and nearly reached shouting volume. Cass could hear Gibbs objecting while Bombay stood firm. Bombay returned to the room without Gibbs.

"What I've just told him is what I am going to tell you, Cass," Bombay said. "Forget about Harkem, forget about all of this reincarnation bullshit, and above all, forget about Agent White. You will surely never see him again."

"Forget about Bircher as well?"

"Not entirely. I'm sending Gibbs down to Herceg Novi to train a new agent fresh from the States. The new agent is replacing you, Cass; I'm assigning you to accompany me to Warsaw."

"Warsaw." Cass said flatly. She wanted to protest, she wanted to say that she had worked so hard on her current assignment in Bosnia that she wouldn't give it up. She wanted to say that it was unfair, yet she remained silent.

"If by some very small chance Bircher is able to avoid capture by the Agency, and is able to avoid death at the hands of Harkem, then there is a chance he might just get to the Ambassador in Warsaw. I need you there, Cass." Surprisingly, Bombay sounded sincere.

Cass shot him a skeptical look.

"It will all be explained to you on the flight," Bombay said. "Our plane is leaving within the hour."

He saw the look of protest in her eyes. "Your apartment is being packed up as we speak and your belongings will be there before you arrive. How is your Polish?"

"Zajebiscie," Cass said, translating under her breath into English. "Just fucking great.

III

It was raining. The front of the storm had passed above Warsaw two days ago, but the rain continued and seemed in no hurry to leave. The scenery was drab: massive apartment blocks that the storm had washed into a dull gray color spanned the horizon as far as the eye could see. An assortment of weeds and grass grew up from the concrete sidewalks and a city bus idled on the corner. It was so dark outside that it could have been midnight, yet it was only four in the afternoon.

A bus waited on the corner. Nearby, at the top of an apartment building, there was an open window. Past that window frame, an even tone of darkness filled the apartment. The flat seemed empty and the only proof that anyone lived there at all was a piano in the corner, a brown sofa in the living room and a tea kettle on the stove next to the refrigerator. The kettle was boiling.

He sat on the sofa extinguishing the ashes of his cigarette in an empty jar that only hours before had been full of peanut butter. He loved peanut butter, and in Warsaw, finding a good jar of peanut butter was harder than trying to find a few grams of cocaine. He had spent considerable time trying to find both.

The whine of the kettle finally stirred him to move and he struggled to rise, as the sofa was far too low to the ground. While the whistle continued, he paused to recall why he had even bothered to stand. Eventually his mind caught up with his body and he removed the kettle from the stove. The apartment was silent again.

His tea was weak. The only real taste it provided was the flavor of the rust floating around at the bottom of the kettle.

Finishing his tea, he simply stared forward at a wall and tried his best to think about nothing. It was not working. There was no need for a clock. Inside his mind he experienced every second as a driving pulse, each one longer than the last. He hated waiting. It had only been a few hours since he had last masturbated. He debated starting the process again until his eyes fell onto his other favorite way to pass the time.

Art.

It was the blank canvas, the uncut stone or the paper yet to be inked. These were the vessels of freedom, another kind of power that came from the ability to create. Despite his true love for the endless possibilities that were limited only by the creativity of an artist's mind, he would not have traded all of the works from any museum in the world for his favorite piece of art sitting in the corner - his M-14 7.62 millimeter rifle.

No critique was needed, nor any interpretation. Its purpose didn't have to be debated by critics or crowds, and it was not destined to be on display, framed by soft light or soothed by jazz music quietly being played from a perfectly balanced sound system. Simply put, the art was the steel, the wood, and the way in which after you shot someone in the face, the bolt cycled back and sounded just like an old-fashioned cash register being opened.

"The Golden Rule," he said, smiling at Fibonacci's theory while extending his hand and running his fingers from the barrel down to the charging handle.

The rifle was shouldered with a snap. The safety was disengaged and the crosshairs rested on the head of a small child seeking shelter from the rain at the bus stop some two hundred meters away. The man in the apartment held his breath until his heartbeat began to slow into a soft rhythm. It took a few moments until the crosshairs settled between the eyes of the child. Taking the slack up on the trigger, the man in the apartment released his breath; the child did not stand a chance.

The phone rang.

Suddenly the screen on his mobile next to him lit up the darkened apartment and after four rings it vibrated itself off the windowsill and landed at his feet. At first it did not distract him. The crosshairs never moved, his eyes never blinked and his finger held fast to the trigger. An eternity passed while the mobile vibrated on the floor. Finally, he released the trigger and set the rifle down.

"Good afternoon," the polite and proper voice of a secretary said warmly. "Am I speaking with Mr. Swan?"

"Yes," he said coldly. He hated the name. Swans were meant to float around in quaint ponds at parks and be fed popcorn by little children. He was not a swan. He was a killer. He was a hawk or a falcon striking down upon the weak from above. How he had the misfortune to be born with a last name like that was beyond him. "You are nine minutes late...."

"The Chief of Security would like to apologize that he will not be able to review the intelligence briefing with you today," the secretary said. "I have specific instructions from him to fax you the briefing, and will do so within the hour, Mr. Swan."

"Brooks?" Swan spat as he paced around his apartment. "Where the hell is Brooks? Put him on the phone!"

"The Chief of Security is not available," the secretary said calmly. "He has already departed to attend the European Defense Summit this weekend in Basel."

Swan was furious.

"In addition to the fax, the Chief of Security has also provided me with a detailed overview of..." The secretary sounded distracted.

"What are the results?" Swan demanded.

"Mr. Swan," the secretary continued politely. "In the last twenty-four hours there have been no updates or security threats concerning the Ambassador, his daughter, or Embassy staff."

"Is that from Brooks?" Swan asked as he looked back to the rifle in the corner.

"It is my interpretation, sir," the secretary said.

"What?" Swan cursed. "Your interpretation! What about Brooks? What about my goddamned job to protect the Ambassador!?"

"Mr. Swan, there is one more detail I would like to forward to you," the secretary gently intruded upon his rant. "In account for the National holiday, our office will be closed tomorrow. We will be unable to provide you with any further intelligence briefings until four o'clock on Monday."

"Sixteen hundred!" Swan corrected her. "Sixteen hundred! I can't do my job if you don't provide me with..."

"Have a pleasant evening, Mr. Swan." the secretary disconnected the line.

"Bitch!" Swan yelled. He threw his phone across the room. It hit the couch, landed on one of the uncomfortable cushions, and bounced onto the floor with enough force to cause the battery to fall out and skitter across the room.

Swan hated the couch. He stood now in full draw; a pistol retrieved from his holster shook in his hands as he held the couch in his sights. Despite the shaking in his hands he felt confident he could take the shot. Swan's eyes were on target and a vein ran thick with blood in his forehead. He lowered the pistol.

"Hearts and Minds," Swan babbled out loud. "Hearts and Minds."

Holstering the pistol, he sat down on the couch. "Let the damned Army win the Hearts and Minds, but don't expect my Marines to be giving candy to kids and posing for pictures with some godforsaken Hajis."

Swan's hair was cut high and tight. His combat boots were laced around his feet and a hidden K-bar was sheathed within a pants leg. His uniform was pressed neatly and rested in the closet next to the piano. He had worn it years ago and the civilian clothes which it had been traded for, he wore with utter disdain. As he had told many people, there is no such thing as a former Marine: once a Marine, always a Marine.

It was the waiting that bothered him the most. It gave him too much time to think about the dreams and the war as well as his last days in the Corps.

Swan cursed all of those who had fired upon him with their Kalashnikovs. He cursed them not because they shot at him or because they had tried to kill him, but because they had missed. He found it amazing that out of all the rounds fired in his direction, none of those bullets had found their target. Swan longed for a glorious death and the war had been his only hope at attaining one.

His last day in the Corps was served down a dead end street in a dead end village somewhere between Mosul and the Turkish border. The night before, an IED had lit up a NATO convoy and a local source confirmed that the bomb maker was in the village. Swan and his Marines searched house to house. The source had lied. They found nothing.

It could have been the forced marches or the eighty pounds of gear strapped onto his body. Whatever the cause, a few minutes after the last house was cleared, Swan's knee could take the strain no longer. It snapped.

A helicopter landed in Kuwait within the hour. Ten hours from then, Swan lay on an operating table in a military hospital in the German city of Landshul. There were no medals or plaques in post offices, no bands playing upon arrival or tearful family members waiting to share an embrace when he got back home. His chance at glory was gone, replaced only with the lonely memories of war and a year of rehabilitation therapy.

The doctors had set his disability rating at sixty percent. He would never fight again. Swan tried for years to appeal the decision, he trained so hard right up until his knee almost snapped again. There was no hope. The subsequent years had been hard on Swan and he had drifted through life, drinking and fighting at any opportunity. He was nearly lost until one day, the phone in his small New York apartment rang. Swan was offered a job.

Based just outside of Austin, Texas, AESOP International was one of the largest defense contractors in the world. The corporate website showed pictures of smiling children in some forgotten African nation, doctors helping landmine victims in Cambodia, and a businessman shaking hands with a villager in the Middle East. AESOP International's mission was listed: *To provide logistical support and security for the promotion of peace and prosperity in developing nations worldwide.* It was a nice way to say *Mercenaries for Hire.*

The majority of contracts awarded to AESOP International were from the Department of Defense in war zones such as Afghanistan and Iraq. Security was costly and AESOP International charged its clients accordingly. Despite the expensive contract cost and objections from the Office of Diplomatic Security, the State Department subsidized the security services for certain high-level officials - the Ambassador to Warsaw, included.

Swan accepted the job and was on a plane to Warsaw the following evening to guard a man who he thought was the world's most unimportant Ambassador. It mattered little whom Swan was guarding so long as it kept him busy and his mind focused. Now Swan found himself pacing back and forth in his apartment, the words of the secretary haunting each step he took.

With the National holiday nearing by the minute, Swan knew he would have three very long days without purpose. It would be too much for him. The next time he shouldered his rifle, there could be a round in the chamber and he might actually pull the trigger. The four walls closed in. Swan had to get out.

Berlin was calling.

Swan was not German; he had no connection whatsoever to the country or to the city, and he generally found the majority of Germans that he encountered to be egotistical bastards. The sole reason that he began packing his ruck was because the train to Berlin was the only one out of town that night. He knew that anything would be better than sitting in his apartment sharpening his knife and losing his mind.

The rain continued as Swan shouldered his pack and laced his boots. He checked the stove at least a dozen times to be sure it was off. He adjusted the magnet of a lamb on his refrigerator, rolled up his George Michael poster that was next to the couch, and placed his tea cup in the sink. He put his rifle inside the piano and poured flour onto the carpet by the door. Out came his K-Bar to slice a hair from his arm. He placed the delicate fiber between the door frame as he shut and locked the door. He was ready.

It was the first time he had ventured outside that day. The trees along Madalinskiego Street were full with heavy foliage and protected him from the weather as he walked. Swan turned right onto Independence Street and eventually he disappeared down a flight of stairs into the Pole Mokotowskie metro station. Within a few stops he exited the tube and arrived at Warsaw's Central Station. Swan bought a ticket and got on the train.

A few blocks away from the train station, past Jerozolimskie Avenue and down Ujazdowskie is the United States Embassy. The long line that stretches around the corner, even in the rain is composed entirely of Poles hoping to get their J1 Work and Travel Visas for the summer. Past the entrance, through a long corridor and into the Embassy is the large office of the Chief of Security, Mr. Brooks.

"I notified Mr. Swan of your departure to Basel for the conference." The secretary smiled at Mr. Brooks.

"Thank God; you're a dear, Effie," Mr. Brooks said, loosening his tie and setting his cup of black coffee down on her desk. He called her Effie because her feminine yet slightly boyish face reminded him of the character in *The Maltese Falcon*. "The fact that the State Department even bothers hiring these contractors is beyond me. Let alone one like Swan."

"I am certain he will voice his frustrations next time you talk to him," the secretary said.

"Why can't he just go drink himself to death under a bridge? After all, Warsaw has plenty of them," Brooks said, looking down at the secretary. "Has anything else arrived since my meeting?"

"As a matter of fact, yes, I received communication from our Embassy in Sarajevo."

"Bosnia?" Mr. Brooks questioned as he looked over the report that his secretary handed him.

"Central Intelligence?"

"The CIA is not operating at this time in Bosnia," Mr. Brooks answered, shaking his head. "Probably the intelligence is from one of the private contractors that they employ there. Damned contractors. They are everywhere!"

"You don't seem concerned about the report, sir?" the secretary queried as Mr. Brooks retrieved his coffee cup and placed the report back on her desk.

"Just someone covering their ass," Mr. Brooks said. "Someone down in the Balkans must be up for retirement soon and they didn't want anything coming back on them."

"Would you like me to research the suspect that they mentioned?"

"Who?" Mr. Brooks thought for a moment. "Bircher, Bircher...I have never heard of him. To hell with the report, it can wait until Monday."

"Are you certain that you would not like me to inform Mr. Swan?" the secretary insisted "You know, sir, that he will certainly observe the date on this fax and will almost certainly..."

"It can wait," Mr. Brooks politely interrupted her. "Swan can wait as well."

"Goodnight, sir."

"Goodnight, Effie," Mr. Brooks called politely as he put on his coat and retrieved his umbrella. "Enjoy your holiday, and don't worry about that report. I will take care of everything on Monday."

IV

A Kalashnikov rested in the corner. A picture of a naked woman was taped on the stock. The hand guard had initials carved into it and a crude outline of a Barbie Doll was etched onto the dust cover. The safety was off.

The room was empty except for a wooden stool and a few discarded papers scattered across the floor. The walls were concrete. There was no heat and a soldier stood motionless outside, looking into the night. Lying in the snow at his feet was a German Shepherd named Sasha.

The soldier had started a fire in a rusted oil drum to warm his hands. It was not helping. His post was over a thousand meters in elevation and surrounded by the wilds of the most inhospitable mountain in the Carpathians. It did not matter that in the valleys below, spring had arrived nearly a month earlier; within only a few hours the snow had accumulated to well over a meter. The branches of the pines around the checkpoint touched the ground, pinned in place by the heavy weight of the snow and forming a barrier of shadows and darkness which fueled the soldier's imagination. Even the reflections from the fire dared not wander too far off into the storm. The night itself seemed cursed.

Behind him, somewhere out beyond where his vision ended, spanned the massive prison complex known only on secret government maps as *Svoboda*. The prison was violent and corrupt. It would likely be one of the most notorious in the world, except that outside of the knowledge of a few intelligence agencies, no one else on earth knew it existed. The prison was nearly forty kilometers from anything resembling civilization. The small Ukrainian village that was chartered nearby was a closed city in the truest Soviet sense. No one entered or left without permission, and no one wanted to be there.

The visibility decreased exponentially with each frosted breath the soldier took, while the curtain of night drew around his shoulders as if at any moment he would be under attack. His hands rubbed together vigorously, a constant ebb and flow of his palms striking together in hopes of warmth, yet his hands were nearly frozen. Sasha remained at his feet and the Kalashnikov remained in the corner of the small concrete checkpoint behind him.

"Did you see the last one?" The soldier recalled Yevheniy's words from only an hour before. "They say he did it with his bare hands! Can you believe it! His bare hands!"

"The orders to release the prisoner were sent directly from both the Ministry of Justice and the Ministry of Defense." The soldier tried to calm Yevheniy "The deaths are not of our concern."

"How many will he destroy once he is free?" Yevheniy exclaimed, pacing frantically in the snow. "I will tell you this, Commander, he is a ghost if he is not the devil himself!"

"You are a fool, Yevheniy!" The soldier lost what little patience he had for his comrade. "Curse you and curse this night! Your fears of Tanga Wanga are better suited for little children and old hags!"

Yevheniy stopped pacing and was about to push the matter further.

"It will be morning soon," the soldier said. "I am relieving you tonight of your duties at this checkpoint. Go to the village. The mail train will be arriving in the morning: wait for it."

"With this weather?" Yevheniy protested, hoping for a pardon of his new assignment. "It's nearly a kilometer to the village!"

"Then it will be more than enough time for your imagination to run its course, instead of driving me mad!" the soldier barked before dismissing him. "Also, the baker will be pulling fresh rolls from the oven in a few hours. Be sure to get a dozen."

Yevheniy knew better than to protest a direct order longer than he already had. The violence resided not only behind the steel wire and concrete walls of the prison but also on the outside. The slightest violation of duty could bring swift and abrupt punishment, the severity of which was left solely to the discretion of the Commanders.

The intensifying storm redirected the soldier's thoughts to his gloved fingertips which ached and burned under the sharp bite from the cold. A part of him wished that he had kept Yevheniy around on such a terrible night. The other part knew his tolerance for such company was at its limit, as the soldier had long entertained pleasurable thoughts of taking the often hysterical Yevheniy out behind the guard booth and shooting him in the face with his Makarov.

What unsettled him the most wasn't the ranting of Yevheniy, but the hard reality that he was afraid, deeply and truly afraid. The recent murders inside the prison walls didn't cause concern because those who perished at the hands of the prisoner who was being released tonight were undesirables better buried in the dirt than spending another day alive. The violence of the attacks was also not able to shake his resolve, despite the animalistic ferocity with which they were carried out. Yet every shadow, every noise or motion in the night, shook him to the core, and it bothered him that he didn't know why he was afraid. This was a primal warning from centuries before. It was the reason he stood outside, for inside the building of the checkpoint, he felt like he was trapped. He felt like cornered prey.

It had been nearly eleven years since his conscription into the Ukrainian Land Forces. He had served his first four years with the 28th Guards in Chornomorske before being transferred to a nuclear facility at Zaporizhia. Checking papers, saluting visiting

Generals and drinking copious amounts of vodka had been the soldier's three primary duties at the facility.

He had longed for a woman.

When he finally found her, she was a dynamo. A power pack. She was a walking pornographic magazine, and with each step of her legs, she turned the pages of his mind further into debauchery.

She was from a small city north of the Black Sea known as Kostopil. They met by chance, passing on the streets during a late summer evening. She had a lovely smile, a warm heart and a glorious pair of breasts. He was in love and whether or not she was mattered little to him at the time. There was talk of romance, of a small dacha in the forest, and even marriage and all that was only on the first date.

The cold violently snapped him from his memories and his eyes refocused. The fire in the barrel was nearly out and his hands and feet were completely frozen. A heavy dusting of snow covered Sasha and her long fur coat. The soldier wondered whether he skinned her if her hide would be large enough to make himself a new winter jacket. As if reading his mind, Sasha looked up at him in defense.

"Don't worry, Sasha," the soldier said, smiling to the dog. "You know I would never do anything like that. You can trust me."

He had already decided that the coat would have been too small.

The soldier looked up from Sasha and peered into the storm. The blue and yellow banded gate that guarded the road before him had long ago vanished under the snow. It was the tempting road to freedom, the one he could guard but never venture down. The prisoner would soon be free of chain and steel, but the soldier would remain sentenced to his post behind the bars of pines and spruce.

After three years at Zaporizhia, the soldier was summoned to Kiev. An officer known as Pavlovsky met him with a firm handshake and kind words from malted breath. The officer talked of war, armaments and men, and of power and might. He dwelt on hardship and despair and all the modern day plagues a soldier faces upon his return to society. Then he talked of a prison named Svoboda.

Pavlovsky's speech was one that he had given many times over to countless young men. The soldier didn't know this, of course. In fact, he was so taken by Pavlovsky's passion and bluster as well as his sense of duty and nationalism that he never thought to ask a single question about his new post. The soldier was young and foolish; he had visions of luxury and leisure, ideas of exotic locations and exciting opportunities. Maybe one day he would be a spy, a diplomat, or even a general. Young and foolish.

As with any event in the Eastern Bloc, no matter how minor or important, there were endless amounts of paperwork to be signed, stamped, and sealed. It took him slightly less than an hour to finish processing after he had left Pavlovsky's office. Three more hours passed before he was directed to a small room with a long rectangular table and a few chairs arranged in no particular order around it. There was one light hanging far too low in the center of the room and no windows, only bricks mortared in around the sills on one wall where the panes had previously been.

He waited there for another forty-five minutes before a secretary entered the room with a folder straining to contain all of the papers between its folds. She spent considerable time detailing non-essential policies concerning the processing that he had completed earlier, and suspiciously, she made no direct reference at all to his new position. Time passed painfully, the way it does in any small room without windows. When the briefing was finally complete he knew even less than when it started. The only thing that the soldier had learned was that he was leaving within the hour on a train to a place he had never heard of. He had no time to tell his family and friends, and no time to say goodbye to his lover from Kostopil.

When the train finally ran out of track at his new post, there were no fancy cars or expensive wines. There was not even a promotion waiting there for him. There was just the guard booth at the end of a road, where he had stood day after day, which had slowly and painfully turned into year after year.

A bright search light screamed out of the night with such surprising vibrancy that the soldier snapped to attention and his sad recollections of his past again retreated back to the shadows. His retinas burned as his pupils dilated and for a few moments his vision was lost. Soon the entire prison stood before him, its imposing silhouette framed by the thousands of bulbs that now pulsed to life. He no longer felt alone or full of regret from the past. He straightened his back, adjusted his belt, and stood ready to do his duty.

Metallic clicks could be heard as doors unlocked and gates were opened. Somewhere from behind the lights and inside the walls shouts and orders could be heard. The soldier could see the main yard, surrounded by a fence ten meters high capped with razor wire. Past the yard was the main gate, which was bordered by the road that went past his checkpoint and onward down into the village. The last lights to flicker to life were the dozen lamp posts along the road. The prisoner was being released.

A whistle blew and then a final metal door opened. The storm churned in the sky above as the prisoner took his first step to freedom. His figure was distant and obscured, but from where the soldier stood, he could see his stride was great and his size imposing. The prisoner vanished for a moment, turning at the main gate before appearing under the first lamp post at the end of the road. The soldier swallowed hard. Sasha grew restless.

There were no forms to sign or documents to file. The soldier was merely ordered to raise the gate and let the prisoner pass into freedom. Waiting to perform his duty, the soldier looked down the road as the prisoner passed under the second and third lamp posts. The soldier pushed his chest forward. He tried to feel strong, brave, and confident, and for a moment he was almost able to fool himself into believing that the most dangerous man in the world was nobody to fear.

Then the power cut out and everything turned to black.

It happened with a powerful clap that cracked into the night as if one massive breaker had been tripped. The only light that remained was the core from the filament of the searchlight, but it soon joined the prison in disappearing so quickly, it was as if it had never existed at all. Darkness raced in upon the soldier from his flanks, nearly crushing him to the ground with the weight of sheer terror.

"What the hell?" The soldier spoke aloud.

A high-pitched whine came from Sasha, followed by a crazed growl. Through the storm he could just make out Sasha and was frozen by the sight at his feet. She stood rigid, immobile, her black lips curled back while her canines snapped forward. The red coals from the fire burned like damnation in her eyes as she stared wildly down the road.

"Sasha." The soldier said this more for himself than for the shepherd as he felt fear rake its fingers across his spine. "Please Sasha....please."

She sensed something cursed was upon them. It was something evil, dangerous and deadly. It would be useless for her to run or to hide. Facing death itself seemed an easier task than to attempt to fight whatever force was now upon them. She might not make it through the night and she knew there was nothing she could do about it. The soldier knew this too.

Then he heard a sound.

It was soft and steady, but it was the most frightening sound he had ever heard: the sound of footsteps on the newly fallen snow. The soldier's legs ignored any orders from his brain screaming at him to turn and run. He suddenly and wholeheartedly accepted the fact that he was going to die. It took all of the strength that he had left to do the only thing he could. The soldier shut his eyes.

The steps were deep and powerful and each one brought the prisoner closer to the soldier. Suddenly the footsteps stopped and all was quiet. It was the loudest silence he had ever heard. The soldier could not hear the falling snow or Sasha growling at his feet. He could only hear his heart as it raced to beat its way out from inside of his chest.

The prisoner was a force of nature, a driving presence, an unyielding powerhouse that now stood before the soldier ready to impart death upon him. Even though his eyes were closed he could feel the shadow of the prisoner looming over him. The anticipation of death was too much to bear and if the soldier had not entirely lost control of his body, he would have reached down to his holster, pulled out his Makarov, and put one under his own chin. He was certain that the prisoner was smiling and that at any moment he would deliver the fatal strike.

"Sorry." The soldier began babbling out loud like a child lost in the woods. "Sasha, I'm sorry."

He did not know how many times he repeated his apologies to Sasha or how long he had stood there. It could have been minutes, hours, or even years. It mattered little. When he finally found the courage to open his eyes, the morning sun was already cutting through the trees. The storm had passed, the night was over, and the prisoner was free. The coals of the fire were long extinguished. Sasha was fast asleep and the white snow warmly and peacefully sparkled in the dawn. Everything was calm, and crisp, as is often the case on mornings after a storm. The night before seemed but a dream.

In an instant they were upon the soldier: heavy and powerful footsteps sounded from directly behind. It was too late to resist. They arrived without warning. Pulling his arms above his head, the soldier screamed as the shadow from behind filled his vision.

"Good morning!" Yevheniy exclaimed, proud to display the warm rolls in a basket he had brought back from the village. "Oh, Commander! I am so sorry. I did not intend to startle you!"

From within his defensive contortion, the soldier looked for a moment at Yevheniy. It took seconds to register and a few more to react. The soldier released his tendons from their locked positions, straightened, and despite his embarrassment, was truthfully overwhelmed with joy to see his comrade.

"Good morning," the soldier replied, adjusting himself.

"Have they released the prisoner according to the Minister's orders?" Yevheniy questioned, determined to sound proper in an attempt to recover his stature from the night before.

"The prisoner has been released as ordered." The soldier regained his cold tone. "You must have passed him on your return from the village, yes?"

"I am sorry, Commander," Yevheniy shook his head sheepishly. "I did not. My footprints were the only ones in the snow."

"The only ones?" The soldier looked uneasily at the fortress of trees surrounding him.

"Yes," Yevheniy said, reaching into the basket in his hand. "Surely the only route the prisoner would have taken was into the village?"

"Surely," the soldier agreed.

"Unless he was planning on climbing a few thousand meters over the Tatra Mountains guarding the Polish city of Krakow in one of the worst storms in history!" Yevheniy attempted humor.

"You're sure there were no footprints?"

"None, Commander," Yevheniy answered, extending his hand. "Would you like a warm roll?"

V

Josie entered the courtyard. It was past midnight, the town was deserted and a desolate silence held fast between the wind. There was a Bel-Air up on blocks rusting in the sand to his left, an old church to his right, and up ahead a solitary tumbleweed was getting kicked around by a stale breeze riding the breakers rolling in from the Adriatic as its waves struck the shore.

It reminded Josie of Mexico, of some dog-eared border town on the Rio Grande full of cowboys and desperados. Josie walked up to the steps of the church. The facade was worn, choked with sand and pock-marked from the constant barrage of the salt blasting in from the sea. At the top of the church above the squared roof was a wooden beam, and under the beam a bell was suspended and appeared to be in worse shape than the church. Josie turned away from the church and walked back through the courtyard as a single gull silently drifted overhead, riding the thermals from the waves below.

A narrow street waited for Josie at the end of the courtyard. His destination was only two blocks further. He paused, held a private conversation with himself, straightened his back, loosened his neck from side to side, and just for comfort, reached down and touched the cold steel of his forty-five.

The two blocks passed quickly and Josie found himself standing in front of a white corrugated-steel gate. Despite the perforations in the gate, he could not see what lay beyond, but he was certain that from where he stood he could be seen and he was sure that he was being watched.

"Tell me, traveler," a coarse voice questioned from behind the gate after Josie had waited there for a few minutes. "How many meters was the shot taken from?"

"It's impossible to know," Josie said, turning to look back down the narrow street. "Surely it was less than a hundred meters."

A long silence greeted his response.

"An accident, perhaps?" the voice said coldly. "Do you believe that she really had it in her to kill him?"

"Without a doubt."

"Because he was going to leave her?"

"No," Josie said, casually taking note of the two men who had appeared from the courtyard and were now standing at the far end of the street. "It had nothing to do with him at all."

"A bold statement!" The voice coughed. The sound of a match being ripped across a box crackled from behind the gate. "You're telling me she did it for herself?"

"Isn't that why everyone does most things?"

Josie leaned up against the wall next to the gate, glancing at the two men who were watching him. "It was there in those final moments before her husband died that she realized every waking hour of her life had meant nothing at all to anyone, especially to her. If she had any sense of dignity, she would have simply shot herself instead."

Josie nodded his head up the street discreetly in the direction of the two men. "Some of yours?"

"Some of mine." The voice affirmed. "What of the new man in her life?"

"She had no illusions about him, or about any other." Josie leaned against the brick wall next to the gate. "She knew that in time he would leave her, just like all the others."

Silence held the conversation for a few minutes. Josie waited patiently.

"The gate," the voice said. "It's unlocked."

Josie turned back to the courtyard. Both men were gone. He opened the gate and stepped inside.

The bitter smell of vanilla drifted from a pipe and hung like laundry on the line, heavy and wet, pinned in place, and not to be disturbed until morning. The offending pipe rested firmly in the rounded hands of a man sitting on a stool, his back pressed up tightly against the stucco wall of his home. He made no effort to rise, but with a sweeping motion of his free hand, he indicated another stool. Josie walked forward and sat down.

Between the stools there was an old wooden barrel that served as a table and looked as if it had just been pulled from the surf. Here a candle rested, paired with a box of matches and a full bottle of single malt scotch.

The candle illuminated the man across from Josie. He was aged and weathered like a sailor, yet his shoulders were wide and his frame was stout and youthful, his thick legs and chiseled calves rising above a pair of sandals while a white and neatly trimmed beard rounded off the man's face. He called himself after the man he had spent his entire life trying to emulate: Papa

The table that the two men sat at rested alongside a wall. Past the wall was an open wooden door. Opposite the door and out into the night Josie could see a small garden and an outdoor brick oven, the kind so commonly found in Croatia for cooking the beloved Odojek. The entire fenced property was completely protected under a canopy of terraced citrus and kiwi leaves; their stems grew wildly in all directions.

Movement within the garden suddenly caught Josie's eye. He was not alone with Papa. In the corner of the garden just past a vine of tomato plants sat a large brown rabbit. It was well fed and chewed lazily on some greenery while regarding Josie. Its ears were unlike any that he had ever seen. They were so obnoxiously long that Josie found himself smiling. The cheer from the rabbit put Josie at ease about the favor he was going to have to ask.

"So, I see you're still alive," Papa said, coughing once before clearing his throat.

"And happily so are you," Josie said, indicating the bottle of scotch.

"Don't flirt, boy! I'm a professional drinker!" Papa waved his hand. "Nothing wrong with a little indulgence."

Josie nodded gently towards the open door along the wall. "Your wife?"

"Two years ago," Papa said. "She left me."

"A very smart woman, then?" Josie replied. "Your girlfriends?"

"They have left me as well."

"And what of Pilar?" Josie asked, leaning his back up against the wall.

"She was a damned fine boat, Josie. Damned fine," Papa said, dipping the bowl of his pipe for emphasis. "Had to sell her."

Josie looked genuinely surprised. "What about Boca Grande? The Tarpon? The Hammerheads?"

"I believe that a phrase you once said yourself suits those questions best," Papa said, now nipping on the pipe's stem. "In another life. In another life."

"Don't be a bastard," Josie said, dissatisfied with the evasive answer. "Why did you have to sell the boat?"

Papa nodded and adjusted himself higher on his stool. "The Krauts. Goddamned Germans bought up everything in this city. Prices doubled across the board, taxes too. If I hadn't sold her I would have been forced out of Zadar just like everyone else. True enough, it's a shithole, but it's my home, my city. I've got nowhere else to go."

Josie let the matter drop but Papa held it tight.

"You try to give the Krauts another go, one more chance to prove that they aren't all a bunch of paper hanging sons-of-bitches." Papa poured a glass of scotch. "Give them that chance and I'll be damned if they don't start wearing their uniforms, polishing their boots and marching around telling everyone in Europe what to do."

Josie smiled.

"You asked about Pilar?" Papa questioned with a serious look in his eye. "Have you come for another voyage on the sea?"

"No chance in hell," Josie said bluntly.

Papa smiled. A serpentine chain of smoke rolled from his nostrils and he said, "Still haven't made peace with Neptune, my boy?"

"Peace, no. An agreement, yes."

"The terms and conditions?"

"Simple," Josie said, tapping his fingers on the table for emphasis. "All I have to do is stay the hell off of the damned ocean. If I do, then Neptune and I have got no quarrel."

"Good thing you didn't join the Navy," Papa said, smiling.

A polite silence separated the two men. Neither looked directly at the other; instead, each chose a distant corner and focused intently on it. Minutes passed.

Papa finally spoke, motioning his head towards a figurative mountain on the horizon. "The hills, Josie, they are right there in front of us."

"Like white elephants, Papa," Josie said. "I suppose we should get on with it?"

"Don't rush me, boy. We'll get to it soon enough. I'm an old man, Josie. Hell, I haven't even gotten into a fistfight for at least a year. All I got left are stories. I never was one to live through another man but now I've got no choice. The last story I heard worth a damn was about a young Ranger that escaped from prison. The fact that you are sitting here, Josie, means that you must have another story to tell."

"Yes, I do." Josie nodded and poured a glass of scotch for himself. "But before I start, let me tell you that escaping from that prison years ago wouldn't have meant a thing if it wasn't for a brave captain and a boat named Pilar that got me the rest of the way to freedom."

Papa called Josie a son-of-a-bitch, turned his eyes away, and bit his lip hard.

"Just tell the damned story," Papa said finally, trying to hide his choked up state with a fit of coughing.

Josie told the tale.

Josie didn't have time to be Victorian or elaborate, but the man across from him deserved a story with detail: he chose his words with care. He described his arrival in Yemen and the airstrike that nearly killed him, as well as his passage at Najran across the Saudi Arabian border with the Mujahedeen.

Papa relaxed his jaw in thought and gazed upwards, lost in the vision of Josie's tale. As the story continued, the dawn began to cast deep shadows, shifting the night back. The stillness that precedes each sunrise settled around the two men.

Josie told Papa of his arrest in Syria, his escape into Turkey, his push through the mountains of Bulgaria, and his arrival in Visegrad. Why Josie finally stopped in the city of Mostar was even beyond his best guess, but he had little time remaining and drew his words to an end, concluding at the encounter with Gibbs from the day before. Josie had done his best.

Papa ran his fingers roughly through his white beard, while his thumb tapped the bowl of the pipe. His head remained tilted at an angle as if he were looking to some distant star. He was somewhere out there between Yemen and Bosnia: he felt Josie's words as if he himself had endured the trials. It was a good story.

"The pigeons? The Serb?" Papa said after finding himself again. "How was it arranged?"

"Arranged? It wasn't."

"There was no sniper then?"

"Of course not," Josie said. "Plus Serbs are too damned unpredictable. Probably would have ended up touching off a few rounds just for kicks once he got bored while waiting."

"And the birds?" Papa's voice had softened and his coughing eased as the bottle of Scotch rested now nearly empty beside him.

"Pigeons are pigeons," Josie said shrugging slightly. "If Gibbs wouldn't have been so nervous and took a minute to look closer, he would have seen a whole flock of them lined up on the roof."

Papa smiled. "You think he will understand what you told him, Josie?" He asked in a way that implied he had a stake in the outcome.

Josie nodded. "Eventually."

"And what of Zadar?" Papa began working one of his kneecaps with his fat fingers. "How did you get across the border?"

"I waited. I learned to do it quite well when I was in the Army. We were always waiting: waiting for chow, waiting for orders, waiting for this or that. Always waiting."

"You're telling me that you simply went back home and turned on the television?" Papa asked, looking stern as if Josie was hiding something from him.

"Not quite," Josie smiled. "I had to stop first at a kiosk a few blocks down from the Old Bridge to get a very special photograph printed."

Papa chuckled.

"Not even the Agency has enough resources to post an agent at every Bosnian border crossing from Ivanica all the way north to Bihac," Josie said. "I would even bet you that there wasn't one waiting at the main crossing outside of Metkovic."

"In America, you have what is called an All-Points Bulletin." Papa rubbed his beard. It remained perfectly shaped. "You don't think the Agency would post such an alert?"

"They could have," Josie nodded. "But as you well know, this isn't America. This is the Balkans and nothing ever goes the way it should. Even if the Agency issued such an alert, the majority of border checkpoints in Bosnia don't even have a fax machine, let alone a telephone."

"Since you're such a smug bastard, why didn't you just get on a plane in Dubrovnik and fly out directly?"

"It was an option!" Josie laughed. "Yet, in the off chance that someone working for the Agency actually did their job right for once and flagged my passport, I decided against it."

"My balls are still blue, boy, don't be a bitch about it!" Papa protested, growing restless with Josie. "Surely you crossed into Croatia at Neum?"

"In the height of summer?" Josie shook his head. "I would still be waiting there at the border with all those busloads of tourists."

"Further to the north?" Papa offered, extending one fat index into the air.

"Posusje." Josie smiled. "After all, it is a Friday night!"

Papa was worn. He was old and he was out-of-date, but he was sharp enough to know quite well the tales of the hordes of migrating Bosnian women into Croatia, a migration that happened every Friday night.

"Croatia has some of the best discothèques in the world. Thousands of women, wait, let me rephrase, thousands of *beautiful* women cross at Posusje every weekend in search of the Brit, the Kraut or the Italian man that can fall in love with their short skirts and push up bras and take them the hell out of whatever tiny Bosnian village they came from."

Papa smiled, clearly impressed.

"Lifted a bike just outside of Mostar," Josie quickly summarized. "Picked up a girl on the way and made a run for the border."

"How did you manage?"

"Well," Josie said, pushing away from the wall he had been leaning on and firmly planting his feet on the ground. "I didn't even have to stop. The border guard didn't bother to look out from his booth; he just sat there watching the Velez Mostar football match and waved everyone through."

"What of the motorcycle?" Papa asked.

"The Ducati?" Josie reached into his pocket and threw the keys down onto the top of the barrel. "It's parked a few blocks down on Zlatarska Street; it won't float, but you can name it Pilar."

Papa nodded. A few minutes of silence passed. Josie rocked forward on his feet.

"It's time then, isn't it, boy?"

Josie nodded. "I want in."

"In?" Papa looked squarely at Josie.

"I want into the Fortress, Papa," Josie said. "Fortress Europa."

"The Schengen." Papa nodded.

"I can't count on all of the border crossings further in the north to pass as easily as the one at Posusje. I would go it alone if I could, Papa, but I just don't have the time."

"Time," Papa said quietly, as the stiff salted breeze dried his throat. His voice was hoarse again. He poured another shot. "How much time do you have?"

"Two days, maybe three."

"Until?"

"Until it's too late."

Papa leaned back against the wall. His hands stretched behind his head and scratched at the few scraps of hair that remained. He yawned. Papa was tired and he was drunk, but he had already decided that no matter what, he was going to get Josie across the border.

"There is a girl," Papa said. "I can only promise that she will get you across the border. Nothing more. After the crossing you will be on your own."

Josie accepted gratefully. "Through Slovenia?"

"Hungary," Papa corrected. "The Slovenes are too much like the Krauts. They polish their buttons and shine their shoes and they patrol the border like they are defenders of the faith. The Hungarians are fat and lazy, but still, it won't be easy."

Josie reached into his pocket while Papa continued talking.

"The girl. I don't know what to think. There is a man, some musician - reggae music, I think. What can I do? She won't listen to me. I tell her to think about her life, to think seriously."

Josie listened.

"It's not important." Papa waved his hand and stopped his rant. "She will get you across the border, but it will cost you. She is a livewire, Josie, watch her!"

"How soon can she be here?" Josie asked.

"She lives just south of here in the city of Sibenik." Papa focused his eyes, as if doing a complicated series of mathematical computations. "Fifteen, twenty minutes. The last time we parted ways, Josie was on the Libyan coast just outside of Benghazi." Papa referred to where their voyage on the Pilar had ended.

"I can tell you, Papa, that this encounter has been much more pleasurable." Josie helped Papa stand up.

"Well, this time you didn't spend two days leaning over the side of a boat!" Papa's laughter turned into a sharp raspy cough, followed by a few heavy breaths.

Josie extended a roll of banknotes that he had retrieved from his pocket.

"Don't go and ruin it, boy." Papa wrinkled his brow and brushed him off. "I don't know where you're going or what you've got to do. I don't need to. I know it isn't about the pistol tucked into your belt and I know it isn't about the killing. It's about making things right. Well boy, go set it right."

"Thank you," Josie said his hand on Papa's back to balance him.

Josie knew Papa was the kind of man that you could look in the eyes and know just by one slight nod that he was with you to the end, that he could be trusted and that his word meant more to him than damned near anything else in the world. A handshake from a man like that meant a whole hell of a lot, too: it was not just a promise or a pact, but something more that couldn't be described to anyone who had never experienced it, and as Josie released his grip from Papa's extended hand, he did his best to hold back the emotion that held itself high in his throat.

"Okay, Josie," Papa said. "Shall I call her, then?"

"Please."

VI

He was blindfolded. Black plastic zip ties served as shackles around his hands and feet. He wore a tan vest, a white robe, and a pair of sandals. A large set of Bose headphones fit securely around his ears. His face was strained and tight. His hands were clenched and his knuckles were white.

Cass was sitting next to him.

The charter jet idled on the tarmac just outside of a private hanger on the eastern end of the Butmir Airport in Sarajevo. It was late at night and all of the Lufthansa and Aer Lingus planes that normally occupied the terminal had departed long ago. For the most part, the airport was silent and empty. Cass bit her lip.

It was the silence that bothered her. She could deal with the insomnia, the restless nights, and the way she constantly felt detached and lonely, no matter how many people she was surrounded by. What she couldn't deal with was looking out the window of the jet and seeing the airport empty. Of all places, an airport should be busy. There should be people moving about, arguing about delays, and little vehicles pulling racks of luggage around. There was nothing out of her window, just a black runway, a few blinking lights, and the desolate feeling that her mind always seemed to focus on.

Even as a child, Cass had hated the silence. When she heard *Silent Night* on the radio at Christmas, she would always weep without restraint. Between the tears, she would ask why the night is so silent. What happened? Did someone die?

"Why is the night so fucking silent?" Cass said under her breath as she leaned back and buckled her seat belt.

As the jet rolled forward and taxied to the opposite end of the runway, Cass tried to focus her thoughts on Gibbs and the confrontation that he had had with Bombay back in the safe house. Cass knew there was something about Gibbs behind the paranoid, nervous and often erratic man, although she couldn't figure out what it was. There was a strong masculine force in him, yet he never cast a curious glance her way, which, for Cass, was both insulting and flattering at the same time.

Cass had known that Gibbs was getting close to finding what the Agency was so desperately seeking. Bombay knew it too. She thought that their argument in the hallway must have had something to do with it. Why, when Gibbs was so close to completing the mission, was he being sent to Monte Negro to train a new recruit? An even better question, she thought, was why was she suddenly reassigned to a new operation which she didn't know anything about. She was focused now and continued to think everything over as the jet stopped for a moment.

The flaps extended, the turbines roared and the jet was airborne.

In the Agency, there was always some angle or edge, always someone playing politics and someone getting screwed over. Games were played, rules were broken and everything was usually so convoluted that nothing ever really got accomplished, but it was a government job, so what did she expect? Cass played along; she had to no matter how much she loathed the self-serving hypocrisy of it all.

The work that she was doing in Bosnia had nothing to do with helping some farmer in Kansas sleep safely at night, nor did it give a poor kid in the Bronx a better life. The work that Cass did was to make someone powerful, rich, or dead. The more she passed it back and forth in her mind, the more she realized that she was a hypocrite too: she could talk about morals and values all she wanted, but at the end of the day, she took their money, cashed the check, and didn't do anything to stop them.

"Yusuf Abdul Qawi al-Dhi'b." The man sitting in the seat in front of Cass spoke as he turned around and smiled.

Cass nodded her head to acknowledge his introduction and replied without emotion, "Pleasure."

"No, no, no!" He laughed, while gesturing a thumb to the man with the blindfold next to her. "That is al-Dhi'b, my name is Lang."

Cass nodded again. Her eyes searched for any way out of the current dialogue that threatened to turn into a conversation. There was nothing within arm's reach to read, not even a safety manual. Her mobile phone was unhelpfully and unusually quiet in her purse. It was too late.

"The President had to go and tell everyone that we don't waterboard detainees anymore," Lang said, seemingly pleased to know that she was trapped and forced to talk with him. "What is this country coming to if the CIA can't even pour a few gallons of water on some terrorist?"

As much as Cass had no desire whatsoever to engage in conversation, part of her knew it distracted her thoughts, so she allowed it to continue.

"*British Steel.*" Lang tapped his ears and motioned towards the headphones on the man next to her.

"Excuse me?" Cass asked. "He is a British national?"

"No, no." Lang waved his hand. "*British Steel,* it's an album!"

"An album?" Cass raised an eyebrow.

"Priest," Lang smiled, tilting his head up and down. "Judas Priest. Hajis hate heavy metal."

Cass looked ahead between the seats in front of her and noticed another man sitting in the window seat. The man seemed content and calm. He sat quietly with a child's coloring book on his lap. Cass watched as he carefully selected a crayon from the box on the tray in front of him and made exact, intricate marks in the book.

As the man continued to color, Lang began a lecture on Heavy Metal and 80's music while the detainee winced in pain from the volume of the music. Cass tried to focus on his words but soon her eyes glazed over and her empty thoughts returned.

"Ratt, Dokken..." Lang continued to rattle off names of his favorite bands. "Manowar, Quiet Riot...."

A long finger cut like a knife through the air and interrupted his speech. It was Bombay. Cass looked up. Lang paused, stared at Bombay and then back at Cass, smiled and found a seat further down the aisle. Bombay sat down.

"Who was that?" Cass whispered as Bombay adjusted the seat in front of her. "CIA?"

Bombay shook his head. "Just ignore him."

"I was," Cass said sadly.

The man with the coloring book took no notice of the new tenant in the seat next to him. He simply continued to color.

"Department of Defense," Bombay said. "He is an Intelligence Analyst."

Cass knew that translated to *interrogator*.

"Al-Dhi'b," Bombay motioned to the man next to her. "For the last year he was detained at the U.S Army base in Kosovo."

"Processing?"

Bombay nodded.

"Wouldn't it have been easier to interrogate him there?"

"Are you scared he is going to behead you, Cass?" Bombay chided sarcastically.

"I'm quite comfortable," Cass replied in defense. "At least he isn't trying to chat me up. I just don't understand why he is being transported to Poland."

Bombay replied in a mocking tone of formality. "Al-Dhi'b is being transported to a secure military base to receive proper medical evaluations and treatment."

"I don't work for Reuters." Cass returned his sarcasm.

"Truth be told, the Poles want a crack at the Agency's new interrogation techniques. The Department of Defense put out a contract, took the highest bidder, and here we are. Al-Dhi'b drew the short straw."

"What can he tell us about Bircher?" Cass asked, adjusting her seat. "Will he be able to provide us with any information?"

"Possibly," Bombay said, trailing off for a moment as he received a text message on his cellular phone. "Though it will be of little value now. I expect the most they will get out of him concerning Bircher would be how he crossed from Yemen and made his way into Europe."

"A little late, then." Cass nodded.

The Adriatic passed below as the Gulfstream turned sharply to the East. Bombay answered two calls as he organized a folder in his lap that had been clutched in his hands when he had first sat down. Lang turned every so often to see whether Cass was alone yet, while the man next to Bombay selected a violet-blue crayon and kept coloring.

"Traditionally," Bombay began again after he ended his second call. "Traditionally, Warsaw has been very difficult for us."

Bombay handed her the folder.

"Hell," he continued. "It's not just been difficult for us. Everyone, even the Russians and the Israelis, have a hard time setting up shop."

Cass took the folder and opened it to the first page.

"Why?"

"Who knows. The Agency sets up networks in Georgia and Iran like it is setting up picnics, but we just can't get established in Warsaw."

Cass noticed the folder contained nearly one hundred pages of intelligence reports and briefings. She was tired. It was late and the flight was not going to be long enough to sort through all the documents. She hoped Bombay would summarize.

Breezing through the folder, ten pages in, Cass turned to a five-by-eight color photograph.

"Rodham," Bombay tapped his fingers on the photo. "He is your only contact. He is the only one we have."

"British?" Cass said.

"Correct," Bombay replied. "He is the only one who hasn't been turned a half a dozen times....well, at least we think he hasn't."

"By who?" Cass demanded. "The Russians?"

"Sometimes yes, sometimes no." Bombay shrugged. "Doesn't matter really, does it? Back to Rodham."

Cass listened while fingering through the pages, taking little notice of the words her eyes scanned.

"Rodham owns a large industrial shipping firm on the west side of London. United Industries."

"Weapons?"

"Hardly." Bombay shook his head and let out a laugh that made Cass feel foolish. "Heavy machinery and construction equipment."

"Legitimate?"

"Yes," Bombay said. "Entirely."

Cass looked through a few more pages then caught something. "His main office is based in Kent; the firm is in London, so why does he live in Warsaw?"

"Valid point," Bombay acknowledged. "The majority of Mr. Rodham's shipping destinations are to ports in Eastern European nations."

"Russia... Ukraine..." Cass listed them as they appeared on the next page.

Bombay nodded. "With favorable corporate tax rates, a growing market and a secure economy, Poland was the best location for Mr. Rodham to establish a European office in."

"The Heart of Europe," Cass offered.

"Yes," Bombay replied.

"Why is he working for the CIA? Judging by the assets and holdings of his company, surely he doesn't need the money."

"He doesn't work for us," Bombay said. "And you're right - he certainly doesn't need the money."

Bombay watched Cass drift through a dozen pages apathetically. He was aware that Cass had no patience for the often tedious briefings like the one contained in the open folder on her lap. Besides, his style of leadership was one that was powered by control and dominance. Briefing Cass directly was an extension of this style.

"Let me ask you," Bombay said. "Have you ever tried to buy a tool here in Europe?"

Cass shot Bombay a curious look.

"Perhaps a hammer or even a screwdriver?"

Cass shook her head. "No."

"Well, if you did, the first thing you would notice is that the tool would be ridiculously expensive. The second thing you would notice is that the quality would be terrible."

Cass thought for a moment. "I've never noticed."

"Rodham did," Bombay said. "That's why he is worth nearly a quarter of a billion dollars."

Cass listened more intensely.

"Imagine if you bought a hammer back home in the States for twenty dollars, then were able to sell that same hammer here for over one hundred. Now imagine if you bought a forty ton piece of machinery."

Cass understood. She searched for a connection or an angle that would explain why Rodham would need to cooperate with the Agency.

"Export Tax," Cass declared.

"Exactly. In the early eighties we had already established a relationship with his corporation, in using their services to deliver Land Rovers to the Mujahedeen in Afghanistan."

Cass raised a finger and said, "So, through this partnership I would assume that his corporation is..."

"Entirely exempt from taxation," Bombay said.

Cass looked through the remaining contents of the folder quickly, skipping large sections; she didn't find what she was looking for. "Even in Bosnia we had an expat on the ground. You're telling me there is not one single American contact in Warsaw?"

Bombay shook his head. "There was one, about five years ago. He was good."

The jet began to descend noticeably. Cass opened her jaw and popped her ears.

Bombay took another call while Cass waited to find out more.

"One of Ethan Allen's boys," Bombay sighed. "Who in the hell would have guessed that one of the best we ever had working for us would come from a state known only for maple syrup."

"Vermont." Cass smiled.

"We set him up as a student at the University of Warsaw," Bombay said. "His major was International Relations."

"Access to important people," Cass said.

"Exactly," Bombay answered. "Within two semesters he had established contact with dozens of high value assets. We nearly had a network set up but then...we lost him."

"Murdered?"

"Hardly. I'm sure he is still alive, somewhere out there."

Cass waited.

"The freedom got to him." Bombay spoke evasively as the jet hit a high pressure system coming off of the Carpathians as they entered Polish airspace.

Cass started to ask for more information before Bombay interrupted her.

"Listen Cass, forget all of the bullshit in that folder. This is just like Bosnia; you get in, set up and do your best to get the job done. Rodham is going to put you in touch with people, important people. If Bircher makes it to Warsaw, these people will know it, and as soon as they do, it's your job to send up the flares. Our window of opportunity is very short here, Cass. You're going to have to focus!"

Bombay was cut short in his speech by yet another incoming call. Turning without saying anything further to Cass, he walked back to the front of the plane for a more private conversation with whomever was on the other line. Lang seemed to be comfortable in his new seat, and despite taking notice of Bombay's departure, he made no attempt to return to his original place to start another conversation with Cass.

The jet was due to land in a few minutes at a military base that the CIA used frequently. It was also the base where Bircher had been kept prisoner for years. Cass reached into her purse, arranged some items in preparation for landing, checked her mobile, and adjusted her seatbelt. Once she landed, Cass planned to catch some sleep and then spend the evening on base going over localization procedures. The following morning she would be driven south to the city of Kutno, where she would catch the twelve-fifteen Intercity PKP train to Warsaw.

She repeated the names of landmarks, streets and metro stations that she would encounter the next day. Luckily, the city was relatively compact, with one main avenue and only two metro lines. Judging by Bombay's confidence that Bircher probably wouldn't even make it to Warsaw, Cass contemplated her mission little, preferring to dwell instead on her questions of what had happened back at the safe house.

The landing wheels kicked out from the belly of the jet, and with a short and sharp protest, they hit the tarmac and the plane landed. Cass stretched her arms wide above her head as she took long steps to recirculate the blood in her legs. It was still early in the morning, well before dawn, and the sun had not yet begun to appear on the horizon. The air was cold and crisp. Although Cass was incredibly tired, it energized her as it flooded into her lungs.

Another day had passed, and for the most part she had avoided the silence, save for those brief thoughts at the airport before departure. One night without them was better than nothing; she took what she could get.

"Welcome to Poland," Bombay said sarcastically.

VII

"Billy Idol?"

Josie made his inquiry from the Opel Vectra's passenger seat.

"Yes," Tatjana replied as *Eyes Without a Face* played on the radio. The car passed north of the city of Lucko and headed for the Hungarian border on the A65 motorway. "Would you prefer I change the station?"

"Not at all, Tatja," Josie said.

"That is Tatjana." She corrected the informal use of her name.

"Of course." Josie raised his hands apologetically. "Tatjana."

She was cold.

Maybe she was in a bad relationship, had a rough night or maybe Papa was right about her.

Josie looked out of the window into the darkness that passed alongside the empty highway. When Tatjana had arrived, she had not bothered to acknowledge Josie, speaking instead only a few short words to Papa. He had shrugged, shook Josie's hand with an iron grip, then returned beyond the gate to his garden, his scotch and his long-eared rabbit.

Tatjana's features were strong and athletic, boasting sharp feminine cheekbones and toned muscles. Like the majority of Croatian women, her skin settled closer to pale than to tan. Josie had always found it curious that within one or two days of the relentless Balkan sun, his skin darkened drastically, yet the women seemed not to take any color at all.

There was one aspect of a woman that had always piqued Josie's interest. It was not the fullness of the bust or the curves of the hips; rather, it was the sharpened muscle above each knee that ran its way along a woman's legs and sensually tightened up around the inner thigh. While the word *hamstring* admittedly didn't have a sexual or romantic ring to it, it was the one feature that always got his attention, and Tatjana had a splendid pair

"You kept me waiting back in Zadar for over two minutes," Tatjana said. "You were late."

"I was with Papa," Josie said, returning his gaze to her. "We thought you would knock on the gate when you arrived."

"I said I would be there and that I would wait for you outside!"

"Perhaps you were early?" Josie tried a playful tone.

"Perhaps you were late." Tatjana maintained her coldness.

"Maybe you were just eager to meet me?" Josie increased the tension.

"If," Tatjana said, "I was early, the only reason was to get this over with sooner and to get back home to my boyfriend."

"You're driving nearly ten kilometers under the speed limit," Josie observed, gesturing to the speedometer. "Are you sure you're in such a hurry?"

"Would you rather I get pulled over by the police?" Tatjana countered.

"Your boyfriend." Josie ignored her excuse. "Tell me about him?"

"I love him," Tatjana said. "That is all you need to know, that I love him."

"You said it twice. It sounds like you are trying to convince yourself."

Tatjana did not respond.

The Opel turned north, hooking around Zagreb and passing through Sesvete on the way to Ljubescica and the border. Josie watched the small villages pass by in tight groupings separated by large fields and rounded hills. The landscape had changed drastically since Zadar; the sharp, towering limestone cliffs and barren sea-washed shores had been replaced by gentle rising slopes of cultivated land and forest.

"Is it normal to ask such personal questions where you are from?" Tatjana was clearly frustrated by Josie's last remark. "To ask of things which are none of your business?"

"Where I am from? I am not from anywhere, at least not anymore, Tatjana."

"Well, wherever you were from, they must not have taught you anything," Tatjana said. "Anything on how to be polite."

"You have my apologies," Josie said. "And for what you are doing, my appreciation."

"No, I have your money." Tatjana bit back with a sharp inflection in her voice. "You can keep your appreciation. It is not required. I'm not doing this for you, but for my father. He has told me much about you, and while I could care less if you are alive or dead, you mean something to him."

"But mostly it's about the money."

"Of course."

"Your father has also told me about you. He is very proud of you."

Josie had softened her a bit with the remark. He watched as each time he mentioned her father, her defensive posture changed; her eyes watered and she gripped the wheel tighter. She was guilty. Josie knew that as soon as she got him across the border she was going to turn him in.

"If your father has told you about me then I'm sure you could figure out that there is a reward for my capture?" He tested the waters.

Tatjana stared out through the windshield in silence as she drove.

"If I might ask, how much?"

"One hundred thousand." Tatjana's answer was instant.

"Dollars?"

"Dollars."

Josie was genuinely disappointed that the amount was not higher. Quickly calculating, he said, "That would be a little more than a half a million Croatian kuna."

"I'm not having second thoughts, Mr. Bircher," she lied, tapping the steering wheel with her fingers.

"Josie," he said.

"I'm not having second thoughts, Josie," Tatjana repeated.

"I trust your father."

"He trusts you, but he trusts too many people."

"And you are a woman. So you don't trust anyone?"

"Correct."

"Just yourself, then?"

Tatjana didn't answer. Her hands were starting to shake. She was starting to have second thoughts. Maybe her boyfriend had convinced her to do it, had told her he needed the money and to turn Josie in. Whatever the reason, it was too late to turn around and the tighter she gripped the wheel, the more guilt she felt.

"I'm paid to get you across the border," Tatjana said. "Nothing more. I can't promise your safety. I will only get you across."

"You wouldn't happen to have any chewing gum, would you?" Josie changed the subject suddenly.

Tatjana looked confused. "Gum?"

"Yes."

She reached behind the seat and retrieved her handbag. It was dark and she struggled to maintain the Opel in the proper lane, swerving back and forth between the lines as she fumbled through her bag. Keys rattled, plastic tubes of face crème hit against lipstick containers and eyeliner brushes. The bag sat in the center console on top of the emergency brake. Josie acted as if he took little notice but an important question had just been answered. She did not have a gun.

"Here," she said, finally producing an entire pack of gum. "Anything else?"

"Just the gum," Josie said as he unfolded the wrapper and began to chew. "Thank you."

Dawn grew restless at the horizon and the highway was deserted as they passed the exits for Varazdin and Cakovec, the last major cities before the Hungarian border.

"I'm sure my father mentioned that it's not possible to cross through Slovenia." Tatjana said, breaking the silence.

"I believe he called them..." Josie started.

"Bastards." Tatjana answered for him. "They act like they are the guardians of Europe, the Slovenes. They were never part of us, they were never real Yugoslavs. You know they are almost as bad as the Germans."

"I see you share at least that sentiment with your father."

"Have you ever been to Germany?"

"Yes," Josie confirmed, his eyes looking at the changing sky. "A long time ago."

"How long?"

"The Wall was still there."

"My father did not tell me that you were a soldier.

"I was - in another life."

"What were you doing in that other life?"

"Back in Berlin?" Josie paused for a moment. "I was making plans to cross The Wall."

"I see you never made it, as I'm sure the Stasi would have shot you on sight if you had even attempted."

"Actually," Josie said with laughter in his voice. "I did make it across."

Tatjana glanced at Josie in the shadows of the car as the light from the small villages shone across his face in long bars broken by the edges of his cheekbones.

"You were risking a lot," Tatjana said. "Was it a woman, then?"

"Not quite. It was for love, but not my own."

Tatjana loosened her fingers on the wheel. Josie could hear her breathing begin to slow and noticed her outstretched limbs soften.

"It started a few weeks after the Allies took Berlin. The Soviets shot down a P-51 Mustang they claimed had crossed into their airspace. They were lying."

"Propaganda? How can you be so sure?"

"My grandfather was the pilot," Josie said. "He crash-landed into a small field outside of Feldheim."

Tatjana looked down.

Josie waved his hand. "He survived."

Tatjana nodded.

"She didn't have a name, but I know he loved her. He told me that he watched her crash into that field below him as the winds underneath his parachute pushed him back towards the West. He never saw her again, and as a child I remember the way he used to tell me those stories as if she were still out there flying somewhere above the front lines. He wouldn't admit she was really gone." Josie paused and cast his eyes down for a moment before catching a reflection in the rear view mirror. The mountains that guarded the coast had just been summited by the first light of the dawn. The border was close. He still had time.

"Of course, as a child you don't understand that it's not really about the plane. It's about the war, about watching all of his friends get shot to hell and finally, it's about being an old man and realizing everyone and everything that you have ever known is dead, and no matter what you do, they won't ever come back."

Tatjana had changed. She had softened completely. She looked at Josie and listened.

"I made promises as a boy," Josie said. "It's the only thing you can do when you are helpless. And the promise I made was that one day, one way or another, I was going to get that plane back."

"Berlin?" Tatjana asked.

"The Glorious Shrine to Soviet Victory in the Great Patriotic War," Josie mocked. "Well, that wasn't really the name of the museum where they displayed my grandfather's crashed Mustang, but it is close enough. The building was less than a kilometer away from where I was stationed. The only thing that separated me from getting back that plane was The Wall."

Tatjana turned as if to ask him another question but stopped short.

"He was dead by then." Josie answered what was on her mind. "Didn't matter, didn't change my promise."

"You really crossed The Wall, then?" Tatjana signaled and took an exit off the highway. "How?"

"Passport. I traded a pair of Levi Strauss jeans for it at a disco a block away from the Brandenburg Gate." Josie smiled. "I was an Olympian, the pride of East Germany."

"An Olympian?"

"Took the Silver in '84," Josie said casually.

Tatjana looked at him and raised an eyebrow.

"Why not the Gold, you ask?" Josie said. "Some freedom-loving American beat me."

"If I remember correctly the Olympic athletes in East Germany led very privileged lives," Tatjana said.

"Very true. They also had one thing many East Germans never had, and that was the freedom to cross The Wall."

"It was raining," Josie continued. "I remember the rain more than anything. Everything was grey - the street, the buildings, the sky. It was like a painting."

"Caillebotte?" Tatjana asked.

"Not quite." Josie laughed. "Once I crossed through the border checkpoint I walked a block or two, turned around, and for the first time I realized that I was looking at something most Americans had never seen: the other side."

The Opel Vectra drove across the Trnava River. Tatjana was calm and relaxed. She was right where Josie wanted her.

"The first time that I was standing there and staring back, it really hit me. Only then did I understand what I had gotten myself into. Everyone else was trying to get the hell out of the Bloc; I was the only fool risking his life to get in!"

"Once you knew that the plane was there at the museum, you must have known that The Wall wouldn't last forever. Couldn't you have just..."

"Waited?" Josie asked. "I was twenty years old; the word *wait* wasn't even in my vocabulary."

A small road sign announced that they had entered the village of Domasinec. The border was less than a kilometer away.

"Besides a few school children and an old curator, the museum was empty."

"You found the plane?" Tatjana asked.

"At the top of the stairs, make a right, follow the hallway until it stops, and make a left," Josie said, his finger tracing the path against the dashboard. "All that the Soviets could pull from the wreckage had been neatly placed in a dimly lit display case that was in need of dusting."

He wound his window down to allow the crisp morning air to enter. Fog began to lift from the soil and the trees surrounding the village cast dark shadows. For a moment, it seemed uncertain if morning would ever arrive.

"There was a painting above the case of a P-51 in flight." Josie took a breath of the fresh air. "After all those years, after all of those stories, to see it right in front of me made it seem as if it all had happened in only a day or so. It seemed..."

"It seemed impossible for you?" Tatjana asked.

"As a child, yes." Josie agreed. "It was distant and abstract. While I stood there separated only by a small panel of glass....well....to be honest, it was a bit disappointing."

"It was too easy?"

"Yes," Josie shrugged. "In a way it was. There was no shootout with the Stasi, no international incident, not even one intercontinental ballistic missile was launched. There was only the rain outside, the worn faded carpets, an old water heater that ticked constantly and a few scraps of steel in a case from my grandfather's Mustang. It was almost like a movie set: each prop was perfectly in place, yet everything was so anticlimactic that if it had been a film, I would have wanted my money back."

Tatjana looked as if she understood.

"There is a small plot of land," Josie finished. "A grave actually. It faces a mountain just outside of a small village in Alaska. Not many people know about this grave, but I do."

Tatjana held her breath.

"On the headstone there is a small square piece of steel. It is the last bit that was left of the propeller of the plane. I put it there. I kept my promise."

Tatjana fought to restrain a tear.

There were no more signs for the border and the road had long ago turned into dirt. The village passed and nothing but forested lots and open fields misted through the dawn.

Josie let the silence clear for a moment before he asked, "Are we close to Letenye? I believe your father said we would cross there?"

"We are not crossing at Letenye," Tatjana said, clearing her throat. "It's too much of a risk. There is a better crossing."

"Possibly one not on the map?"

"Exactly. During our fight for Independence, we were forced to find alternative sources for even basic items like food and medicine."

"Weapons as well?"

"Of course. The largest manufacturer of Yugoslavian arms was Zastava in Serbia. We had Karlovac of course, but the Serbs quickly destroyed the city."

Josie reached down and tied his shoes as he listened calmly. He double knotted the laces.

"Hungary was the only entry point for us. Truthfully, the Serbs needed the crossings just as much as we did. They got their heavy weapons from Russia, we got ours from the Germans, and the Hungarians made money."

"You were a driver?" Josie understood.

"I was," Tatjana replied and then nodded. "I guess I still am."

A vast field of sunflowers cut through the mist and soon towered high alongside the roadway surrounding the Opel, their leaves brushing up against the door panels.

"The Hungarians made the most from the war, from these crossings, from what they let pass into Yugoslavia. Where we will cross was our main crossing point fifty years ago, before the highway from Budapest to Zagreb was ever even thought of."

"I would venture that the villagers know."

"They do," Tatjana said, her eyes peering straight ahead. "How else do you think they could make any money in a place like this?"

A large concrete foundation came into view alongside the road. Next to it was what seemed to be an old radio tower that had collapsed long ago. What the vegetation hadn't entirely claimed was left bleached and covered with graffiti. There was a guard booth further along; classically shaped, it looked better suited for downtown Miami with its art deco lines rather than sitting here in ruin in the middle of a field in Croatia.

As the Opel passed by the booth, Josie was reminded that the only borders that exist are the ones created by men. The soil beneath the tires of the Vectra was the same - the trees, the sky and the air, it was all just an imaginary line, but it was a line that people would give their lives for even though it meant nothing at all. The crossing happened so fast that if Josie had chosen to blink he would have missed it. Line or no line, Josie had just entered the Fortress.

"Tatja," Josie said as the Opel continued along the dirt road through the field. "They won't shoot you, will they?"

She turned her face to Josie. She was crying. She shook her head. "No."

Josie nodded.

"How long have you known?"

"A couple of hours now," Josie said. "As soon as I mentioned your father, as soon as I mentioned admiration."

Tatjana looked down as the car slowed.

"What can I expect?" Josie asked. "How many of them are there?"

"I don't know." Tatjana brushed a tear from her cheek with the back of her hand. "Six or seven."

"Who are they?"

"Ustashe."

"Militia." Josie stated. "Searchlights?"

"Yes."

"Kalashnikovs?"

"Yes."

"Dogs?"

"Maybe," Tatjana said. "I'm not sure."

"Where are they?" Josie asked.

"Do you see where the road turns up ahead?" Tatjana motioned to a corner only ten meters away.

Josie nodded.

"How could you?" Tatjana asked. "How could you tell me about your grandfather even though you knew what I was going to do?"

"You're too hard on yourself, Tatja." Josie shrugged. "My grandfather died before I was even born, never met the man. He lived in Pittsburgh on the same block his entire life and I would be damned if he ever flew in a plane."

"Then why..." Tatjana started.

"First, I needed you to relax. You were so damn nervous I wasn't even sure that you could keep the car on the road, let alone keep it between the lines. Secondly, I needed your trust, and thirdly, I needed your guilt." Josie was smiling. "How else do you think I was going to get you to tell me where they were waiting?"

Tatjana tried to act brave and act furious but she couldn't because the feeling of guilt was still there. She felt used and naked, and as much as she hated the man across the center console from her, she hated herself more. Her father had trusted her. She had let him down.

"You've done your part," Josie said. "As you mentioned, your job was to get me across the border - nothing more, nothing less. You've done all I have required. The money is yours."

"How can you be so casual?" Tatjana hissed. "You're not exactly a free man yet."

"Casual? When I was a child, one of my first memories was watching two men play chess together at a park in the Upper East Side of New York City."

Tatjana listened. The corner of the field was only a few meters away.

"I remember that one of them told me that all I had to do to win the game was to think four steps ahead. After that it was a guarantee."

"Four steps ahead?" Tatjana repeated.

"So from that day forward I always told myself if I was four steps ahead, I would always win."

"In chess?"

"In life," Josie responded.

"It's impossible," Tatjana said, her hands shaking now on the wheel. "Life is not a game, Josie, it's not your game of chess! You can't plan everything in life."

"Almost everything."

"Except?"

"The weather, of course," Josie shrugged. "The weather and the Russians - you can never tell what the hell they are going to do."

"On a rainy day in Moscow, then?" Tatjana asked.

"Well," Josie said. "Sometimes all you have left to count on is luck."

Massive sunflower heads loomed high above the damp road, wrapping the car in darkness and blocking the dawn's early light. In the distance, back on the Croatian side of the border, a church bell rang out once and then everything was silent again. Tatjana was still crying. Josie produced the small silver paper that his gum had been packed in, opened it up, and spit his gum in it.

A brilliant white spotlight filled the car with a clear penetrating light, creating a momentary sensation as if the vehicle was on fire. Tatjana shielded her eyes as men began shouting and the unmistakable sound of a Kalashnikov bolt being charged back and slapped forward was heard.

At least five men rushed forward, each of them wielding an assault rifle with their fingers on the triggers. Amid the shouting and commotion, the one sound that could not be heard was the baying of dogs, as there were none present.

One man stood before the rest next to the Opel. He was massive; he wore a leather jacket, denim jeans, cowboy boots and a pair of chrome spurs. His jacket was unbuttoned and the glint of a stainless steel revolver rested at his side. It took only seconds, but his eyes adjusted from the spotlight and focused on the car right in front of him. Tatjana had her head down on the wheel crying. The passenger side door was open. Josie was long gone.

VIII

Al-Dhi'b sat on the floor. Black zip ties were locked tight in place around his wrists and a blindfold was secured to his face. These and the headphones positioned tightly against his ears had remained in place for hours since the flight. He was in the middle of a concrete cell; a wooden table was before him and a steel door was to his right. Directly behind him was a pane of one-way glass.

Cass was behind the glass, at a plastic table with a cup of black coffee in front of her and a Turkish cigarette in her hand. Two Polish intelligence officers were sitting at the table as well. One of them was leaning back in his chair with his legs crossed, while the other tapped his fingers on the table in an offbeat pattern that annoyed Cass. Neither of the men had tried to start a conversation with her. They probably didn't speak English and she was not going to volunteer the information that she spoke their language.

The two men observed the prisoner. Cass, on the other hand, let her eyes wander in no particular direction. The lack of sleep was apparent around her swollen eyes. The pulses made by her eyelids reminded her how tired she was; despite her best efforts, when the jet landed, she had been unable to sleep. She was too exhausted to think about anything but rest, and hoped that the interrogation would be over quickly so she could try to find some place to close her eyes and try her luck with the Sandman one more time.

Minutes passed inside the cell and nothing changed. The prisoner moved little, only occasionally swaying from side to side in obvious discomfort from the music. Cass extinguished the first cigarette and lit another as the two Polish officers started a heated conversation about a soccer match between rival teams Wisla and Legia that was being played in the evening.

Footsteps arrived from down the hall. They belonged to Lang. Seeing Cass, he smiled and pulled up a metal folding chair next to her. She had a feeling that her chances of getting any sleep before the train ride to Warsaw were rapidly diminishing. She looked at Lang apathetically; Cass felt that he was nice enough - but that he was just bad at reading human emotion, a curious trait for an interrogator. He was the type of person who couldn't take a hint, and who didn't really care if you were listening so as long as he could hear himself talk.

Cass wondered why she did this to herself. Why did she push people away? Why was the thing that she so desperately needed in life the one thing that she never gave people a chance to provide? She judged everyone, built up walls, and kept everyone else on the other sides. The only person who had ever gotten past the walls was Juka, the man she had cancelled dinner with the night before in Mostar.

"Wolves," Lang said, tapping his fingers above her knee, dangerously close to her thigh. "We got it out of him right after the plane landed."

Cass was silent. The two fingers that held her cigarette rested on her temple as she closed her eyes for a few moments.

Lang continued.

"Sometimes it's boats or planes." He shrugged. "Other times - quite understandably - it is snakes or spiders."

Cass opened her eyes and took a long sip of her coffee.

"You know," Lang laughed to himself, "two years ago, we picked up some bomb maker outside of Tikrit, and for him, it was butterflies. Can you believe that shit? Goddamned butterflies!"

"Everyone is afraid of something," Cass offered, understanding where the conversation was going.

"Almost everyone," Lang said. "There was one...Harkem...we never broke him."

Cass raised an eyebrow. Lang had gotten her attention.

"It was in his eyes," Lang said.

"What?" Cass asked, trying to sound casual. "What was in his eyes?"

"Nothing," Lang answered. "Nothing at all. There was no pain....no fear."

An uncomfortable silence grew. as Cass stared at him. She wanted to ask Lang everything he knew about Harkem, but before she could start, Lang continued his monologue on fear.

"The Agency catalogs fear," Lang said. "All of the torture in the world won't get you anywhere unless there is fear."

"You mentioned al-Dhi'b is afraid of..." Cass gently prodded, shifting forward in her chair as she began to take interest.

"Yes," Lang picked up. "Wolves. There is some Middle Eastern tale of a wolf that takes human form during certain times of the year and eats little children that wander too far off into the desert at night."

"Something like a werewolf?"

"Something like that. His father told him these tales when he was a child. Inside his mind he retains that childhood fear.

"The new technique," Cass asked, disappointed in the simplicity of the method. "It's fear?"

"Of course. It even works better than LSD!"

Cass looked at him in disbelief.

"While certainly pain and discomfort will get you the results you need, you'd be surprised but it's actually quite a long process. Of course there is some fear and apprehension for the detainee, but it's just not the same. What we are talking about here is different. Its primal fear."

"Primal fear?" Cass echoed.

"It's the fear that has been passed down through your genes, your DNA. The stuff that kept your ancestors alive: picture the man in the cave clutching a wooden club and hiding behind a fire from whatever waits for him out there in the night."

Cass nodded as she finished her cigarette.

"The problem is that now, there is no use for these fears. No real place for them in society. Look at how many people back home in the States are medicated - over two hundred million, all of them walking zombies. Listen, the last saber tooth tiger died thousands of years ago, yet plenty of people are still afraid of open spaces."

"Open spaces," Cass thought out loud. "Where they would be exposed and too far from shelter."

"Exactly," Lang said.

"Another example?" Cass was inwardly surprised at her curiosity.

"Here is a perfect one," Lang replied, shuffling excitedly in his chair. "An Army Sergeant, EOD, gets a call about a roadside bomb discovered on a highway going into Baghdad."

Cass listened intently.

"His team pulls up to the site, gets out and sets up a perimeter. The only problem is there is not an IED to be found. So the Sergeant walks back to his Humvee and does a radio check to verify the location."

"HQ gets back to him and confirms that his team is in the right place. He puts the radio away, turns around and just happens to glance down between his boots. Sticking out of the dirt under his feet are six 155mm artillery shells daisy-chained together. Now what do you think the first thing he did was?"

"Freeze?"

"Close, that was the second thing he did. The first thing he did was piss himself. Literally."

"Primal fear."

"Of course!" Lang smiled. "Do you know why people piss themselves when they are frightened?"

"I've never given it much thought," Cass admitted.

"It's so that whatever is about to eat us will find us suddenly unpalatable," Lang said. "Growing up as a boy in South Carolina, every damned snake I ever picked up pissed himself for the same reason. Humans are no different."

Cass shifted in her chair.

"Back to my point," Lang continued. "There is no longer a requirement for this fear. It's outdated, useless. Those artillery shells were not going to eat him, and whether he pissed himself or not, it would have had nothing to do with preventing that bomb from atomizing the Sergeant and everyone else within a few city blocks.

Lang paused to tap Cass's knee again, a bit higher than the last time, then continued, "Luckily for us and the Agency, there is still enough fear to exploit."

As if on cue, the door behind the prisoner opened. The man with the crayons entered the room. He looked apathetic as he put his briefcase down and set up a small projector on the table. After getting the projector in operation, he walked over to the prisoner and removed his blindfold, signaled and the lights abruptly went off in the room. The projector displayed its contents on a concrete wall before the prisoner.

The images were troubling, and even slightly nauseating to Cass. The slideshow continued for nearly twenty minutes. Each scene of wolves hunting and consuming their prey was progressively more detailed that the last. Cass noticed that from time to time that the man with the crayons would roughly grab the back of the prisoner's neck and shake it from side to side.

Eventually the projector stopped and the lights were turned back on. The prisoner's blindfold had already been returned to its place.

"It's called priming," Lang offered.

"The prisoner doesn't seem to be suffering too much," Cass noted.

"He is suffering much more than it seems. I will bet my bottom dollar that this Haji will be telling us all we need to know within the hour. If not, we'll wait till tonight, take him out into the forest, past the hangar, and tie him to a tree. Out there, those images will be with him when he is all alone."

"Why was your partner touching his neck?"

"Primal reinforcement. Wolves, and as a matter of fact most predatory animals, kill their prey with one swift bite to the neck. By grabbing the prisoner's neck, an attack is simulated, and this triggers adrenaline to surge from his brain, reinforcing the images that it is receiving from his eyes."

"So how is this method any easier than waterboarding?"

"In every way," Lang said confidently. "Anyone can get information in a matter of seconds by inflicting severe pain."

"The issue?"

"The issue with it is that they will tell you anything to make it stop. With just a wooden Popsicle stick I could get anyone to admit that they shot JFK. I could even get a Haji to admit to eating pork!" Lang said.

"So..." Cass started.

"Simply put, no matter how much pain you put a prisoner through, there are still secrets that they keep, not because they wouldn't tell you, but because we wouldn't know to ask about them. With this new method we don't even have to ask. Plus weeks upon weeks of interrogation takes its toll on everyone, and sometimes you don't have that long."

"How long is this new method?"

"As I mentioned, the hardest part was finding what he was afraid of. After that we will have everything we need within twenty four hours at the most."

"Does the prisoner recover?"

"That is the other benefit. They typically recover in a week or two," Lang said proudly. "During development we may have pushed it a bit too far and a few of them hung themselves after they were interrogated, but we have gotten that all sorted out now. The last thing this President needs is more pictures to get leaked like they were from Guantanamo. Essentially this fear was already present in the detainee, we only amplified it."

"So this was it? That is everything?"

"Not at all. What I have told you is for when we want him to tell the truth. Right now we just want to get him used to talking."

Cass shot Lang a look of annoyance.

"Think of it again as priming," Lang said.

"So you are going to torture him?"

Lang shook his head back and forth as if debating with himself. "Some would say it is... others wouldn't."

Cass looked back to the window.

The man with the crayons walked up to the prisoner once more and Cass took a breath in anticipation of some violent act about to be inflicted upon the blindfolded al-Dhi'b, but the interrogator simply reached down and adjusted the prisoner's position, tucking one of his legs under the other. He then sat down in the chair and began to color.

"What in the..." Cass released her breath.

"Paresthesia," Lang offered. "Pins and needles."

"Pins and needles?" Cass asked as if it were a joke.

"It's worse than it seems," Lang defended.

Cass rolled her eyes.

"Seriously," Lang insisted. "We start with the legs, and then move up to the arms, then onto individual joints and muscles. By the time it's over, al-Dhi'b will be in tears begging us to stop."

Cass looked over to the man with the crayons. He had his coloring book out again. She watched as just as before in the jet, he carefully selected each color from the carton. His strokes were slow and careful and never strayed over the printed boundaries. The crayons triggered something in her suddenly. It had been awhile since her last episode, but now she felt the room begin to spin. She stood up, nearly lost her balance, and knocked the empty cup of coffee over in the process of running to the door.

The bathroom was at the end of the hall. She had to stop herself twice in panic to take a breath and keep herself from gagging. The black and white checkerboard tile flooring made her dizzy and the smell of the industrial cleaner on the floor made her cough. She barely made it in time.

After she purged herself she limped to the sink. The water spat and protested as it came out of the faucet. It was dirty, cold, and smelled like sulfur, but Cass did not care. She reached her hands under the water and returned them to her face with a freezing splash. Kneeling on the bathroom floor, she pushed the top of her forehead into the edge of the sink.

It was something that reminded her of what her mother had done when Cass was a child. She would pick Cass up and push her chin onto her forehead. It was peculiar but it worked. It was Cass's security blanket, one she still needed from time to time as an adult and for now the edge of the sink would have to do. She began to cry as memories overwhelmed her.

Cass was only nine when she found the telescope in the attic buried underneath a mountain of rock wool insulation. It was dated but it had a tripod and a few eyepieces with it. While the telescope would hardly reveal the craters on the moon, its aperture was large enough to keep a child entertained. Cass spent the first few days studying the birds in the trees and making small sketches. Later, she watched the mailman on his route through the neighborhood, and within a little over a week, she turned the lens into the bedroom of the house next door.

She never looked at the birds again.

It was a childhood curiosity that turned into an adult obsession. While she had always debated with herself whether it could be classified as an addiction, she could usually convince herself that it was harmless and that she was in control. She knew she was addicted. Like most voyeurs, Cass didn't require nudity or intercourse; just watching someone in the privacy of their own home was erotic enough that it satisfied her needs.

As a lonely child looking out of her bedroom window, she learned many things from behind the lens. She learned about life, love and about pain. In that house next door, there was a young girl. Cass would watch her play with her dolls, comb her hair, brush her teeth or color with crayons. Cass felt at times as if she was in that house playing with her best friend.

Cass also learned about violence through that lens but she was helpless, herself just a child, and there was nothing she could do to help her friend in the following weeks or the coming years of abuse.

Years later, when Cass was in Junior High, her mother told her that the family next door was moving. Parents and teachers tried to ignore the truth; they said anything they could to stop the rumors, behind which Cass was chained to the truth of what she knew. It would be two weeks before the police issued a report to the local newspaper that the girl Cass had watched all those years had been found alongside the railroad tracks. She had committed suicide by stepping in front of the morning freight train.

When she heard the news, Cass ran to her mother, rested her forehead on her chin and cried. They did not speak, only embracing for as long as Cass had needed. She had to cope with her first experience of death and the lonely thoughts that come with it. When tragedy strikes, some people tend to form pacts or write promises to themselves to do such things as enjoy life each day, never be afraid, or to always stand up for what is right. Such pacts are soothing and true in the moment, and on that night so many years ago, Cass made a promise never to stand by again while others suffered.

As time passes the pain often fades, and while Cass and her telescope continued to search the night, she had nearly forgotten about her childhood, until she saw the crayons. As the water rushed from the faucet in the bathroom, Cass remembered her promise. She gripped the edges of the sink, rose from her knees and swung her head forward, staring hard into her own eyes in the mirror. Cass knew what she had to do. She had to keep her promise. She couldn't stand by while others were going to die. She had to kill Harkem.

"Cass," Bombay intoned, standing in the doorway. "Your train leaves soon, it's time to go."

A string of floss raced back and forth between his teeth as he leaned on the frame of the door. She did not know how long he had been there, how much he had seen. She did not care.

"Yes. I'm ready," Cass answered. She turned off the water and brushed past him into the hallway.

Bombay did not mention the incident in the bathroom as he followed her. Instead, he focused on the mission, and after he finished one more of his lectures, he said, "You will remember what I've told you about Rodham?"

"Of course," Cass acknowledged. "I understand. He is not to be trusted."

"Good," Bombay said as they walked out into a parking garage. "The damn Brits have their own agenda. He is no different. We need him to give you the names of those contacts."

Cass nodded while opening the door to a dated red Lada. She glanced from it to Bombay.

"It's the best they could do on short notice." Bombay shrugged. "Get in."

"How long are you staying in Poland?" Cass asked as she buckled her seatbelt.

"I will be flying out within the hour," Bombay lied. "As soon as I return from the train station."

"What about Gibbs? I haven't heard from him."

"Don't worry about Gibbs. The mission. Focus on the mission. Focus on Bircher."

"The briefing did not mention the duration of my stay in Warsaw."

"You will be there as long as it takes until we get Bircher."

"Will I return to Bosnia after?"

"No." Bombay offered no further explanation.

"What about Harkem?" Cass asked, nearly spitting out the name.

"He is not your concern." Bombay brushed off the question. "The Ambassador is safe."

Cass pushed further. "Why isn't he dead by now? Why haven't we taken him out?"

Bombay was caught off guard. "Harkem?"

Cass glared at Bombay.

"Bircher," Bombay said. "Focus on Bircher. We've got to get this bastard!"

She watched the morning sun rise high above the small villages as the Lada drove down a long dirt road. Each little town they passed was poor and drab. The grass itself seemed depressed and lonely, as if frustrated that the winds had carried its seed to such a place. Even the villages in Bosnia reminded Cass of something closer to the twentieth century than any of the ones that passed by her window now.

Bombay took a call and cursed a clutch of chickens obstructing the road. As they approached the city of Kutno, Cass tried again.

"Harkem."

"Drop it," Bombay ordered in a patriarchal tone.

Cass was furious but she said no more.

Kutno was grey and the air was heavy with smoke and diesel fumes. Graffiti was the only decoration on every building: no brick seemed untouched. The train station was nothing more than a raised concrete platform with a blue and white framed sign denoting the name of the city. A few switch houses rested off the end of the platform and the entire area was deserted except for an old vagabond lying on a bench. He could have been sleeping. He could have been dead.

Bombay had stopped the car by a set of metal stairs leading up to the platform. Cass took the ticket and her backpack and stepped out from the Lada.

"Remember, Cass," Bombay said, his eyes focused on his phone as he sent a text message. "Remember about Rodham!"

Cass wanted to slam the door. She wanted to rip the phone out of his hand and throw it into the field by the tracks. She wanted to reach into his shirt pocket, grab the pack of dental floss and crush it under her boot. Instead, Cass shut the door softly and Bombay drove away.

She climbed the stairs. Bombay was right. She knew that she needed to focus. Focus on her mission. Focus on killing Harkem.

The Agency issued automatics had always left her desiring more power, and long ago she traded her Glock 17 for a .357 Magnum with a Secret Service agent she had met in Germany. The Magnum was small and snub-nosed and it was more easily concealed than the Glock. While Cass did not know how she would even find Harkem, she felt confident that the jacketed hollow points would do their job. She would not order Harkem to stop or to raise his hands. She would not handcuff him or take him in and most certainly she would not look into his eyes. Cass did not care if she had to shoot him in the middle of downtown Warsaw during rush hour. She was going to do it for all of the people that he had killed, for the world, for her own loneliness, and for the promise she had made to that little girl who she couldn't save all those years ago.

IX

Two men stood on the corner. The younger one towered over the older man, his hands clenched into fists and shouting. He wore a black tracksuit; it was a Chinese knock-off of an American brand, and instead of having the correct number of stripes, it had a single white band running down its entire length. Everyone in the village privately referred to him as the Skunk in reference to the comical appearance the tracksuit gave him. The Skunk was not comical, however. He was a dangerous and unpredictable enforcer for a man known as the Mayor.

"Tell me, you old fool!" The Skunk demanded. "When did you hear the news of the stranger in the village?"

"This morning," the old man answered nervously, looking down to the sidewalk and avoiding eye contact. "Yes, yes it was this morning. The women who live by the border told me."

"Where did he come from?" The Skunk cracked his knuckles.

"No one knows. The women said that he arrived this morning from the mountains."

"From the mountains?" The Skunk scoffed. "There is nothing out there for nearly one hundred kilometers!"

"The women have said that..."

A clenched fist caught the old man in his chest mid-sentence and he fell to the sidewalk, gasping for air. Two sharp kicks followed and nearly knocked him unconscious, while the people walking by on the street looked away.

"See what happens when you listen to old women?" The Skunk spat and stepped back for another kick.

"I've seen him!" The old man exclaimed, holding his hands high above his head.

The Skunk restrained his kick. He knelt down and helped his victim to his feet. "You said you have seen him? Why didn't you tell me before?"

"I have seen him," the old man confirmed again, finding his balance. "Just for a moment. Only a moment."

"What did you see?" the Skunk asked, continuing to fake kindness.

"His eyes," the old man replied, his voice shaking. "It is all that I can remember. There was no life in those eyes, nothing. Only darkness."

The Skunk stepped back and began to crack his knuckles again. "I don't believe you. What did he look like?"

"*The eyes. Only the eyes.*"

"What else?" The Skunk tightened his body as if to spring upon his victim again.

The old man shook his head.

"Tell me!" The Skunk demanded, hitting his fist into his palm.

Silence.

"Nothing?" The Skunk stood in disbelief. "Nothing at all?"

The old man shook his head again. His frail hands tended to the flowers in his cart that he sold on the corner.

"Bastard!" The Skunk said. "You are useless! It doesn't matter. The Mayor will find him. You will see."

The old man felt confident that the only reason he was not struck again was because he had maneuvered around his small flower cart and was momentarily out of reach. His body ached where he had been struck, but his mind was far from the thoughts of pain. He felt the eyes of the stranger staring at him from every corner on every street, from out on the fields and behind the shadows of the forest. He was afraid.

"You have sold some flowers today?" The Skunk tossed a few cut stems at him.

"There were two funerals this morning."

The Skunk paused for a moment as he struggled to complete the basic addition in his head. Settling on a number, he extended his hand, demanding his fee. "Fifty zloty."

"I have only made thirty-two zloty today! It is all I have!"

The Skunk closed the distance, rounded the cart and grabbed ahold of the old man with both of his hands.

The Old Man was no longer frightened, just sad. He remembered how the village was once beautiful, and that everyone knew each other and all of the children would laugh and play upon the very street where he stood. It was a memory too distant. He also remembered his first girlfriend, television, and first Western movie he had ever seen. He remembered peace and happiness.

The Mayor changed all of that.

In the ruins of communism, the Mayor simply appeared one day without announcement or explanation. The villagers who raised objection to his unelected post were at first bought off, and then those who continued to protest were one by one met with unfortunate accidents.

Soon houses became vacant and covered in graffiti, garbage littered the street, windows to local businesses were broken and walking outside after nightfall became a gamble of personal safety. The police had been bought and paid for by the Mayor and took little notice of the protests from the villagers. Rumors spread from family to family and all were certain that a curse had fallen upon the village. In reality there was nothing mysterious or cursed about the Mayor. He was simply a typical Eastern Bloc bully with too much power and no one around with the will to stop him.

From a population of over three thousand before his arrival, the town was reduced to a shadow of its former self with only a hundred residents electing to stay. Most had left quietly, hoping for a fresh start in the cities of Katowice or Wroclaw further to the north. Those who stayed were either too poor to move or too scared to do anything but wake up each morning, put their heads down, and hope to make it through another day.

Most thought that the Mayor profited from the protection money that his men such as the Skunk collected from the local vendors. Even those within his inner circle felt confident that his wealth was acquired from such business. No one knew that the Mayor was actually not even Polish. He was a Ukrainian paid to keep the only road that led across the border closed. The road led to the prison, Svoboda.

The old man was still in the hands of the Skunk, who took nearly all of what he had in his wallet. The old man remembered watching those American cowboy Westerns as a child. He wished that a lone rider on a pale horse would one day ride into town with his Peacemakers and shoot the Mayor and his men down in the street. In every possible way he wished that he could be that man. But he sold flowers on the corner, sadly he was not a gunfighter.

Hours later, long after darkness claimed the village, the Skunk sat behind the wheel of a Mercedes G-Class SUV. The Mayor sat beside him in the passenger's seat and behind them both, nearly filling the entire backseat of the Mercedes, sat a massive bear of a man wearing a leather jacket. A black nightstick rested in his palms.

A dense forest of pines encircled the parked vehicle. There was a clearing in the distance, empty save for a pair of old rails that ran through its center, serving as the last reminder that years before, there had been prosperous mines further up in the mountains.

"You're sure he will pass here? Maybe he will wait back in the village until morning?" the Skunk asked, breaking the silence.

The Mayor did not reply.

"Maybe he turned around? Maybe he..." The Skunk's increasing nervousness was apparent in his voice.

"Patience." The Mayor held up a finger. "Patience."

The Skunk restrained himself from asking more questions. Silence returned to the vehicle.

"When the stranger arrives," the Mayor said, after a few minutes had passed, "just be ready."

The Mayor knew that the stranger was last seen in the forest heading up to the old mines. From there, he could follow the rusted rails north to lead him past the very clearing which they were staring at through the windshield. If the stranger made it past them, there would be nothing stopping him from reaching Krakow. From there, he would be free.

Aware that the stranger had been released from the prison across the border, the Mayor wondered what was going on. No one had ever been released before. Ever. Something must have happened. Someone must have played politics or have wanted someone else dead, and while the Mayor didn't have an answer to these questions, he did have an answer for who the stranger was.

Harkem.

The Mayor had never seen Harkem, but had heard plenty. The stories did not impress him. Hardened criminals and government agents alike shook at the mere mention of Harkem's name, but the Mayor cared only about being the meanest son-of-a-bitch around; if someone else laid claim, to that title then it was his duty to bust him and put him in the ground. A golden opportunity had presented itself for the Mayor and his ego, and was plenty confident that he would take Harkem down. The ten bore side by side shotgun that sat across his lap provided extra insurance.

A pressure system had developed in the afternoon and had pushed the clouds east, allowing warm winds to arrive. The air was clear and the stars were out. The humid night made the winter before seem like a bad dream.

"The old fool," the Skunk said. "He is starting to forget how much the price of safety is around here."

"You charged him fifty, yes?" the Mayor said, adjusting the shotgun in his lap.

"Yes. He told me that he only made thirty-two zloty today, but you can't trust that old bastard. He was probably lying."

"He wasn't," the Mayor answered.

"He is starting to talk, to cause trouble in the village," the Skunk said, nervously tapping his fingers on the steering wheel.

"Trouble?" The Mayor laughed. "Go ahead and bust him if you want, but wait until after the holiday."

"I'll bust him good," the Skunk said. "Why wait?"

"He is in business," the Mayor said, staring straight ahead. "He will sell more flowers in the next few days than he will for the rest of the season. We can still use him. Think!"

The Skunk nodded in approval. His mind passed from the old man to the match tonight on television. After these uncomplicated thoughts, his eyes drifted to his reflection in the driver's side mirror. He curled his lips, forced a frown across his face and squinted hard, doing his best to appear menacing and tough. The Skunk thought it worked. Everyone else, including the Mayor, thought that it made him look like an asshole.

The Skunk thought about his scowl.

The Mayor thought about Harkem.

The man in the leather jacket behind them thought about nothing at all.

Suddenly a figure appeared out of the night.

The Mayor calmly opened the glove box and retrieved a Tokarev pistol. He put it on the dashboard and then tightened his grip on the shotgun. The Skunk sat rigidly and held fast with both hands to the seatbelt locked around his chest. The man in the leather jacket cracked his knuckles and stretched the muscles of his massive neck. He was neither afraid nor nervous; he was just waiting for the command.

Turning back to face him, the Mayor gave it. "Crush him."

As he opened the door and stepped out into the dark, the man in the leather jacket appeared to double in size. His frame stretched above the Mercedes and his shoulders seemed to be continually expanding outward. With the nightstick held in his meaty hand, his steps shook the vehicle as he walked in front of it and into the clearing. The figure was now facing the vehicle. He was coming.

The Skunk breathed heavily and tried to tame his runaway heartbeat.

The Mayor started his instructions. "Wait, easy, easy..."

"Now? Yes?" The Skunk was wound tight and ready to act.

"Wait," the Mayor repeated sharply. "Be ready, only ten more meters. When he passes over those rails, hit the lights. It will blind him instantly, he won't stand a chance. With any luck we can dispose of his body in the old mine and be home before the match has even started."

The words from the Mayor brought some reassurance to the Skunk. He looked in the mirror and pursed his lips like an eighties rocker. "It's almost too easy."

"Almost," the Mayor conceded. "Wait, just a few more steps."

The Skunk fingered the keys in the ignition. He could see the two men out there in the night, their forms now distant and vague, yet in only a matter of a few seconds their forms would collide as one violent black mass illuminated by only the stars above.

"Now!"

The Skunk jumped. His right hand reached foolishly across the controls.

The windshield wipers streaked across the windshield.

"Now!" The Mayor hit his fist on the dashboard, nearly knocking the Tokarev onto the floorboards. "Now, you bastard! Now!"

Nothing.

"The lights!" The Mayor was belligerent. "The fucking lights!"

The Skunk looked down in confusion at the controls flanking the steering wheel of the Mercedes as if they were placed in the cockpit of a MiG 29. His brain lost the battle with the adrenaline that flushed through his system. Sweat poured from his shaved head as he finally found the control for the high beams.

"Now!" The Mayor's face was flushed a bright shade of red.

"Got it!" The Skunk cheered.

The lumens from the Mercedes raced out into the night with a searing blast of focused halogen light. Both mens' pupils dilated instantly. Moments passed before their eyes adjusted from the sharp change of black to white. They looked forward to the rails in shock.

The man in the leather jacket was there, just at the far end of the light's reach. He was not in the middle of a brawl, violently delivering the final strikes to Harkem, nor was he standing victorious. In fact, he was not standing at all.

His bloodied and lifeless body rested on the earth. His leather jacket had been torn from him and his legs were sprawled underneath him in the most unnatural position imaginable. He was broken. It was nauseating. The Skunk started dry heaving.

The Mayor rapidly searched the scene before him. Harkem was missing.

The rising body temperatures and perspiration from the two men inside the vehicle misted over the windows and quite suddenly they could not see outside of the Mercedes. The Skunk looked desperately down to the door handle next to him. Fight-or-flight instincts pulsed through his body, and after seeing the busted body across the rails, fighting was not an option. He pulled the keys from the ignition and strained against the seat belt.

The Mayor reached out and grabbed him, pinning him back down in his seat. "Start it!"

There was no response.

"Damn you!" The Mayor grinded his teeth. "Start it! Start the vehicle!"

The Skunk stared forward. Fear glazed over his eyes and they developed a clouded marble hue, almost as if he were dead. The Mayor shook him violently and began shouting. It was of no use. Finally resorting to the butt of his Tokarev pistol, the Mayor struck him in the face.

The vicious strike opened a small laceration across the Skunk's head. He turned to face the Mayor. His eyes were wide and so distended that it appeared as if they would fall free from the sockets.

"Now!" The Mayor screamed, hitting the horn with his fist.

That did it. The Skunk suddenly snapped out of it and reached to the ignition.

The Mayor watched him put one hand on the wheel while the other reached down for the transmission. Just as the Skunk was about to shift the Mercedes into motion, everything seemed to explode.

The vehicle depressurized with such force that all of the air was sucked from the Mayor's lungs. Blinding fragments of metal and glass filled the cabin of the Mercedes so thickly that it was impossible to breathe. The Mayor shielded his face from the exploding driver's side window, thrusting his hands up instinctively with clenched fists.

Struggling to catch his breath as if someone had poured a shockingly cold bucket of water on him, the Mayor inhaled sharply. The vehicle rocked on its struts for a weightless moment before returning to the will of gravity. The Mayor lowered his limbs and opened his eyes.

His arms were pock-marked with red welts where the glass from the window had embedded itself. His ears allowed only a high pitched drone to enter and he was fairly certain his left eardrum had been ruptured from the explosion. The Tokarev was clutched in his hand and it gave him courage. It was his only hope to make it out alive and back to the village to live and fight another day.

The Mayor looked to the driver's seat.

The Skunk was gone.

"Bitch," the Mayor said out loud in disbelief.

Did he cut and run? What about the explosion? Where was he now? More importantly, where was Harkem?

The door remained shut. The keys were in the ignition. The Mayor looked at the blood-soiled glass of the window and noticed that the seat belt was still buckled in place, but where it connected to the frame of the vehicle, it had been torn free.

The Skunk had been dragged out of the window.

It played back in his mind like a slow motion highlight of a great soccer goal. He saw the keys turning in the ignition, the hand about to shift gears, and now, the shadow that had loomed outside of the window the moment before impact.

The windshield and the passenger window were still misted over. Now the Tokarev mattered little as fear rushed into the station of his core like a locomotive behind schedule. He wanted to reach down to the ten bore resting in his lap but in the tight space of the vehicle, its use would be severely limited. The Mayor held onto his Tokarev so tightly that one of the Bakelite grips cracked.

The eyes...I only remember the eyes.

The Mayor recalled the reports from the old women in the village earlier in the day, and he could feel those eyes now.

They appeared from behind every twisted branch and knurled trunk of the pines around him. They were waiting to strike.

A hand streaked across the windshield inches from his face. The Mayor cursed.

Silence.

A scratching sound raced up along the passenger's side, starting from the back of the vehicle and stopping just outside of the Mayor's frosted window. Then a heavy panting came out from the blackness and echoed inside the car, bouncing into the Mayor's ears and destroying any resolve he had left.

The faint noise of glass crunching underfoot could be heard before ceasing at the driver's side door. Seconds passed until the Mayor felt Harkem rapping his knuckles up against the door beside him. The Mayor heard a low wicked laugh, and then he heard the sound of his own door handle being lifted.

All the Mayor had to do was shift his body over the center console, throw the vehicle into drive and step on the accelerator - and he would be free. He knew it was impossible. The broken window framed the blackest night that any man had ever known. Harkem was out there and would rip him apart before he was even planted in the driver's seat. Nonetheless, the Mayor reached out, fumbling with the controls and trying to convince himself that he could actually make the switch and save his life. He hit the wipers and they cleared the window. The lights were still on and shining across the tracks. The Mayor looked forward again at the twisted frame of the man on the rails, then he looked into the rearview mirror. Harkem was in the backseat. The Mayor screamed.

No one could be certain of how long he was there. Some of the villagers thought it had only been one day, while others thought it surely must have been at least six or seven. Whatever the duration was, when they found the Mayor, he was alone in the Mercedes. What was left of his head rested against the passenger window and an empty shotgun shell was found between his legs, but the ten bore that had once rested there was missing, and so was Harkem.

X

A white van with Albanian plates was parked alongside the highway. The passengers were sitting near it in the grass as the van was being searched. Seats were torn free, the spare tire was removed and anything that wasn't bolted in place was soon spread out along the ground. A line of cars with impatient drivers idled behind the van, all waiting to cross into Croatia. They had not moved for what seemed like hours.

Gibbs arrived at the checkpoint, taking note of the van and the large line of vehicles waiting across the border. The Croatian at the guard booth did not bother look up at him as he stamped his passport and handed it back to him. Gibbs was soon racing down a series of long and winding turns as he approached Monte Negro. Getting out of Croatia had been quick and easy, but he knew that getting back in would be difficult and could take hours if not days.

Driving down into the valley below, Gibbs thought about the conversation with Agent White back at the safe house in Mostar. Gibbs was disappointed with himself. Why hadn't he stood up to White? Who the hell did he think he was, anyways? What about Bombay, who knew how close Gibbs was to finding what the Agency was looking for? Why would he waste time and send him to Herceg Novi to pick up the new recruit?

Gibbs rolled down the window as a wash of paranoid thoughts pushed the sweat from his pores. A thick forest of skyscraping Spanish pines flanked the road and eclipsed it, but the dark shadows failed to cool his distressed body. Reaching the floor of the valley, he felt additionally hemmed in by immense walls and sharpened peaks of limestone – and garbage. The coarse road was littered with scraps of steel and bolts of iron that had strayed from the lampposts, burned automobiles, and countless tons of concrete rubble located off the shoulder. Gibbs ignored the debris as it passed by his open window, downshifting when the sign for the border told him that Monte Negro was around the bend.

Despite all of the years he had been searching for it, and all of the countries he had been in, he knew little about what he was actually supposed to find. Some within the Agency referred to it as 'The Site' or 'The Complex,' and in any official intelligence briefings, the location was described by a series of digits that meant nothing at all to him.

There were whispers that The Site was a secret Soviet base that had been abandoned in the nineties and that it held a nuclear tipped intercontinental. Other rumors that circulated by the water cooler were that The Site was actually a series of underground tunnels used by Al-Qaeda to store massive quantities of opium smuggled into Europe. The most outlandish tale that Gibbs had heard was that the location housed an archive of Third Reich documents and secret weapon prototypes.

He didn't believe any of it.

Many leads had led to dead ends. It was easy to find an informant who would tell the Agency anything for a crate-full of US taxpayer-funded greenbacks. Gibbs had followed countless numbers of these leads, each one equally and frustratingly as useless as the last. He merely desired to find the location and complete his mission so that he might finally get the hell out of the Balkans and back to his home in California.

His hope was placed in a Bosnian named Amir.

The vendors of Mostar's Ceberova Street market sell a wide variety of souvenirs, from tin or copper impressions of the Old Bridge and repurposed pens of bullet casings, to pepper mills and handbags. Amir sold t-shirts. It was the stylized *Nightmare on Elm Street* one that caught Gibbs's eye: for an instant in time, he became the distant teenager who had suffered many sleepless nights after a viewing of the movie, but he also recalled riding his bike, walking his dog, and the seasons of childhood. He bought the shirt.

Amir was a character. Gibbs thought with admiration that all Yugoslavs were. Amir talked little of the war, using it only as a plot device in his stories. He talked about how after the Serbs took his house, he broke back in one night and stole back his poster of Christina Applegate. He talked about how during the war he was too scared to get an erection, but after paying for a prostitute and not being able to perform, she tied his manhood to a Popsicle stick so at least he could get inside. Amir had many stories to tell.

Gibbs passed the market often and had numerous conversations with Amir. On one such occasion, Gibbs noticed that when Amir retrieved the car keys from his pocket, there was a curious object attached to them: a square aluminum stopper, the type used by mountain climbers for protection in the event of a fall.

"Number Six?" Gibbs had offered.

"Number Seven," Amir corrected, noting the size of the stopper. "Do you climb?"

"In another life!" Gibbs laughed.

"Before the war," Amir said, "Yugoslavia had the best climbing in the world."

Gibbs regarded his statement with doubt.

"The landmines. All the best routes are still too dangerous to even approach."

On his visits with Amir, The Site was far from his mind, but on that particular day, Gibbs realized that Amir had much more to offer than vintage t-shirts and dirty stories. Amir said little as he set up his shirts on the exterior of his kiosk, his shoulders down and his feet shuffling in the dirt.

Without explanation, Amir shook his head and said sadly, "Spring."

"Spring?" Gibbs had tried to cheer him up. "It's been summer for far too long!"

Amir shrugged and continued unpacking boxes and folding shirts.

Gibbs was confused by the change in Amir. "Has business been slow?"

Amir ignored the comment.

"Women?" Gibbs prodded.

"There is a village," Amir said. "It is to the north."

"She is from the village, then?" Gibbs asked.

"A mountain," Amir said putting up another t-shirt. "A cave."

"A cave?"

"My cousin and I, we nearly died. The cave was the only reason we survived."

Amir had never spoken directly of the war. Gibbs was caught off-guard.

"I remember hiding there in the shadows," Amir said. "Looking out at the sky, which was the same color as it is today. It is a sad color."

Gibbs was uncomfortable. He never had been a good shoulder to cry on. The only reason he stayed was because Amir had reminded him of home and the man he used to be. Gibbs stood there in an awkward position without offering condolence.

"You know the darkness in that cave was so strong, our small fire was barely enough to see each other. My cousin, she once crawled on her knees as far back as she could go. I thought I might never see her again."

Gibbs listened. He had already decided that as soon as possible, he would find a way out of the conversation and never come down Cerbova Street again.

Amir shook his head. "Do you know what was back there? A door! In the middle of a mountain."

"A door?" Gibbs snapped to attention. "Did she open it?"

"She said it was locked. She said it was wide like a bank vault and smooth like stainless steel. When the sky looks like this, I always wonder what was behind that door, if it would have saved her."

Gibbs waited silently, his mind racing.

"My cousin, she didn't make it through the spring. My mother is the only one left. Days like today, Boss," Amir had said to Gibbs, using the nickname he called any American. "Days like today, I wonder about that door."

"You've never returned?"

"No." Amir shrugged. "No."

Gibbs nervously tapped his fingers on a wire hanger sitting on Amir's kiosk.

"It was a tough climb. Somehow we made it. As you Americans would say, free solo. No ropes."

"Why don't you go back up there and have a look?"

"I would. Maybe you would like to be my climbing partner?"

Gibbs caught his breath. Suspicions blared in the American's thoughts like sirens. Was it a setup? Amir could have been Russian, Iranian, or even another American planted here at the kiosk. Maybe Amir's goal was to take him up there and leave him hanging from a rope or torture him for information about The Site. Alternatively, maybe Amir was telling the truth and in his desperation to find The Site, Gibbs ultimately took his chances.

Abruptly, his thoughts shifted from Mostar to his present position at the Montenegrin border. Two men sat playing cards in white plastic lawn chairs off to one side of the guard booth. As Gibbs watched them, an argument unfolded; the chairs were scattered wildly and the two men became engaged in a brawl. The larger of the two quickly gained the upper hand and would surely have finished the fight if a third man had not appeared and stopped the bludgeoning.

Within a few minutes the two sat back down, picked up the cards and continued playing. Gibbs had his passport stamped and left the checkpoint shaking his head. *Wild place.*

War-torn houses greeted his entry to the country. Everything was coated with a coppery ash. Women and children sat by the roadside, their sunken eyes pleading for relief but their hands unextended. Serbian flags hung from the windows of any house with occupants and Cyrillic letters spray-painted on buildings served as road signs. Herceg Novi was a few kilometers away.

The city was one of the largest tourist attractions in the country. Gibbs could not see why. Even the Russian tourists looked uncomfortable in the cheap and tacky atmosphere. It was as if one large dollar store in Jersey had exploded in the center of the city and distributed its contents throughout the area. Gibbs had recalled reading a tourist brochure from the Ministry of Tourism that stated: *Monte Negro! Not Monte Carlo*! Gibbs pitied anyone who would have gotten the two confused.

A group of men in their mid-fifties sat in the corner of the lot where Gibbs finally chose to park. They were unshaven and wearing sweaters and tight denim jeans. He locked the his black Land Rover. The group of men were eyeing it up and he felt that it very well could be the last time he saw the automobile.

"Screw it," Gibbs said, shrugging his shoulders. If it was stolen he would have to endure another lecture from Bombay about government property, but he would have another vehicle issued to him. Maybe the new one would at least have a working air conditioner.

A wide boardwalk bordered by mimosa trees looked out into the bay. The water was dark and deep, better suited for a port than a tourist destination. Massive carved slabs occupied anything that resembled a beach and lay deposited in a way which suggested that they once served as breakers.

The boardwalk was entirely devoid of tourists. Evenly spaced and ornately decorated lights shone along its length, but all of the bars and restaurants were empty and dark. Only a few small kiosks were open. They sold postcards and magnets. Gibbs leaned on the railing under a light and scanned the horizon out over the dark water below. He felt like he was trapped in a carnival where all the rides are moving, yet there wasn't one person there to enjoy them. It was haunting.

He checked his watch. The new agent was already thirteen minutes late. Gibbs was always on time. The alarm clock in his apartment was ten minutes fast, the one in the car was seven, and the watch on his wrist was more than five minutes ahead. For Gibbs it was a simple mathematic formula, and he had no use for anyone who could not solve the equation.

His thoughts drifted like the waves around the breakers while he waited, erratic and without direction. Gibbs thought about Amir for a few moments before Josie drifted through his thoughts.

While he was always the center of attention, Josie was one of those men who made everyone feel special. He was the best Ranger that Gibbs had ever known. Despite the stiff neck from their last meeting, Gibbs felt a quiet satisfaction that Josie was alive and all the guilt that had plagued him for what happened in Yemen was finally being released.

"Yes?" Gibbs answered his mobile sharply, expecting the caller to be the new agent calling from some brothel or casino down the boardwalk with apologies for being late.

"Boss! Boss, it's me, I need help!"

"Amir? Where are you? What's going on?"

"Someone is here," Amir said clearly distressed. "They are in my house. They are looking for me!"

"Amir?" Gibbs yelled. The connection was poor. "Amir?"

"Boss," Amir said in a hushed voice. "Listen to me! They are coming!"

Gibbs's heart raced. "Who? What are you talking about?"

"The cave." Amir started speaking faster, "The village, the mountain. Do you remember?"

"Yes. What is going on?"

"My mother. You must take care of her, there is no time left for me! She lives in the village, the village with the cave!"

"Jesus Christ!" Gibbs hit his hand on the railing.

"Do you remember?" Amir asked again. "Do you remember the door?"

"Yes, yes of course."

"The name of the village is..." Amir started.

"Not over the phone!" Gibbs protested.

"There is no time!" Amir exclaimed. Shouting could be heard through the static. "The village....the name..."

Gibbs held his breath.

"Cvitina!" Amir said.

"What!?" Gibbs yelled. "I'm coming for you, just stay there!"

"Cvitina!" Amir yelled again.

Gibbs heard him this time.

The call disconnected.

"Shit!" Gibbs cursed. His heart was in his throat. Gibbs turned from the railing as his phone rang again.

"Amir!" Gibbs answered.

"Hello, yes?" A voice in broken English asked. "Yes, hello. I call to you."

"What?" Gibbs said. "Who is this?"

"I call for lesson," the voice repeated. "English lesson, you are a native speaker, yes?"

"English lessons!"

"How much for one hour in week for..." The voice trailed off in Gibbs's mind.

The boardwalk was empty. The lights were on. Gibbs was out in the open. Pigeons circled above a rooftop in the distance. A piece of cloth was tied to a lamp post behind him and drifted slightly, indicating the direction of the wind. Everything snapped to a standstill before accelerating violently: *The phonecall. Mostar. The Bridge. Josie. Pigeons. Lens, scope, rifle.* It was a setup.

"Sniper!" Gibbs cursed under his breath.

Gibbs turned to leap for safety as a rifle cracked out from the night.

XI

There were thousands of them: each was unique and delicate. To count every single one would have been impossible. The spider webs were fastened between the hand railings that flanked the river Spree as it flowed past the Central Station in Berlin. Despite their numbers hardly anyone noticed them.

Josie noticed.

He had survived by paying attention to details and took every opportunity to use observation as a tool. He was constantly sharpening his observational prowess. Those small webs one day could be the difference between life and death. That day could be twenty years from now or within a few hours. Either way, he was ready.

The walk by the Spree was just what Josie needed. He took short strides and nursed his Achilles that he had torn from sprinting through the sunflower field back in Hungary. Having doubled back, he crossed the road behind the Opel and waited there for a few hours, tucked up against the abandoned border post. He was lucky the man in denim didn't have dogs; if he did, Josie would have had to resort to his forty-five. Josie hated killing, especially dogs. In the morning, Josie changed his clothes, walked into town, caught a bus from the village of Letenye to Budapest, and from there it was as easy as waiting for the train to Berlin.

The cobblestones beneath his feet were damp from rain that had arrived after midnight, but now they started to dry in the stale wind. Josie studied the tight, orderly patterns that the stones beneath his feet had been arranged in. The only intrusion into the design was a single row of pavers running in the opposite direction of all the others, and much like the spider webs, they were easy to pass over without taking any notice. Even if anyone had noticed them, their true significance would not be obvious. When a pedestrian would step back and glance from a distance to see how the pavers run their course, they would understand that those little cobblestones represent one of the most important borders in history, the Berlin Wall.

Josie did not need the reminder at his feet to visualize the imposing expanse of The Wall. His memory produced a picture as crisp as the day he crossed it with his forged passport and his stainless steel forty-five. Josie still thought about it. He thought about it all too often and despite how he wished his memories would crumble like The Wall, they stood there serving as a barrier that he could never forget.

People had died trying to cross that line on the ground, while now, only a few decades later, it meant nothing at all. Times had changed. Berlin was no longer the pride of the German nation. It had simply been forgotten.

Josie turned from his walk along the Spree and began his search. The bitter taste of hashish hung in the night air. A young couple fornicated behind some bushes only a meter from the sidewalk, and a junkie stirred from his sleeping quarters on a park bench.

He thought about the man he had killed that day so many years ago. Josie was certain that if he hadn't pulled the trigger back then, he could have looked the man up in the phonebook, given him a call and had a good laugh about how none of it had really meant anything at all. The only problem was that Josie had pulled the trigger, and the man was dead.

Josie didn't understand it at the time that The Wall was not just a border between East and West. A border within himself had also been crossed. When it happened, there was no long or elaborate explanation. Simply put, there was no foreplay. There was only a Stasi officer sitting in a brown leather chair at a wide oak desk in his office. His pleas were silenced by four blasts from Josie's pistol.

Josie remembered that within hours he was back walking close to where he was now. That night as he walked alone, death no longer troubled him. It no longer haunted his dreams as some impossible or abstract idea. It was real and all too easy. Josie realized that the killing didn't bother him. What did get under his skin were the ones that boasted about and romanticized the act of killing. They were the dangerous ones.

A prostitute rubbed up against Josie as he turned down Orienburgerstrasse. She wore knee high black leather boots with pink fishnet stockings. Her tight, corseted top was packed full and her skirt was so high it was practically non-existent.

"How about a little fun tonight, Big Boy?" She whispered dangerously close to Josie's ear.

A young female Aussie tourist sitting at a café along the sidewalk leaned out and slapped Josie on the ass to encourage him.

"Fun?" Josie asked while he continued walking. "Fun...like checkers or chess?"

"Checkers, chess, or your wildest fantasy," the prostitute smiled, running her long nails along Josie's back.

He smiled and politely wished her a pleasant evening.

"Wait," she frowned. "This is my city; please, I want you to have a good memory tonight. A good memory of Berlin!"

"I've got plenty of memories from Berlin," Josie retorted, "and not a goddamned one of them is good."

The red light district was clean and orderly. Josie found the lace and leather clad women of the night to be entirely charming, sweet and easy-going. All were beautiful, most were intelligent, and the rest had a great sense of humor.

The majority of people in the passing crowd were there to look and not to buy. It was an attraction that anyone visiting Berlin should not miss. Why bother to visit the Reichstag or

Checkpoint Charlie when you could walk down a street packed with more eye candy on a single block than there was on any other place in the world? Not in Amsterdam. Not in Thailand. Nothing compared to Berlin.

Josie continued his search.

At an outdoor café, Josie ordered tea and baklava, then found a table securely tucked behind a big tree. Two men sat across from him at another table. One read a magazine. The other stared at Josie. They were two of the largest men Josie had ever seen. They were there to protect the girls, not to start a fight with a possible patron.

The prostitutes came and went. Josie found their shifts were short in duration. Some of them worked for only an hour or two while others worked for three or four. There was a door behind the café where they would enter when their shifts ended. They would re-emerge within moments, clad in jeans and loose-fitting retro shirts. Josie was surprised at how quickly they transformed back into society. It was as if they were all actors in a play.

Josie had brushed off the first prostitute earlier because she had been too loud and attracted too much attention. She had been too aggressive. Josie had heard that the more attractive prostitutes were typically in the middle of the street, as the less desirable ones were placed closer to the edge in hopes of convincing a man to spend his money before he had the time to see what else was available.

Finishing his tea and licking his fingers free of the baklava's honey, Josie ordered a coffee to go, paid his tab, and walked down the street. The dozens of women he spoke with along the way were sharp and full of wit. Josie laughed and flirted and feigned interest in buying every girl, because if he did not present himself as a potential client, the girls would signal the others further down the street not to waste their time with him.

He found her standing alone underneath a doorway. Two men passed by, but she offered no solicitation. A bit out of shape, and seemingly a bit under the weather, she was almost bashful as she hid her face with her long blonde hair. Josie approached her.

"Perfect," Josie said.

At first she did not look at him as he stood there, but when she finally turned her eyes up to him, she shook her head in disgust and said with a sharp Slavic accent, "You are dark...too dark."

"I am dark because it is dark," Josie offered. "It must be nearly one in the morning."

"You're Turkish, yes?" she accused. "Yes, I see it. You are a Turk."

"No, no!" Josie waved his hands. "I'm Irish!"

"You're too dark for Irish." She had her arms crossed.

"I may be the only Irishman who will admit it, but it will be our little secret..." Josie pulled closer and whispered to her. "We're all just a bunch of Spaniards. Centuries detached, of course."

She uncrossed her arms and looked cautiously at Josie. "You're not Turkish?"

"I'm not a Turk. My name is Patrick, Patrick Keene."

"King?"

"*Keene.*"

"Guten Tag, Mr. King," she said, misunderstanding his last name.

"Guten Tag, fraulein." Josie smiled and inched closer. "The Turks, they beat you, don't they?"

She nodded. "Most of the girls won't accept them. It is too dangerous."

Josie motioned to the two sparrows inked above her breasts. "Those are very beautiful tattoos you have there. Would you happen to have anymore?"

"For sixty euro, Mr. Irish, you can see the others." She smiled and arched her back but kept one long segment of hair over the left side of her face.

He knew she was the right one. The going rate for two girls was only forty euros, plus it came with an open bar. She was on her own. Josie knew she only set her price high so that there would be room for negotiation. Prostitutes never negotiated.

"Sixty is much more than the other girls charge."

"The other girls, Mr. Irish, won't let you do what I will let you do." She said. "I've had men pay me hundreds."

"I am certain that you have." Josie smiled. "I too would be one of those men but I only have forty euros. There must be something we can arrange?"

"I must pay for the room, for the bar and for the union dues," she protested.

Josie knew she did not even have a room to offer and that she certainly was not a unionized prostitute.

"Please, there must be something we can work out?" Josie acted strained.

She paused. She stretched her arms high above her head and leaned up against Josie as if she would kiss him, pushing her pelvis directly up against his.

"Despite your odd ear, you are the best man I've seen here tonight, Mr. Irish." She said indicating Josie's cauliflower ear. "Forty euro, but we must go into the park and we must be quick."

"There?" Josie asked, peering into the darkness. "Is it safe?"

She ran her fingers down his shirt and around his pants taking a firm grasp of the bulge just below his belt buckle. "Do you want to see my other tattoos, or not?"

Josie paid her.

The park was an immense forest of shrubbery and hedgerows. There were no street-lights or nearby turns in the road that would allow the high beams of passing cars to intrude. The dense foliage of the perimeter oaks provided perfect cover, and despite the other patrons of the Berlin night, the park was entirely empty.

Josie struggled to remove the prostitute's hands from his belt buckle. As they stood tucked behind a few shrubs, she looked up at him wildly when she realized he wasn't going to have sex with her. He could see that she was afraid and confused. Perhaps she thought he was going to kill her.

"Here is one hundred euro." he said. "Please don't scream, just listen."

"What do you want from me, Mr. Irish?" She reached cautiously for the money.

Josie relaxed when he realized she was not going to scream or in any other way draw attention. He removed his pack from his sore back and found a comfortable spot of moss invisible to anyone passing by.

"Do you want to undress yourself?"

"I want to go to sleep," he replied. "There is a thousand euro in it for you if you stay until morning with me."

"Morning?" She clearly didn't like the sound of this.

"Morning." Josie confirmed. "All I need you to do is to stay awake."

"You are a criminal? You are hiding from someone! Maybe you really are a Turk! I don't want trouble with the police."

"I do not want trouble either. All you have to do is stay awake. Think of how many people you would have to fuck tonight for a thousand euro."

She paused and thought for a moment. "Why do you trust me?"

"I don't trust you at all. You're a prostitute and that is why I am paying you."

"Oh." She looked down as if she were about to cry.

"Look, I'm not here to save you or to tell you how to live your life, to preach to you or try to sell you some dream of running away together. Don't think that this is going to be something more than it is." Josie adjusted his pack behind his head. "I'm no knight in shining armor. I'm here to sleep. I need you to keep watch."

Josie handed her the coffee that he had bought before he left the cafe. "It's for you."

"I just woke up a few hours ago. I don't need it."

"At least hold it close to keep yourself warm for the rest of the night," Josie advised. "It's warm enough now but soon the moisture will rise out from the ground and you'll be cold. I can't have you moving around all night."

"What if I decide to run away? What if I try to leave?"

"I'm a light sleeper. Plus, I think you would prefer to earn the money by sitting here, rather than the alternative."

She nodded, taking hold of the coffee. She held it close.

Josie shut his eyes and took a deep breath, hoping sleep would arrive.

"You know that I am not like the other girls?" She asked him after a few moments passed.

Josie kept his eyes closed. "You don't have a penis, do you?"

"No," she smiled. "It's my eye, it is glass."

"The left one."

"You knew, Mr. Irish?" She asked.

"I knew. That's why you were perfect. No one would be waiting for your return."

"Perfect?" She repeated, lost deep in the word she had obviously never heard applied to herself before.

"Do you see Jupiter?" she asked him pointing as if he was looking. "It is in the east."

Josie kept his eyes shut.

"Don't you think that it is amazing that we can see something so far away, Mr. Irish?" she asked. "When I was a little girl I always looked up at the sky."

Josie turned even further away from her and hoped that she wouldn't talk all night.

"I never liked to sleep. I always had so much energy," she said. "Sometimes I think that is why I am what I am now. Even as a child I could never sleep. I would lie awake looking at the stars and listening to the radio."

Josie realized that the harder he focused on going to sleep, the more awake he became. He began to listen.

"Now," she continued, "now I can't listen to the radio. It's like when I hear it no one else exists in the world. It's the loneliest sound, Mr. Irish."

"When I hear the radio at night when I am alone in my flat it makes me feel..." She paused for a few moments. "It makes me feel that I am still out there somewhere, as a child listening to the same station. It makes me feel like that little girl has a chance to be something different. I wish I was that little girl again."

Tears dropped off of her long eyelashes and she started to sob.

The cup of coffee slid out from between her fingers as she fell onto Josie's chest. She rested her head in the pocket of his shoulder and he wrapped his arms around her. She could have come from a poor family, been a junkie, or maybe she fell for the same old trick of a new boyfriend telling her that he needed the money, and that if she really loved him, she would sell her body for cash. The answer really didn't matter. She was a person. A human being that was far too used to being treated as something else.

"I have never met a man I could trust, Mr. Irish. You are a good man."

"Josie," he offered. "Call me Josie."

"Anna," she returned, as if she knew the name he had first given her was a lie. "My name is Anna."

Josie held her and felt her sobs slowing and her heartbeat returning to its standard.

"Are you really Irish?" she asked.

"American." Josie said. "I used to be an American."

"And now?"

"I don't know. I just am."

"I don't understand. You can't change what you are."

"Maybe you can."

She nodded her head, knowing that he was saying it more for her than for himself, and held him tighter.

He looked up for a moment through the darkness and shrubbery to Jupiter, then he closed his eyes and fell asleep.

XII

The train left Krakow at two in the morning. It was already forty minutes behind schedule. Aside from a few students, two soldiers, and a businessman, the train was vacant. The passengers had cast subtle glances at each other as they queued on the platform, waiting for the train. The only one worthy of any interest was an old man struggling to carry a suitcase full of Oscypek cheese, which he was bringing from his mountain village to the markets in Warsaw to sell in the morning.

The tickets listed seating assignments, but not one passenger obeyed them as they boarded. The wagon closest to the engine was chosen by all, leaving the remaining seven empty. The sole method of travel more dangerous in Europe than taking a night train in Poland was flying in a Russian-built Tupolev. The passengers on board knew that their safety depended on numbers and that even then, it might not be enough.

The final whistle blew, one more passenger ran along the platform and boarded the train as the engine bolted forward, locking the wagons behind it and pulling them out into the night. His name was Kuba. He was short and stocky and walked with the wide, sauntering gait of a boxer entering the ring. Unlike the others, he did not seek the safety of the first cabin; instead, he took a seat far back near the mail wagon at the end of the train. Kuba didn't care that the train was late or about safety in numbers. Kuba cared about the bottle of chloroform tucked into his jacket and the amount of money he was going to score tonight. Kuba was going to rob the train.

He would freely admit that the scheme was not original. It was one used frequently in the early nineties in Belarus and

Ukraine. Kuba had only modified the general properties slightly. The majority of the trains in Poland were of Soviet origin, with a standard hallway running the length of the wagon on one side, while a grouping of six enclosed cabins seating eight passengers each were stacked on the opposite side. Despite the notoriously poor manufacturing tolerances in the Eastern Bloc, each individual cabin was well sealed. This is where the chloroform came in.

The entire routine was simple. Kuba would first walk down the entire length of the wagon, ensuring that any windows in the hallway that had been left open were promptly shut. At the end of the train, there was an air and heating intake panel located just off of the floor. Kuba didn't have an exact measurement; usually half of a liter of chloroform was enough to put every single passenger on the train out cold. From there the robbery was easy.

The critical aspect of the entire plan was timing. The night train express stopped at two stations during its course to Warsaw. Kuba would have to estimate the train's location between the two stations, making sure that the occupants would be sleeping while the train stopped and he could depart, or he would miss his station and be trapped on the train all the way to Warsaw. Waiting was the hardest part. So instead of waiting, Kuba drank Rectified Spirits. The spirits were intended to be used as an industrial floor cleaner, but Kuba filtered the alcohol through a slice of bread and sipped gently on the purple colored liquid.

The night slowly rocked past his window in a way that made it seem like the train wasn't moving at all. The soft motion of the cabin was enough to put most of the passengers to sleep without any added assistance. As the engine crossed a road its whistle could occasionally be heard from inside the wagon, but it seemed distant and trailed off as if it were miles away. Except for a few barren fields and poor villages, the train was alone, moving cautiously through the dark the way one does when walking alone past a graveyard after midnight.

The first station passed without incident. No one boarded and no one left. Kuba was high, but despite his stupor, he stood up, reached into his pack, took out the chloroform and a gas mask and started to walk down the hallway. It was time.

Kuba emptied half of the bottle of chloroform into the intake panel. It would take a few minutes to circulate through the system, condense into a vapor and then pump through the ducts into each cabin. As he waited there at the end of the hallway, he looked at his reflection in the window. The Israeli surplus gas mask that he had stolen from a soldier fit almost too well. The rubber seal clung tightly to his face and each time he put it on he felt trapped and deprived of air. Luckily, he was too drunk tonight to care. He looked intimidating, like a man ready for the end of the world and all the death that came with it.

The passengers slept.

When Kuba had first entered the wagon he made a quick note of which cabins were occupied. The first was occupied by the two soldiers, the next held the businessman as well as the man from the village with his cheese, and the students occupied the third. Kuba quickly did some calculations and hoped to pull in at least four or five hundred zloty from the heist.

Opening the sliding glass door into the first cabin, Kuba tripped over one of the soldier's outstretched legs. He caught himself on the door, then adjusted his balance and quickly went to work. The soldier that he had tripped over had only a few banknotes in his wallet. The briefcase next to him yielded some formal military documents and a half-eaten kanapka wrapped in wax paper. Turning to the other soldier, Kuba found that the man had no money at all in his wallet; the only thing of interest on his person was a fake Omega watch that had probably cost him ten zloty from some Chinese vendor outside of the train station. Kuba took the watch anyways.

He fared better in the next cabin. The businessman carried over two hundred zloty and his wrist yielded a much better watch. The man from the village had a few coins in his pocket but his suitcase full of cheese in the rack above was tempting. Kuba was drunk enough to nearly take off his mask to sample the irresistible cheese, but at the last moment he pulled the straps tight when he realized his temptation. A few harsh words to himself and a vow to not drink before the next robbery were muttered out loud before Kuba moved on to the next cabin.

There were five students in total: two boys and three girls. Kuba wasted no time searching the backpacks stored in the overhead racks, then quickly scored fifty zloty from one of the boy's wallets before taking another twenty-five from his friend next to him. Two of the girls didn't have anything, but in the purse of the third girl, a new Sony cellular phone and twenty zloty awaited his eager hands. Quite satisfied with a successful night, he turned to leave the cabin, but as his hand reached the sliding door he looked down at the young girl sleeping nearest to the door.

She was beautiful. Her mouth was open, it was as if she was calling to him from her dreams.

Standing above her, looking down, Kuba was a bad man, and being a bad man he began to have bad thoughts. Just as he was about to entertain those thoughts with his eager hands, he heard a noise.

His head snapped around and he paused with it cocked to the side as he listened again.

Nothing.

Focusing his eyes, he looked out into the dark hallway to try to hear the sound again.

Still nothing.

The next ten seconds passed like hours but his heart was the only noise that echoed in his ears. Kuba again scolded himself for drinking, then he checked the bottle in his pocket to ensure that he had used nearly a liter of chloroform. He told himself that every window had been shut, and that he had at least another twenty minutes until anyone would begin to stir free of slumber. Kuba returned his focus to important things like the beautiful student; he told himself that he had heard nothing at all.

Kuba heard the sound again.

Spinning wildly on his toes, he faced the hallway. He slid the door open, left the cabin, and inched along the wall until he could lean forward to peer into the next cabin.

The night trains typically had all of the lights in the hallways turned off to help people sleep. It had never bothered him before, but now it put him on edge and he struggled to see even a few feet in front of him. He began to breathe. His mask suddenly felt tighter, and hotter. The Plexiglas shield began to fog up. Rubbing his hands over the lens of the mask only made it worse. It was too dangerous to take his mask off because the chloroform had not settled yet and the vapor was still being circulated through the air intake system. Even though he was well past plastered, he was afraid of something in the next cabin.

Bracing himself against the wall of the hallway, Kuba stretched out his hand to grip the cold aluminum handle of the cabin door where he had heard the noise. His arm was tight and tense; a bulging tricep stood ready to fling the door open and he readied himself to spring forward in a surprise attack.

Again, the noise.

This time he heard it clearly. It was the metallic echo of a stiff coupling which separated the first wagon from the second, rocking back and forth each time the train passed over a motorway. When he had been inside the cabin with the girl, the sound must have been distorted by the walls. Dropping his shoulders and taking as deep a breath as the mask would allow Kuba relaxed.

With little effort the door to the cabin swung free and Kuba stepped inside. It was empty. A rolled up newspaper perched on one of the seats and a Styrofoam cup rested by the window. Kuba paid little attention to a small canvas bag in one of the overhead racks; it was common for one of the engineers or ticketmasters to keep a change of clothes stored in the wagon closest to the engine.

Kuba shook his head, laughed a bit to himself and tasted the alcohol on his breath. Within a few more minutes he would depart at the last stop before the train continued on to Warsaw. He could stumble into town and with some luck find a field to pass out in for the night. Kuba glanced over the debris in the cabin one more time: the paper, the coffee cup by the window, the *open* window.

"It was shut," Kuba said out loud. "Yes. I shut it. Wait? Was it shut? It couldn't have been open."

Rocking back and forth on his heels, he felt the sedative effect of his drunken stupor. Walking forward to the window, he steadied himself before finding the latch and pushing the window up to close it. Then he leaned forward and rested his head on the glass.

Kuba let his eyes wander and stare out into the countryside beyond the pane of the window. The landscape was an endlessly rolling plain, empty and black. Scanning casually through the void, he seemed to see a flash of movement, a form out there on the plains. He stepped back from the window slightly and focused his eyes and strained through the lens of his mask to see what was waiting there in the night. Whatever it was, it moved from obscurity to dangerous clarity in an instant. Suddenly Kuba realized that the figure was not outside the train, but a reflection on the window from behind him.

"Behind you!" Kuba cursed.

It was too late.

A pair of hands latched onto his throat, sprung with such force it was as if a steel trap had been tripped and now dangled from his neck. The gas mask clung tightly against his face and all of the oxygen left his body as he attempted to scream. His legs flailed, seeking purchase in vain, and his hands tightly grasped his attacker's wrist. He tried to scream again, and then he soiled himself.

His brain was calling for blood and his body panicked with alarm as basic functions started shutting down. Weighted down with adrenaline, his limbs were heavy and useless. Kuba's eyes opened wide as the last warnings from his mind arrived in segmented, blinding pulses. Feeling his blood pressure peak and his heart pound, Kuba took one last breath before he lost consciousness.

He awoke on the floor of the cabin, facedown and his body shaking with violent contortions in an attempt to restart itself. He tore the mask from his face, throwing it across the cabin and taking a large violent gasp of air. His lungs burned, his head pounded and he spent the next minute coughing and gagging as if he had just been pulled from the sea.

Looking around desperately, Kuba noticed that the newspaper was missing, as was the coffee cup by the window and the canvas bag in the rack overhead. The window was also shut, and nothing remained to prove that he had been attacked at all. Kuba wondered if his mask had leaked, allowing the chloroform to alter his perception. He wondered if maybe he had tripped while entering the cabin and knocked himself out. He wondered what the hell was going on.

Kuba was lying on his stomach, still struggling to resume normal motor function. His legs were sprawled out behind him; one of them was sticking out into the hallway, caught between the sliding door and the frame. He was about to write the whole ordeal off until he tried to swallow. His hands reached up and felt his neck. There was blood dripping from the finger gouges in his throat.

His ankle was suddenly seized with such power that a loud snap of bone fracturing echoed in the small cabin. He arched his back and screamed as he was ripped free from the doorway. Part of his shirt was torn in passing the frame and his head smashed against the sliding door when his body entered the hallway. Kuba's fingers scratched and pleaded into the carpeted floor, tearing his fingernails free as they desperately clung to anything that passed.

Like a doll, his body went limp as it was ripped down the length of the hallway. Kuba's eyes registered the images as they passed by in a blur, but the one clear image he had was that of the figure looming behind him right before the attack; everything else was black with fear or white with pain.

At the end of the wagon the grip on his ankle was released. Kuba curled up into the fetal position and dared not to move. Each time he opened his eyes he saw a shadow charging forward to deliver the final blow, but as his vision returned, he noticed that he was alone in the hallway.

Struggling to stand on his broken ankle, he fell back to the floor of the wagon as a shot of searing pain registered in his brain from the crushed bone above his foot. Sitting there leaning up against the same service panel that he had opened and poured the chloroform into only a few minutes before, Kuba suddenly became aware that there was something approaching from the other side of the wagon.

"Behind you!" He could do nothing to protect himself and softly exhaled what he expected would be his last breath.

The looming mass of his attacker was upon him, lifting him with one swift motion high into the air, and it was as if gravity had been temporarily suspended. Kuba was thrown through the aluminum sliding doors that separated each train wagon from the other and as he lost consciousness, the final images appeared as a fractured and broken slideshow.

Kuba saw the open door, the night sky, and the countryside passing before him. He saw his attacker's empty and black eyes. Kuba felt gravity take hold and felt the crisp air outside of the train. He saw the tracks before his body hit them. The slideshow was over.

It was after six in the morning when the train finally locked its wheels and sounded its arrival at the Central Station in Warsaw. The students struggled to work the sleep from their bodies as they walked off onto the platform. The soldiers cursed their luck at being robbed. The businessman was already busy making calls. The man with the suitcase full of cheese was struggling to get it off of the train. At the same time in a village eighty kilometers to the south, a farmer found Kuba's body alongside the tracks. Back in Warsaw, Harkem took his first steps into the city.

XIII

Swan sat next to the window watching the countryside pass as the train crossed the Oder River into Poland. The weekend in Berlin had been what he had needed: it had kept his thoughts focused, and even better, it had enticed him out of his apartment and away from the vodka in his freezer.

Tucked into Swan's pocket was a small piece of spray-painted concrete that he had bought from a Turkish vendor on Wilhelmstrasse. The Turk claimed it had been part of The Wall. Swan doubted this, but he had made his purchase all the same. He had actually enjoyed Berlin; he sent a postcard to himself at his address back in the States, ate some goulash from a Hungarian restaurant on Kronenstrasse, and even asked a Japanese tourist to take his picture at Checkpoint Charlie. There was a small amount of time during the trip when he didn't think about Mosul, and at least for those few moments he had been free from his memories.

The vast rolling plains of Western Poland were now passing by his window, and they reminded Swan of the High Plains of Kansas where he had spent his youth. Instead of milo or soybean fields, wild grass grew beyond the train's confines, mixed in with unkempt lots of sunflowers and wheat. Swan curled his lip at the wasted potential of the land.

Leaning the side of his head against the window's glass and settling into the seat, his thoughts drifted back in time. He could visualize the Stutkas, the Panzers and the Blitz; he could see that the open plains before him offered no resistance to the German war machine. He appreciated history and the strategy of war, but his thoughts all too quickly returned to his own war and his desire to have died fighting it.

Swan needed to focus. He retrieved his cellular phone from his pocket and turned it on. He hoped to receive an updated report from Brooks back in Warsaw but took a deep breath of frustration when he did not see any new messages. The battery icon flashed red, and after refreshing his email once or twice, he powered the phone off.

"Fuck," he said, returning the phone to his pocket. Where was the damned report? Was Brooks still in Basel? Did he even go? What about the secretary?

Swan decided that Brooks and his secretary were probably too busy fucking each other to bother sending the report. Swan wished he could be busy fucking someone.

The charger to his cellular phone was tucked in his rucksack, which rested above his head in the luggage rack. He went to fetch it but noticed that the one outlet provided in each cabin was already being used by the passenger sitting across from him.

The man was built in a way that made him seem genetically gifted; Swan noticed that there was no bulk in his frame – nothing excessive, nothing useless. Everything about him was wired and tight, like a fighter who had just cut down to make weight.

The man was wearing black slacks, Reebok running sneakers, and a fitted V-neck. There was a small pack next to him and a book resting on top of it. Swan observed that the title of the book was in Cyrillic, and doing his best detective work, he guessed that the man was probably Russian or Bulgarian. He would have never guessed that the man sitting across from him was an American heading to Warsaw to kill the very ambassador whom Swan was employed to protect.

When Josie had first entered the cabin at Berlin's Hauptbahnhoff Station, he was immediately aware that his travelling companion was certainly military, and absolutely

American. Josie noted the CRKT spring-loaded folder in the man's right pocket, the pistol tucked under his polo shirt that printed itself every time Swan moved, and that the right pant leg of Swan's khakis rested with a slight protrusion. It could have been a wrinkle or it could have been the handle of a boot knife.

Relaxing into his seat and picking up the book next to him, Josie watched as the sliding glass door to the cabin opened and Anna entered. Josie had paid her off in the morning, and expected that that would be the last he would see of her, until she asked him where he was going. He had told her the truth. She had family in a small city outside of Warsaw and it had been more than two years since she had been home. Josie bought her a ticket.

Closing in on the Polish city of Poznan, the ticketmaster passed by the hallway where they sat, counting the passengers already on board while escorting a homeless woman off of the train. She had apparently just relieved herself in the small hallway of the wagon and Swan looked at her as she passed by, her soiled dress clearly visible.

"Shitbirds," Swan said in a barely audible tone.

Josie's ears perked up.

The curse had caught his attention. The specific word identified Swan as a man who had spent a considerable amount of time on a ship. Josie decided that he had served in the Navy, yet Josie doubted he was a former SEAL. SEALs were too busy travelling around the world posing as gemologists while dusting Somali pirates or Mujahedeen for a few grand a day: there was no reason for a one to be in a second class express train headed to a city where there was nothing to do but drink Piwo and look at beautiful women.

The train arrived in Poznan.

It would wait there for twenty minutes so Josie took the opportunity to depart and buy some breakfast. The passageways under the rail platforms were crowded. By the time Josie made it through to the station house and purchased food from a vendor, he had seconds remaining to push his way back to the train.

As he had instructed, Anna crossed her legs when Josie returned. It was a sign that he had not been followed when he had disembarked earlier. After this gesture, she shut her eyes, pulled a light jacket up around her shoulders and went to sleep. Swan was upright in his seat and glancing out the window.

Opening up the pages of his book, Josie enjoyed his breakfast roll and cheese while thinking more about the man across from him. The man didn't have any visible tattoos, service rings or any other obvious military insignia on him. Josie thought that if only he could lift up the man's shirt and see his pistol, then he would be certain of the type he was dealing with. SEALs carried Glocks unless they were real cowboys, in which case they carried 1911s or revolvers. Marines carried Berettas, and everyone else, Sigs. That was the standard, not the rule, but for the most part, military contractors stuck with old habits.

The ticketmaster returned as the train continued on through the Polish countryside. There was some confusion when he entered the cabin because he had not counted Swan on his previous pass and demanded to see his ticket. Swan cursed and protested that he had been on the train since Berlin and that it would have been impossible to miss him. The ticketmaster ignored the tirade; instead, he firmly held out his hand for Swan's ticket.

With a loud exhale, Swan struggled to stand and keep the pistol from bulging out of his shirt as the barrel pushed firmly into his genitals, making each movement painful. He removed his wallet from his back pocket and handed the ticketmaster the folded piece of paper it contained. In the process a few spare coins dropped onto the floor. Josie watched them fall and land on the carpet without a bounce. He smiled.

A grinding click could be heard as the ticketmaster stamped Swan's ticket, offered no apology for the inconvenience, then backed out of the cabin and shut the door. The coins rested near Josie's feet. Swan returned his wallet, sat down, and then stared out of the window again, seemingly unaware that he had dropped anything. Josie was tired of his internal debate about the man, so he offered a test.

"Excuse me," Josie said, trying his best Eastern Bloc accent and pointing directly to the carpet. "Your coins are on floor."

Swan avoided his eyes and continued to look off into the distance without blinking. Josie kept his hand extended to the floor and looked right at Swan until he was finally forced to react. Without gratitude or even so much as a friendly nod, Swan turned and looked down to the coins. His heavy shoulders shrugged and he cleared his throat as he slowly began to lean forward to retrieve them. Just as he was about to touch them, he instinctively stopped.

Josie's question was answered. Marines.

During his Ranger years, Josie had had more than his share of encounters with Marines. They were the self-proclaimed baddest of the bad, the cursed and the damned. They ate babies and pussy for breakfast and would turn you into a human Pez dispenser with their K-Bar. They were also the most superstitious bastards Josie had ever met.

There was Mad Max, the Marine who believed that every time *Highway to Hell* played on the radio, an IED detonated somewhere. Another Marine would eat only an odd amount of food on deployment, such as three carrots, one hamburger or five potato chips. For the record, soups and liquids counted as one. Josie also remembered Big Stanley, the artillery sergeant who suffered a serious mishap from the recoil of a one-five-five millimeter howitzer. His hand took the worst of it; after his return from the hospital, he was able to shake your hand backwards by bending his disjointed fingers around your palm. He only shook hands the normal way on his birthday.

"Superstitious bastards," Josie affirmed.

While each Marine possessed his own special and unique superstition, there was one that was common and shared by all: never, ever, *without exception* pick up a round that has been dropped and hit the ground. It didn't matter whether it happened at the Armory, on post, or even while clearing a jam on the frontlines. Once the brass hit the dirt, that was damned well where it stayed. Leave it or join it, no questions asked.

This intense aversion to picking up brass rounds was quickly compounded, the way most obsessions are, governed by increasingly complex rules to include any type of alloy on the ground. Heads or tails? It did not matter, for it was not a question of luck, but of life or death.

Swan's hand was frozen just above the coins, as if time had stopped. His fingertips began to shake and a small bead of sweat formed on his squared brow, running down to the tip of his nose before dripping onto the carpet. Josie pretended that he had not noticed Swan's discomfort. Swan tried one more time. He couldn't do it.

As casually as he could, Swan eased back into his seat, glancing once at Josie and then to the sleeping prostitute. His heart was racing and his face was flushed red. Why the hell did the man across from him have to notice those coins? Why didn't he just take them for himself? He was furious; he suddenly stood up, opened the sliding glass door and went to the bathroom.

Hours passed, as did the stations of Kutno, Konin and Sochaczew. Warsaw was close. Upon his return, Swan had sat impatiently in his corner seat, looking out the window with his chin resting on his hand, which was in turn supported by his arm's position on his knee. Josie had not made another attempt to speak with him and acted as if the coins on the floor did not exist.

Anna had slept for nearly the entire train ride since it departed Poznan; she shifted only once, and her head now rested softly on Josie's shoulder. He looked down at her and shifted his position slightly so that she would be more comfortable. He would occasionally adjust the coat that covered her to make sure she was warm.

The loudspeaker at the end of the hallway crackled to life and announced the approaching the last stop before Warsaw's Central Station – Zachodnia. Swan organized his pack and pulled out his cellular phone, frustration flushing across his face as he registered that Josie's charger had been plugged into the only outlet for the entire trip. Nonetheless, Swan turned on his phone.

Josie could hear the small chime from Swan's device warning him that the battery was low, but then Josie heard another sound, that of a new message. Swan punched furiously at the small keypad, his eyes focused, his head leaned forward to peer at the screen. His lips moved as he read the email feverishly before suddenly recoiling in disbelief. The phone powered off but he had had enough time to read the intelligence update that Brooks had sent. It was the update about Josie. It was accompanied by a photograph from when Josie was imprisoned. Swan looked up.

"Damn," Josie said, smiling while he gave an exaggerated shrug. "Looks like I almost made it."

"Almost," Swan said, as the color in his face darkened and a vein in his neck pulsed.

Time stopped suddenly with such force that it seemed both men would be ripped free of the train. They locked eyes with each other in the most intense fashion. They were separated by only a foot in distance. The cabin pressurized with a sense of impending destruction; the slightest spark was all that was required to start an inferno.

Josie moved first.

"The last I heard, the price on my head was one hundred grand?" He leaned back, crossing one leg over the other. "Did it change from yesterday?"

Adrenaline surged through Swan's body. It took all of his self-control not to drive forward and attack. He knew he couldn't - not in public, not with a witness, and not like this.

"It's the same," Swan finally said, holding his body in check.

"The girl." Josie motioned with his head down to Anna. "She will get off at Zachodnia. Nothing happens until she leaves."

Swan curled his lips and thought about the offer. He nodded.

Uncrossing his legs and turning through the pages of his book, Josie took stock of Swan's aggressive posture. "There is no need to make this unpleasant."

"Fuck you," Swan said directly and slowly, emphasizing each word. "I know who you are. I know what you've done."

"You're a fast reader," Josie said, motioning to the phone.

"I didn't have to read that much to know that you're a coward," Swan said. "Even worse than that, Bircher, you're a goddamned terrorist."

Josie raised an eyebrow. "A terrorist?"

Swan ignored Josie's protest. "They want you alive, Bircher. Personally, I want you dead but I've got a deal for you."

"A deal?"

"I can promise you that as long as you go nice and easy, and don't cause a scene in front of all the people on this train and in the station, that not so much as a thread on your shirt will be wrinkled."

Josie understood what he meant, but opted to be a smart ass. "I would accept, but you see I've spent the last night sleeping in a park. My shirt is already wrinkled."

Swan smiled. He preferred violence to diplomacy anyway. Diplomacy didn't solve anything: violence did. Violence stopped violence, killing stopped killing, and for all those trust-fund, organic, earth-loving yoga shitbirds who didn't live in a black and white world, Swan had a rude awakening for them. Swan didn't believe in *Live Laugh Love*, he believed in *Kill Hate Fuck*. The situation with Josie was for Swan, a win-win.

"Let me tell you something, Bircher, I'm not going to stand around giving you a handjob like your Ranger buddy did back in Bosnia. When this is over, you're not going to walk off into the sunset like before."

Josie nodded politely as if someone had informed him about the weather forecast.

"What are you going to tell me?" Swan positioned his feet squarely on the ground and seemed ready to strike. "Are you going to tell me that at the next station there is some sniper waiting to shoot me through the window?"

Josie shook his head. "No. I could tell you that this beautiful girl on my shoulder is holding a Draco pistol between her hands underneath the coat or I could tell you that if I don't walk off this train, a man sitting in the next cabin will detonate a suicide vest."

"If you told me any of that, Bircher, I would tell you to get fucked."

"Of course," Josie said, raising his hands. "I could also tell you that the way you favored your left knee when you went up to use the bathroom has me concerned that you're not up to the challenge with that disability."

Josie had hit a nerve.

"I'm not disabled!" Swan spat.

"You know, the way you drag your heel when you walk, it's like the pain is not just physical. Instead, it's like the pain is a constant mental reminder of something you wish you could forget."

"You're still talking. But it ain't gonna help."

"Fine, fine. Truthfully, I never doubted you for a minute. You struck me as the kind of goddamned fool who can't be reasoned with and would settle for nothing less than an early morning fistfight on an express train."

Swan smiled for a moment. "I always hated Rangers. Thought you were all nothing more than a bunch of glorified Grunts with parachutes. I'm going to enjoy this."

Anna stirred as the train stopped and Swan arrested his attack by driving his fingers into the armrest. Josie continued to smile as Swan nearly foamed at the mouth in anticipation. His eyes were bloodshot. His adrenaline took him beyond reason.

Zachodnia station was nothing more than a long platform of benches and walls covered in graffiti. Grass grew up from the bottle-strewn concrete. The skyline's desolate brick factories dominated the landscape. Anna awoke, stood up from her seat, handed Josie his coat back and with one slight but grateful nod, walked out of the cabin and down the hallway.

The train left the station.

Josie had only seconds until the battle, but as he looked out of the window along the tracks ahead, he knew a few more moments of delay would give him the chance he needed. "You know, it doesn't have to end like this."

Swan shot Josie a wild-eyed look and clenched his teeth. Just before he struck, his eyes widened with anticipation.

The train entered a tunnel.

Josie brought the bindings of the book in his hand down squarely upon Swan's knee. In the darkness, he could hear the snap of the knife being opened and could feel the pressure of Swan charging forward. With his back against the seat, Josie shot his foot forward to deflect the hand that held the blade. Following this, Josie felt the crushing pressure of Swan driving up against his chest as he was slammed back in his seat.

As Josie was attacked, he lifted his body to where he could secure a guillotine choke with his left arm. Swan swung wildly, his blows landing wide on the seat's headrest, only inches from Josie's face. Deepening his hold, Josie allowed his weight to sink back into the seat while his feet pushed Swan's legs out from under him. Hanging there in Josie's choke, it took only ten seconds until Swan was unconscious.

Lights appeared outside of the window even though the train was still in the tunnel, and then a wide grouping of tracks could be seen before an entire array of platforms became visible. The train had arrived at Warsaw's Central Station.

Releasing his hold, Josie gently set Swan back in his chair. Grabbing his pack, Josie left his phone and charger in the cabin. The phone didn't work anyway, it never had. The only reason he had it was to blend in with every other mobile phone-addicted idiot. He had no interest in carrying a personal GPS for someone in Nevada to pilot a drone to Josie's location and blast the hell out of him. He had already made that mistake in Yemen. Never again.

A sharp whistle sounded and the artificial lighting blinded Swan as he opened his eyes. He coughed a few times and wiped the spittle from his chin, then staggered to his feet. Running down the hallway of the wagon, he steadied himself against a wall, regained his full balance and then stepped down onto the platform. More out of habit than out of hope, his eyes scanned the massive station desperately. He was out of luck. Josie had escaped.

XIV

A peacock sat under a willow tree. It had called once since Cass had arrived, and for the most part, seemed content to strut back and forth throughout the hedgerows. Stretching out past the bird's parade ground were delicate walkways and perfectly manicured lawns. Despite being directly in downtown Warsaw, the Royal Baths Park was quiet and peaceful.

Cass found every flower in each arrangement to be perfect. From the statues and canals to the theater and the eighteenth-century orangery behind her, nothing appeared out of place. The park was how she had always imagined Europe, like one of those faded, sepia washed postcards found at antique malls back home in the States.

The day before, she had promptly made herself comfortable in the city using the notes she had made on the flight out of Sarajevo. From the train station she walked to Emilii Plater Street, circled the Palace of Culture, entered the Metro at Rotunda, and rode the train until its final, southernmost stop, Kabaty. From there she caught a bus back towards the center and made a few adjustments to her notes. Forty minutes later, she caught a cab at the bus terminal across the street from the train station.

Cass had enjoyed the taxi ride to her apartment. As the cabbie drove past the Russian Embassy, he sarcastically referred to the Russians as *Best Friends* and then he put two fingers to his head in the shape of a gun, dropped the hammer of his thumb, and figuratively executed himself. That got him quite a laugh from Cass. Arriving in the district of Powisle, Cass entered her flat and found that all of her belongings from Bosnia were already there, arranged in the center of the living room in small cardboard boxes.

Now Cass paced back and forth in front of the orangery as she waited to meet Rodham. She was used to meeting in crowded cafés or student bars and welcomed this pleasant change of scenery, but she started to feel exposed and self-conscious in the stillness of the park. She had always hated being the center of attention and found it difficult at times to walk down a street alone; if she felt that someone in a vehicle passing by was looking at her, she would inadvertently trip or move in some odd or awkward way. Maybe her self-consciousness was the root of all of her issues - the reason why she disliked most people yet desperately sought human contact and a refuge from her loneliness.

"Rodham." A proper and firm English voice spoke from directly behind her.

Cass turned and extended her hand. "Cassidy."

His handshake was firm and even a bit aggressive, but lasted only long enough to be considered professional. Rodham was imposing; his attire was impeccable and sharply tailored. His rounded middle and wide shoulders gave him the structure of a bear, but he flashed a warm smile and put Cass at ease.

"Pleasure," Rodham said.

"Pleasure," Cass replied, already mimicking his British accent perfectly. She hated when she did that. There was something in her brain, perhaps from the childhood accident, that caused her to take on the inflection of the person that she was speaking to.

"It's a very beautiful park," Cass said slowly, trying her best to control her tone. "I appreciate that you didn't choose to meet in some disco at one in the morning like some of my other contacts."

Rodham took little note of her last words as if the surprise of meeting in such a place was not worth the reply. "I took the liberty of reserving the orangery for the two of us; I hope that this will do?"

"Yes, of course," Cass said, feeling quite outclassed, the way some Americans do when they speak with someone from England. She felt like one of those foolish Yankees who visit Europe in droves, all wearing their stars-and-stripes hats or "Proud to Be an American" t-shirts.

Holding the door to the orangery open, Rodham extended his open palm, inviting Cass to enter first. A pure, hypnotic scent of citrus and flora met her senses. Dozens of orange trees grew in long rows next to the greenhouse windows. Countless plants, flowers and cacti were potted everywhere the eye could see. In the middle of the orangery, a marble fountain rose from a deck of blue and white tile. Rodham stood at their seating next to the fountain.

One hand held the back of a green iron chair, and the other again warmly extended, encouraging Cass to sit. She walked over, felt like she should curtsey, realized she was the center of attention and nearly tripped, then took the seat.

Cass made herself comfortable while Rodham rounded the table and took his own seat. She was trying to remind herself to be confident and tough but she found the entire atmosphere so disarming that she allowed herself to enjoy the moment as a woman. Curiously, there was a third chair at the table, but Cass was too distracted to notice.

Once seated, Rodham moved the conversation forward formally, remaining in control of the pace as if at a business meeting. Introductions were passed over quickly, and as topics with more substance began to arise, Cass was suddenly aware that she was revealing much more about herself than Rodham was. He politely avoided any serious reply to her questions, and she began to feel that she had to get forceful and try to gain an equal footing in the discussion.

"You were in the British Army?" she asked, pulling on the information from the briefing on the jet.

"Correct, my dear," Rodham said. "That was over two decades ago."

"During the Troubles in Northern Ireland, then?"

Rodham nodded. "I served in Londonderry."

"Derry," Cass corrected.

Rodham smiled politely. "Yes, yes indeed. Derry."

Cass knew she had just made herself look like a bitch for debating the proper name of a city and murmured an apology.

Rodham seemed unoffended. "My dear, we can continue to play this game, but I expect at the end of a very long conversation, you will not have discovered anything more about me than what you have already read in my file, provided to you, no doubt, by the Agency. I also expect that by the end of our chat, your Irish temper will have at some point gotten the better of you, and there is a chance it could spoil our tea."

Cass looked up quickly as if to ask how he had known her heritage.

"Your grandmother was born on the twenty-ninth of November in the year of nineteen eleven."

Cass wrinkled her nose. Her eyes narrowed but Rodham anticipated her pending sarcastic line of questioning.

"Dunegal," he said, naming her grandmother's city of birth. "To be blunt, my dear, there is no need to start a game which you will not win. I would rather we be professional about this."

Cass nodded. Rodham was good.

He leaned back slightly in his chair and with the extension of one thick finger, he summoned the waiter, who appeared balancing a silver platter and efficiently set the table with three small porcelain plates, three delicate cups with gold bands along the rims, three knives, one ornate tea kettle, and one delicious plate stocked high with shortbread and citrus. He filled the cups, each to the exact same level, adjusted one of the knives he had previously placed, and then departed without a word.

"One, two..." Cass counted privately to herself. She was on alert. "Three!"

"Sheryl's," Rodham said, extending his hand to the shortbread. "Best in Scotland, made fresh this morning. Please."

Cass took a square of shortbread and set it on her plate, and Rodham did not give her time to question the third place setting at the table.

"I certainly hope that the Agency has informed you that I am under no terms whatsoever employed by any intelligence branch or government agency. The reason why I am involved in this situation is the complete and total failure of your country to establish an intelligence network in Poland. This has forced them to outsource certain aspects of their operating procedures to a businessman such as myself."

"I am aware," Cass said. Trying to be proper, she picked up her knife and cut a small piece of shortbread, then held it in her fingers. "I am also aware that your company benefits greatly from this relationship."

Rodham nodded. "Just as in any business transaction, my dear, both parties must benefit."

Cass took a bite of the shortbread. Her eyes widened.

"Tops, is it not?" Rodham smiled the warm smile that she had first seen outside of the orangery. It was a dangerous smile, one that Cass could imagine that he had employed many a time for his own personal gain.

"It is," Cass said, catching herself picking up his accent again.

"Your current operation here, to the fullest of my understanding, involves an American known as Josiah Bircher. It is my duty to provide you with a name and an address of a person whom your Agency believes Mr. Bircher will contact when he arrives in Warsaw. A name and an address. Nothing more, my dear."

"Yes. That is all I expect. I'm not here to ask you for anything more."

Rodham retrieved a business card from his breast pocket and placed it face down on the table beside the tea kettle. "Here you are."

Cass reached for it. Rodham stopped her.

"While I understand that you have expressed that you are not here to ask me for anything else, may I be so bold as to suggest that you don't let this opportunity pass. I would advise that you take this time to ask for something."

Cass retracted her hand. By the tone in his voice, she thought he was referring to something sexual. She tilted her head as if she had not decided yet whether to be offended. "I don't understand."

"Questions," Rodham said, lifting the gold-banded cup to his lips and taking a silent sip. "You should be asking questions."

Cass felt that she had lost whatever small percentage of control she had retained in their conversation. She looked down to the card on the table; all she had to do was pick it up and politely excuse herself from the table. It was so easy. Rodham smiled again.

She tried to resist but she couldn't keep her thoughts from escaping her lips. She asked the one question which had been driving into her mind with each step since she had left Mostar.

"What do you know about Harkem?"

Rodham did not even raise an eyebrow. "What would you like to know, my dear?"

"Is it true?" Cass asked, leaning forward in her seat. "Is it true what they say about him?"

"Everything about Harkem is true," Rodham replied with a dry tone in his voice. "Everything."

"The list? Reincarnation?"

Rodham nodded.

"Impossible! Surely such a serious man as yourself can't believe...."

Rodham interrupted her politely, and as only a true Englishman can. "Two years ago I was in America on business. Las Vegas. Finding myself with a day free, I took a drive to the only place I had ever cared to see in your country. Monument Valley."

Cass listened and took a sip of her tea. Her hand was shaking slightly as it held the cup.

"The first step I took out of the car, I knew I had been there before. There was no denying it."

"In another life?"

"Hard to say, isn't it, my dear? Truly, it doesn't matter whether I believe in it or not. The man you have asked about believes in it entirely and he has killed many for it."

"He works for the damned Russians, doesn't he?" Cass said. The reminder of death agitated her, conjuring up the promise she made years ago.

Rodham leaned back in his chair as if he were taking a long pleasant drag on a cigarette. There was a hint of a wrinkle on his brow, suggesting that he was deep in thought and perhaps about to reveal something that he rather wished he didn't have to.

"A better question to ask first, my dear, would be *whom do you work for?*"

Cass sat upright and glared at him.

"Bombay." Rodham did not stir from his casual position in the chair. "What do you know about him? Surely that is not even his real name – it's such a ridiculous name. I also hope that you have realized by now that Gibbs was sent to Monte Negro to die. He was getting too close; he knew too much, my dear."

"Impossible! It's not true, it can't be true."

Rodham raised his eyebrow and motioned to the card on the table. It was as if he were offering her a way out, a chance to maintain innocence in the way the world turns, a chance to still believe in Santa or the Easter Bunny. Cass shook her head. She didn't take it.

"Let me offer this. Did you recognize anyone on your flight from Sarajevo?" Rodham asked.

"No, I had never seen any of the passengers before. Except for Bombay."

"What about the man sitting next to Bombay at the front of the plane?"

"No."

"Are you certain?"

Cass shut her eyes. She had seen the man's face and even heard his voice when he was talking on his mobile as the plane landed. Cass thought hard, and a vague recollection flashed faintly in her mind. "Wait...wait..."

Rodham waited.

"Yes!" Cass exclaimed, her voice rising as she solved the question. "Dartmouth! Yes, it was at Dartmouth. He was a student there, I remember him now. He was in one of my classes, but I can't remember which one."

"International Business," Rodham answered for her. "Do you remember where he was from?"

Rodham gave her time. She thought. She remembered. "Kentucky. Yes, I remember it now. He was from Kentucky."

"Close." The man in question appeared from behind Cass, walking out from a row of dense citrus trees with an orange in his hand. "You have to go just a bit further east. Try Kent."

"Bastard!" Cass thought to herself. She turned quickly in her chair, her hands raised in an almost defensive position.

"My name is Jonathan," the man from Kent introduced himself, sitting down in the third chair, crossing his legs and casually picking up his cup of tea.

"As you are well aware, Dartmouth is the premier Ivy League university when it concerns agent recruitment by the Central Intelligence Agency," Rodham said. "Jonathan was there for one year to establish contact with as many prospective agents as possible."

Cass was pissed. She crossed her arms. "Why?"

"Rather simple," Jonathan chimed in while peeling the orange. "My mission was to build an instinctive trust between as many students as I had time for; one of those students was you, Cassidy."

"Well, you have wasted your time," Cass said. "If Rodham had not pushed the subject I would not have remembered you. Even now that you're sitting across from me, I don't have a single memory of you other than your name and where you had claimed to be from."

"Then my mission was a success," Jonathan said. "While you have forgotten me, I can promise you that your subconscious has not. If in a crisis I called upon you for assistance, even if your mind held misgivings, your instincts would tell you that you could trust me. Except it has nothing to do at all with your instincts, but with well-orchestrated past lies that I put in your mind."

Rodham gently brushed the sugar from his fingertips and then waved his hand to intervene. "My dear, not to push you too quickly, and not to move on from the past, but the question which you should be asking now is why would British Intelligence need to have an inside man for an American operation?"

Cass remained silent. She scowled at Jonathan in the way that only a frustrated woman can.

"What it really comes down to is - whom do you work for?" Rodham said.

"You know who I work for!" Cass allowed her Irish temper to get the better of her, just as Rodham had predicted. "I've already told you!"

"Yes, yes my dear, you have already told me, I believe that you referred to them as the *damned Russians*."

Cass choked. She wanted to stand up, grab the business card from the table, give Rodham the finger and slap the smug little grin from Jonathan's face. She didn't. She sat there and put her head down.

"On even the simplest level you understand that you do not work directly for the CIA?" Rodham asked, noticing her posture. "Your employer is entirely a private corporation, and while they are contracted by the Central Intelligence Agency, and all of your fellow coworkers refer to the company as 'The Agency,' you must understand that it is no different from any other business."

"They need to diversify," Jonathan offered. "A balanced portfolio, so to speak."

Cass studied Jonathan's relaxed features. She was no longer angry. She was simply disappointed. She felt like a child that someone had just played a trick on. What they said made perfect sense.

"You asked about Harkem," Jonathan said, an appeasing posture coming over him as if he were truly excited to offer help. "I can possibly provide you with some more information than Mr. Rodham did. Your suggestion about the Russians was not entirely without merit. The Ambassador here in Warsaw discovered something big that the Kremlin would prefer to keep quiet."

"The Ambassador?" Cass asked guardedly.

"Yes. You were briefed by Bombay that Harkem was released from prison and would be targeting Mr. Bircher. In truth, Harkem was released to kill the Ambassador."

"What about the list? Wasn't Josie on it?"

"Yes, yes I'm getting to that. The list, of course. I can assure you that it does exist, and that there are only two remaining names on it. The names are those of the Ambassador and his daughter."

Cass took an uneasy sip of her cold tea.

"Consider the abstract logic of this madman. Harkem is not simply out to avenge those whom he believes were responsible for his death centuries ago. He is out to kill everyone in their families. He must extinguish the bloodlines."

Cass became aware of the thick, soft tropical leaves of the trees around the table while choosing her next question as if it were her last. The two men sitting across from her would reveal only so much.

"Josie...what role does he play?"

"Why do you think he has revealed himself now?" Jonathan produced another orange and rolled it in his palm. "He knew Harkem was released and that he had little time to get to the Ambassador."

"So Josie is in..." Cass started.

"Bircher is in a race, my dear." Rodham said. "A race to see who can get to the Ambassador first. It doesn't really matter to the Russians which one does, just so long as the job gets done."

"The Russians. My employer," Cass said flatly.

Rodham nodded.

"I'm not asking for your trust," Jonathan said.

"Good, because you don't have it," Cass retorted

"I assume that you have already taken time to familiarize yourself with Warsaw?" Jonathan continued.

Cass nodded.

"Are you familiar with the metro station known as Holy Cross?"

"Swietokrzyska?"

"Yes," Jonathan said, taking the napkin from his lap and touching it to his lips after finishing his orange. "The last metro arrives just after midnight on its final run through the tube. I suggest you make that train."

Cass waited for more.

"Harkem will be there, my dear," Rodham clarified. "More importantly, Bombay will be there as well. You will have all of the proof you will need tonight."

"No easy way around it," Jonathan shrugged. "You're working for the Pinkos."

"Well then, get to it. What do you want from me?" Cass snapped, revealing her exhaustion and sense of defeat.

"Nothing – except your trust," Jonathan said.

"How do you expect me to trust you?"

"I don't. At least not yet. Remember, Metro Holy Cross, just after midnight."

Cass leaned back. Her shoulders were sore from the tension. She turned to Rodham.

He reached down and picked up the business card. This time, he handed it directly to Cass. "Here is the name and the address I was required to provide. You wonder what to do now? Call the number, do your job."

Cass took the card, put it in her purse and met Rodham's eyes with her own. "Gibbs...is he really..."

"Mr. Gibbs is dead, my dear; you have Bombay to thank for that," Rodham said without emotion. "I'm sorry."

Cass turned to Jonathan. "We don't have a deal. I didn't make any promises."

"Of course," he said. "Not yet. First one is for free."

Both men stood as Cass departed the table. Rodham retrieved her jacket and extended it to her as if nothing more had happened than a group of old friends meeting for tea.

"Good evening," Rodham said.

"Evening," Cass replied.

As the sun began to set over the cypress trees and perfect gardens, Cass felt like she had just been released from a pressure cooker. Questions pounded between her temples. Was Bombay really working for the Russians? Was she? What about Gibbs? Was he really dead? Was this all a setup? A test of loyalty? What was Rodham's angle? These questions soon turned into a migraine of stress. Cass felt like an amateur, but the one glint of hope was that she had made a promise, and she was going to keep it. Now she knew where to go.

Back inside the tropical air of the orangery Rodham waited patiently while Jonathan searched throughout his briefcase for a packet of Virginia Loose Leaf tobacco.

Cheers," Rodham said, producing a packet of rolling papers from one of his mysterious inner pockets. "It's damn near impossible to find good tobacco in this country."

"Do you think she believes us?" Jonathan said.

"She believes enough of it," Rodham said absently while licking the paper and rolling a cigarette.

"Your idea about the Russians – quite brilliant," Jonathan patronized his mentor.

"Americans," Rodham said. "They still have enough of the Red Scare in them for our gain."

"Well, we surely couldn't have told her the truth," Jonathan said. "Couldn't have told her that her country, the red white and blue, released Harkem to kill their own Ambassador."

"Very true, but it wouldn't be the first time."

"Libya. Well, at least they tried to make it look like it was the extremists."

"True, but the wars are winding down. They no longer have the need to scare the public with propaganda about blood-thirsty Muslim fanatics wearing sandals and shooting Kalashnikovs," Rodham said. "The Russians have always been the enemy, and after the Ambassador is killed, you can be sure they will leak some forged documents indirectly blaming the Pinkos for his death."

"Are the Russians truly involved in any of this, sir?" Jonathan asked.

"Why do you think I am here?" Rodham asked.

Jonathan laughed nervously as he smiled to his mentor.

Rodham wasn't laughing.

XV

Josie walked through the tunnels that connected the city of Warsaw to the central train station. Chinese vendors and Romanian gypsies seemed to be the sole inhabitants of the underground, and every few steps, Josie had to adjust his stride to avoid stepping in bodily fluids that had been discharged onto the concrete pavers the night before. After a dozen twists and turns, Josie saw a flight of stairs leading up to the surface.

Cresting the stairs on Marszalkowska Street, Josie lifted his head to meet the source of an imposing shadow. It was cast by the Palace of Culture, originally known as Stalin's Palace a gift from the Soviets to the people of Poland. Josie walked crossed an expansive, vacant parade ground reminiscent of Moscow's Red Square, and looked up at The Marriot and the Hotel Intercontinental towering above the dated Soviet building; it seemed to be under attack from the new and looming skyscrapers being built around it.

Josie ventured up the stairs of the Palace and entered through a thick wooden door beyond massive columns. In the reception area there were two sets of stairs, one leading up to a terrace that housed a bank and government offices, and the other leading down to a pair of elevators. Josie went down the stairs.

A small pharmacy occupied the space between the elevators; he entered and began to shop. Josie was disappointed that he could not find any surgical gauze so instead he opted to buy a pair of white socks. He was, however, able to find tape, a pair of travel scissors, Bacitracin, antihistamine, a black marker and a small can of compressed air. He quietly made his purchases and exited the pharmacy, passed beyond the elevators and entered the men's bathroom.

From his pack, Josie retrieved a new set of clothes; after changing into a pair of jeans and a fresh shirt, he laced up a pair of Sambas and then applied a spray of deodorant to his underarms. He arranged his purchases in the stall and carefully selected each item for insertion into a pocket where its imprint would not draw too much attention. The last item was the small can of compressed air, and this went into his back pocket. He pulled his loose-fitting shirt over the portion of the can that stuck out of its hiding place, and checked behind his shoulder in the mirror to make certain that it could not be seen. His pack lay at his feet, and he paused for a moment at the sight of it.

The pack had been with him for nearly a decade. Written on the inside flap was a list of places that Josie had visited with it strapped across his back. Countless cities and nearly a dozen countries were noted in an orderly fashion. There was room for one more mark. Taking the black marker in his hand, he wrote the word *Warsaw*, put the cap back on, stood up and walked out of the bathroom. He left his pack in the stall.

Once out of the Palace, Josie turned north along Bagno Street. An unkempt park was located here; weeds grew freely from between the pavers and a solitary fountain idled in a corner and appeared to have last been in use when Gorbachev was in office. Josie entered the park because while the weeds grew without limits, so did the flowers.

Taking a seat on a rusted bench facing the empty fountain, he casually crossed his legs and leaned to one side while removing the small aluminum can of compressed air from his back pocket. It took only a few minutes until a bee visited a patch of flowers in bloom beside the bench. With a glance around the park to make sure he was not being watched, Josie flicked his wrist, turned the can of air upside down and pressed the nozzle. The bee froze instantly.

With genuine guilt, he gently plucked the bee from the ground where it had fallen and said a silent apology to it for what he had done. He worked his fingernails across the wings and down against the thorax while applying even pressure, and then jammed the stinger into a soft spot of his forehead just above his right eye.

The pain was minor and fleeting, but Josie could feel that his face was swelling. Checking to ensure that the stinger had not remained lodged in his skin, Josie produced the Bacitracin and quickly rubbed it on the wound. He then casually produced the tape, scissors and the pair of socks from his pocket, cutting them into an effective imitation of a cast, which he immediately placed over his left hand. Two pink antihistamine pills were then swallowed and Josie was up from the bench and on his way down into the metro.

Within two stops, Josie's swelling had ceased but a large bruise surrounded the site where he had been stung. Leaving the metro at a station called Pole Mokotowskie Josie wiped the Bacitracin crème from his face and patted it dry with his hand as he turned down Independence Street in search of something he desperately needed: a safe place for the night.

He found what he was looking for on the first try.

The kebab bar did not have a name. There was a large red sign plastered on the window that read *Five Zloty Kebab*. A small counter, roasting lamb, few empty chairs around a hookah, and an Egyptian flag on the wall were all visible from the street. Josie entered.

The proprietor turned around from behind the counter. His chest and arms were well-developed but his shirt revealed a large gut. His skin was very dark. Josie thought his face was warm and rounded, much more like a Greek's than that of an Egyptian's. He waited until the man made eye contact, then turned away, shielding the bruise from view.

The Egyptian asked Josie something in Polish.

Josie tried English.

"You're Turkish?" the Egyptian asked.

Josie almost laughed. He had never thought of himself as resembling a Turk. He did not find it odd to be mistaken for one, and was simply amused that this was the second time in less than twenty-four hours that he had been accused of being Turkish. Josie shook his head, aware that the man was Egyptian and that his response could go one of two ways. He took a gamble.

"Palestine."

The Egyptian pulled back for a moment then bounced to the far side of his small counter to study the other side of Josie's face with great interest.

"What happened?"

Before Josie could reply, the Egyptian bounded back to the other end of the counter and circled out to where he stood. The bar was devoid of patrons and the man eagerly motioned for Josie to sit down. Pulling up a chair next to him, and then tapping Josie's leg for emphasis, he asked the question again.

Josie waited, looked away, and then answered. "Police."

"The hand too?" The Egyptian inquired, noting the makeshift cast.

"Hooligans," Josie said. "I had to fight."

The Egyptian leaned back, slapped his own leg and bit his lower lip while looking off into the distance. In his eyes there was a look of sadness and knowledge of injustice; he seemed as if he were about to cry. Then his face suddenly took on a warm boyish light and he bent his wrist so his fingers were pointed at his chest in introduction.

"Ashraf."

"Al-Khalili," Josie said, choosing his name carefully.

Ashraf smiled an approving nod. He stretched his neck around towards a small curtain that separated the back of the bar from the storefront. Tipping his head further back, he called, "Izak!"

The curtain slid open and Izak emerged. He was strikingly handsome. His hair was perfect, his facial features both delicate and hardened, and his eyes were a deep, penetrating ebony that made him seem timeless and exotic. He reminded Josie of a young Robert DeNiro. Izak pulled up a chair and sat down.

"You're in Warsaw," Izak said, speaking in broken English. "For now how long?"

"Two days," Josie answered.

"Why you move?"

"A woman," Josie said, not looking at Izak as if the memory was too painful to relay. "I met her in Egypt, for vacation. Sharm El-Shiek."

"She is where?" Izak said, crossing his leg tightly as his interest grew stronger.

"I don't know," Josie said.

"So you stay where?"

"Last night in the metro I was on the last train of the night. When the conductor pulled into the final station, he kicked me out and I slept on a bench."

"Hey," Ashraf tapped Josie's leg again. "Listen, we must be careful here. It is not safe alone for us in this country. You know? First time I fly here from the airport I took a taxi, but instead of driving me to Warsaw, he drives me to some village, takes all my money and then calls the police."

"You will stay with us," Izak announced. "You are our brother, there is no going back home. You will have place to stay, to eat and to work."

Josie feigned resistance, then displayed grateful acceptance.

"Your name," Ashraf cautioned. "It will not do, it will scare people from this country. They will think you are a terrorist. You must have normal name for them, Western name, a good name."

Josie pondered but Ashraf was the first to arrive at a decision.

"Yes," He said holding his chin and nodding. "Johnny."

"Johnny?"

"Johnny boy! Yes, yes."

Josie smiled.

Izak extended his manicured hand in greeting. "Brother Johnny."

"You are both Egyptian?" Josie asked, noting the flag.

While Ashraf misunderstood the question and nodded, Izak shook his head and pointed to himself, saying, "Afghanistan."

After a full meal of lamb meat, salad and baklava, Izak took over the counter and Ashraf took Josie out to show him the city. Every few blocks there would be another kebab bar; Ashraf would stop at each one, taking Josie inside for an introduction full of pride and solidarity, as if Johnny Boy was a long lost relative. As the night fell, they toured the streets, all the way from Nowolipki to Pulawska. Ashraf wanted his new friend to experience the city. Josie wanted to scout the Ambassador's residence.

At the end of the night, on the way back to Five Zloty Kebab, Josie paused in the Old Market Square at the statue of Syrenka. He was taken aback by the power of her form. There was strength in her sword and determination in her eyes to fight whoever took up arms against her city. Josie was momentarily transfixed. Ashraf prodded him along, motioning to the clock atop the Palace of Culture. It was time to go.

As Josie lay on a mattress that Ashraf had set for him on the floor of the bar, he laughed over a debate that had taken place earlier in the night and threatened to cause a scene, as it drew unwanted attention.

"Look at this guy," Ashraf had said to Josie, pointing at a street performer. He was a mime of the variety that remains motionless as a statue for hours. "It's Cherry Chaplin."

"Charlie," Josie corrected.

"Cherry," Ashraf insisted, the volume of which intensified rapidly. "No, no it's *Cherry!* What is this Charlie?"

"Charlie," Josie repeated. "*Cherry* is a fruit, *Charlie* is a name as in Charlie Chaplin!"

With this, Ashraf paused as if he were about to argue it and let the entire city hear his point, but suddenly he calmed let out a high pitched squeal of laughter. "I swear all my life I tell everyone its Cherry Chaplin! Cherry Fucking Chaplin!"

With a smile on his face, Josie stretched his arms and legs in all directions, overhanging the modest mattress on the floor. He swallowed the last two of his antihistamine pills, removed his cast and pulled the sheet over his head. It was late by the time he fell asleep and he would be awake long before dawn. After all, tomorrow was the day he had been waiting for, the day he was going to set things right. He was going to kill the Ambassador.

XVI

Gibbs was alive.

In the final second, he had spread his arms wide and taken a leaping dive over the railing that he had been leaning on. The fall of ten meters into the churning water below had a fortunate outcome: he landed in the only spot of surf that didn't contain massive granite slabs waiting to split his skull open. As he fell, Gibbs thought how comical he must have appeared to any possible onlookers. The crack of the rifle and the whistling piece of lead that smashed into the railing a moment after he had sprung over it assured him, however, that his decision was not a laughing matter.

It had taken him the better part of nine hours to return to Bosnia. He stayed along the coast under the cover of darkness, at times swimming out in the Adriatic, until he arrived at Njivice. Here he came across an encampment of Macedonian gypsies. Trading his watch for a piece of bread, new clothes, and a seat by the fire, Gibbs stayed with them through the night. He made an uneventful entry into Croatia, hitchhiked to Dubrovnik and caught a bus full of Italian tourists en route to Bosnia, and after a few more connections, he arrived in the city of Trebinje.

Having no other means of transportation, Gibbs stole a bicycle in Trebinje from outside of a student housing apartment block and made his way to the village of Cvitinie, which was nearly forty kilometers away. Once arriving there and after knocking on a few doors, he was directed to the house he was looking for. The residence was a single story, square house with a slate roof; it sat high in the mountains above the village and shared its terrace with a small farm. A knock on the door and the mention of Amir's name was all it took to be invited inside.

Gibbs now sat by a fireplace, warming his core with the additional assistance of a wool blanket and a cup of Bosnian tea. Rocking back and forth on the hand-carved chair, he made a careful evaluation of all that had unfolded. Every way he approached it led to the same conclusion: Bombay had sent him to Monte Negro to die, and Agent White was to blame.

A voice called to Gibbs from the kitchen. Amir's elderly mother was sweet and kind. Not one of the many hotels, inns, or private villas that the Agency had put Gibbs up in could have met or surpassed her hospitality. She didn't have electricity, the fireplace was the sole source of heat, and water had to be retrieved from the well outside, but her home was the only place that Gibbs had stayed in where he felt truly comfortable and safe.

The conversation between the two was limited. Niska didn't speak English and Gibbs had failed to master even basic phrases in Bosnian despite his extensive time in country. Nonetheless, Niska spoke freely, as if Gibbs could understand every single word that she said. While this was not true, he could at least understand her subject: Amir.

She fetched several framed photographs to share with Gibbs. The first was of a large bank in Sarajevo; she indicated that Amir was working there, and as further proof, she pointed to the photograph of Amir standing next to a brand new BMW and giving a thumbs-up gesture. The next few pictures were of Amir hiking, vacationing in Germany, and sharing an embrace with a very beautiful woman. Niska said that she was from a good Bosnian family and that Amir would soon propose to her. Gibbs had been able to keep his emotions in check until she told him that in just over a week, Amir would come to visit. At this, Gibbs nearly broke down into tears.

He turned and looked deep into the fire, biting his lip and trying to burn his tears away before Niska could see them. His heart raced and sweat began to form around the collar of his shirt. Here was this kind, sweet and loving woman whose only happiness in life came from her son. Gibbs couldn't tell her that Amir was dead because of the very man sitting across from her.

Niska kept talking, oblivious to his demeanor. From time to time, she would go to the kitchen for a few minutes, and then return with more mementos of her son. Gibbs looked through the last of the photographs. There was one of Amir as a boy, pretending to drive his father's tractor. Then a picture of him on the beach in Croatia as a young man, and one captured on the day he graduated from the University of Tuzla. Gibbs ground his teeth with each new picture and choked back the truth as it pleaded to escape from deep inside of his throat. Niska looked directly at Gibbs and told him in so many ways that after her husband had been killed during the war, Amir was all that she had left. He was the world to her.

He wanted to drop to his knees in defeat and take her hands in repentance. He wanted to cry like a child and tell her that Amir was dead because he had sold a t-shirt to the wrong man and had made the mistake to trust a stranger. Underneath the wool blanket, he clenched his guilty hands into shaking fists and hoped Niska wouldn't notice.

She did. She went to the kitchen and brought him a fresh cup of tea.

Despite his lifelong battle with suspicion, fear and paranoia, Gibbs knew that Niska was genuine, not an undercover agent. As difficult for Gibbs to believe, Amir had not set him up. The coincidence of their meeting was just that.

Trying to reason with the guilt, he thought that Amir could still be alive. He had often shown pictures on his phone to Gibbs of poses with a Romanian Draco pistol, the Bosnian emulating the postures and attitudes of his favorite German hip hop stars like Kool Savas or Farid Bang. Gibbs hoped that the Draco had been loaded and that Amir had been willing to pull the trigger when the Agency came for him. Guilt yielded to reality: Gibbs knew that Amir was dead.

Niska finally said goodnight. Stretching his legs closer to the fire, he tightened the blanket around his torso and shut his eyes. Before sleep arrived, he wondered how long it would take the Agency to find the village. Surely they had intercepted the phone call and there could even be a few shooters from the safe house in Mostar already waiting for him high up in the cliffs above the village, just dying to pull the trigger on their three-thirty-eight Lapuas. The Agency would stop at nothing. Maybe they would wait and follow him, perhaps after he had found the location, there would be a Predator drone already cruising at altitude waiting to fire a missile. Maybe it was the same drone that Gibbs had ordered to kill Josie. If so, perhaps Gibbs deserved it.

There was still a chance to run, to get out of Bosnia, and to forget about everything - The Site, the mission, and even Amir. In those final few seconds before sleep took control he acknowledged that while the temptation to flee was great, in the end, he really had no choice of what he had to do in the morning. The reason why he had to follow through and find The Site was because Josie believed in him.

It was the fire in Josie's eyes. The truth and the finality of his statement back in Mostar that left no room for turning back. Gibbs didn't know what waited for him outside of Niska's door, or what to expect when he finally found the entrance to The Site, but what he did know was that Josie was a good man who believed in Gibbs, and a man who had been right all along.

XVII

Al-Dhi'b was in the interrogation room, sitting in the same chair as before. His white robe was now bloodied and soiled, his hair wild, and his eyes bloodshot. His teeth chattered. Most of his fingernails were missing – not from the pliers of torture, but from his own desperate attempt to claw free from his restraints of the night before.

The lights in the interrogation room seemed to brighten each time he blinked. The table was still in front of the chair, except that this time, it was empty. There was no ashtray placed on top of it, nor did he see a glass of water or coloring book even though the man with the crayons stood next to him with his arms crossed, and humming a tune.

Lang walked into the room eating a piece of Boston crème cake.

"Name?" the man with the crayons asked calmly.

"Yusuf Abdul Qawi al-Dhi'b." The prisoner answered with a recognizable British accent.

"Age?"

Al-Dhi'b took his best guess. "Forty-nine."

"Place of birth?" The man with the crayons seemed bored.

"Balat. Egypt."

Al-Dhi'b suddenly tightened up and flinched. His face turned around the room with a wild eyed stare.

"Poor bastard," Lang said, licking the crème from his fingers. "That night in the forest must have worked you over good, al-Dhi'b."

"Egypt," al-Dhi'b repeated to the man with the crayons, anxious to be heard. "I said Egypt!"

"Ibn Khayal al-Zill? We want him. We know that you are aware of where he is. All you have to do is tell us where Khayal is hiding."

Al-Dhi'b wearily showed a hint of rebellion. "What will become of me?"

"If you don't answer the fucking question, you'll be put back into the goddamned forest!" Lang said, kicking off from the wall he was leaning on.

Al-Dhi'b remained defiant. "Will I be executed?"

"Shit," Lang shrugged. "For all I know, you could be released today or taken out on the next transport plane and ditched in the ocean."

"Khayal." The man with the crayons spoke with little enthusiasm. "We want Khayal."

Al-Dhi'b faced his interrogator and answered without hesitation. "Khayal is CIA."

In one stride Lang was upon al-Dhi'b. His right hand closed on the back of al-Dhi'b's neck and began to shake it violently. Al-Dhi'b blacked out.

"Name?" The man with the crayons repeated his query when his subject woke moments later.

Al-Dhi'b cautiously looked around him. His teeth began to chatter again.

"Al-Dhi'b..." He turned and looked at Lang, raised an eyebrow and hesitated as if he would be under attack as soon as he finished the sentence. "Yusuf Abdul Qawi al-Dhi'b."

"Age?"

"Forty-nine." In fearing the loss of his sanity, al-Dhi'b was fulfilling his interrogator's desire.

"Place of birth?"

Al-Dhi'b answered.

"Khayal," The man with the crayons said.

Lang watched the drastic psychological effects that the enhanced interrogation techniques had produced. He could see the primal fear deep inside of al-Dhi'b's darting eyes. It was so heavy on the prisoner that Lang thought it had even taken its own form inside the concrete room, like a separate entity. Lang knew that al-Dhi'b couldn't lie.

"Khayal?" The man with the crayons repeated.

Al-Dhi'b silently started to shake with fear. He felt the words coming up to his tongue and he couldn't halt their progress there.

Lang clapped his hands together and mockingly growled. "Come on! Let's go!"

"Khayal," al-Dhi'b tightened his neck muscles in preparation for an attack. "Khayal is CIA."

Al-Dhi'b was telling the truth. Both interrogators knew it.

"Shit," Lang said, nervously sucking on one of his crème laden fingers.

The only thing worse than having a *60 Minutes* investigative report air a Polaroid of you torturing a naked Haji was interrogating a prisoner who gives you a piece of information far above your pay grade. Lang recalled the interrogation of a German scientist who had been involved in a massive cover-up. He didn't know exactly what it was about – something related to what the US government was adding to the influenza vaccination – but the interrogator hung himself a week after finding out something that he shouldn't have. Lang had been acquainted with the interrogator, who wore Velcro shoes; he could not tie his own laces, let alone a noose.

"After the killings of al-Zarqawi and Bin Laden, Khayal is the next in line. His network extends all the way from Somalia to Iran," Lang intoned, as if trying to convince al-Dhi'b to reconsider. In truth, he was trying to make it clear to the men listening behind the glass window that he himself didn't believe al-Dhi'b's assertion. Somewhere at that very moment, a phone was being dialed and the call was being answered. He didn't have much time.

"Khayal led an assault of hundreds of Mujahedeen against an Army Forward Operating Base in Afghanistan." Lang said, still trying to disprove al-Dhi'b's answer. "Forty ANA troops dead, nineteen Americans, four NATO troops and two agents from Special Activities."

Al-Dhi'b spoke plainly. "He is CIA."

"Impossible!" Lang swept his hand across the table as if he were knocking over a stack of papers. The man with the crayons said nothing, but his detached demeanor visibly altered, his gaze shifting from al-Dhi'b to the interrogation room's door.

"On the sixth of March, there was a drone strike in a valley just outside of the town of Wana in Waziristan," Al-Dhi'b volunteered. "Ten children were among the dead."

"Bullshit," Lang hissed, pacing around the room with his hands on his hips.

"It is the truth. I ordered the children to be taken from the school in the village, shot and placed in the building after the missile destroyed it."

"We should have just water-boarded the fucker!" Lang exclaimed, protesting to no one in particular.

"Propaganda," al-Dhi'b said. "The children served our purpose. Khayal serves yours."

Lang gestured his wrist to the man with the crayons as if he was masturbating.

"The Americans won the war. There can be no doubt," al-Dhi'b continued unchecked. "But then your government realized that you don't make money by winning wars, you make money by losing them. It is the nature of your system. It is the nature of Capitalism."

"You are delusional. Foreign fighters poured across the border, Iran was supplying you with more weapons and training than you had ever had before. Christ, you even had the Stingers we gave you back in the eighties!" Lang sounded desperate.

"Then why was not a single Stinger used? As for the foreign fighters, I was directly responsible for their transport across the border and further training in country. In the total of two years not more than one thousand arrived. It is all propaganda. It's not my fault that even you believe it."

The man with the crayons walked up to a wall opposite from the glass window. He gazed intently at the window, as if he could clearly see through it. He imagined that a car was arriving. A man was getting out. Their time was up.

"Even Karzai knew the war had been won." Al-Dhi'b's occasionally incoherent phrases contained glimmers of truth that found their mark in his interrogators. "He knew the American occupation would be far worse than the occasional suicide bombing in a province far away from Kabul. He was going to pull the plug, tell the Americans they were no longer needed. He was going to tell the world what they were doing."

"Bullshit," Lang said. "That never happened."

"Of course it didn't. The day before Karzai was going to give his speech, Ibn Khayal attacked just as you have mentioned. All you Americans needed to see were your flag being burned and a few dead bodies being dragged through the streets."

"The CIA paid Khayal. They told him where to strike and when. That attack alone allowed billions of dollars to freely be dispersed to the defense corporations that were hand-picked years before the invasion even began. It is so obvious I am surprised you cannot see it; even Eisenhower warned the Americans. He called it the Military Industrial Complex. Bin Laden played the same role as Khayal, except he thought he was safe, and that they wouldn't kill him. Khayal knew better. That is why he is alive today; he knew not to trust the Americans."

"You're a goddamned murdering coward," Lang spat.

"And America is the Great Satan," al-Dhi'b said, shrugging. "The rulers of the world come to Afghanistan to die. Just like the Soviets, the Americans will lose the war, but they will lose it because they never wanted to win. It is all part of the plan. The plan to turn citizens into slaves..."

The door opened before he could elaborate.

"I never would have taken you for one of those conspiracy types," Agent White said, walking into the interrogation room and leaning on the table. "What next? Roosevelt knew about Pearl Harbor? Let it happen just so we could go to war with the Japs?"

Lang was silent. His fears had come true. The man with the crayons walked to the door.

"Of course it's true," Agent White shrugged. "Except the goddamned Krauts had to go and declare war on us. Wasn't part of the plan you see, but nothing ever works out exactly how you want it to."

Al-Dhi'b stared at Agent White.

"Listen, this whole bright idea about Khayal and Central Intelligence," Agent White said, turning directly to face the two interrogators, emphasizing his next point, "it's a damned foolish way to think, and more than that, it's a downright dangerous way to think."

Both men nodded.

"The Poles got some good coffee waiting down the hall for you boys." Agent White smiled. "Let me take a spin here; you'll be alright, boys, go get some coffee."

The man with the crayons opened the door. Lang followed. Outside, two men dressed like Agent White were waiting. Lang thought again about the interrogator who had hung himself. He swallowed hard and hoped he would fare better.

"Listen, forget about Khayal," Agent White tapped his pipe on the table and then chewed on its stem. "I want to know what you can tell me about your time at our little Hotel Kiejkuty."

Al-Dhi'b eased slightly. "The prison? All I can tell you is that one day I was in Beirut, and the next time I woke up, I was in prison. I didn't even find out that I was in Poland until the media broke the news about the black site that the CIA had been operating there."

"I know, I got it. Look, what I really want to know is when you were there did you ever talk to a man named Bircher?"

"Bircher? The one who called himself Josie? The infidel?"

Agent White smiled and ran a palm through his greasy hair. "He was already there when you arrived, wasn't he? You knew him?"

Al-Dhi'b affirmed that he did. "It was surprising for me to see an infidel on our side of the razor wire. I didn't talk to him until he started attending the morning call to prayer. We became friends."

"This is good, but did he ever tell you why he was staying at our little Polish resort?" Agent White scratched an ankle with the heel of his other foot with a growing eagerness.

"He said that your government was responsible for killing our Bosnian brothers in Yugoslavia. He said he knew too much and that he was honestly surprised that he was alive."

Agent White paced. His head bobbed. His slacks appeared shorter as he walked, pulling up to reveal his white socks with each step. "He knew who ordered the attacks?"

"Yes."

"Did he tell you that if he were free, if he ever made it out, what he would do to the man responsible for putting him there? Did he tell you that he was going to kill him?"

Al-Dhi'b shook his head.

"No?"

"Islam is a religion of peace. In prison he converted. He promised me he would never again take a life. He swore it with me as his witness."

"What if I told you that as we speak, he is on his way to kill the very man who ordered those attacks in Bosnia?"

"Then I would tell you that you are wrong."

Agent White listened.

"This man you speak of," al-Dhi'b resumed. "Josie told me that this man has a daughter. Is it true?"

"It is."

"Let me tell you something you might not know."

Agent White shuffled up onto the table and crossed his legs.

"The village you mention is the place where our Muslim brothers were slaughtered. He told me everyone was murdered there - everyone, except a baby girl. The man you mention, the one Josie is after, even this man could not murder a baby, so he took her as his own."

Agent White uncrossed his legs, hopped down from the table and began pacing again.

"Josie told me about another man, a dangerous man. He told me that this one was going to kill the little girl and the man who took her," al-Dhi'b said anxiously, watching Agent White pace closer to him. "Josie said this man was in a secret prison like the one we were in, but that if he was ever set free that there would be no stopping him. He said his name, it was..."

"Harkem," Agent White said, finishing the sentence.

"Yes, yes, it was Harkem. This Mr. Harkem, I was told he believes in life after death, in reincarnation?"

Agent White didn't answer the question. He put everything together. He knew about Harkem's quest to eradicate the bloodlines of those who had supposedly murdered him centuries ago. Now he possessed intelligence that the Ambassador's daughter was not his own, but was instead the only surviving soul of the village that Josie had seen massacred. Josie wasn't going to kill the Ambassador - he was going to try and save the girl!

"Son of a bitch! Here I am, sent to Poland to eliminate that bastard Bircher, but now I'm almost cheering for him!" Agent White slapped al-Dhi'b firmly on the back.

Al-Dhi'b flinched and hunched forward, speaking low, "He told me his only purpose in life was to save this girl, the daughter. The last survivor."

Agent White pulled a pen from his pocket and began clicking it rapidly while taking long deep breaths as if he were about to break free from the four surrounding walls and take flight.

"Am I free?" Al-Dhi'b asked, his voice wavering on certain syllables. "Will I be released?"

Agent White clicked the pen. A few minutes passed before he returned it to his pocket. He took one more final exhale and then walked casually up behind al-Dhi'b. He began to rub the prisoner's shoulders for an uncomfortable duration of time.

Al-Dhi'b stirred under the long driving fingers applying pressure to his deltoids.

"I will make a deal with you," Agent White said, finally releasing his hold. "One more question. It's a big one. All you gotta do is answer it and you can walk out of this door - right here, right now."

Al-Dhi'b waited.

"Baklava," Agent White started. "The wife makes it, but she can't get it right. There is something missing - it's a spice - maybe it is cumin, maybe cardamom...I just can't place it?"

Al-Dhi'b tilted his head slightly and cocked an eyebrow before answering. "Cloves. Is she using cloves?"

"By God, that's it!" Agent White said, slapping his hands against his knees. "Cloves! I lost a fiver on that one!"

That being said, Agent White turned and walked up to the door which had remained open when the interrogators left. He turned back, looked at the prisoner and shook his head, mouthing, "Cloves."

Al-Dhi'b remained motionless as Agent White exited. During this time he could hear a one-sided conversation being held at the end of the hallway. Lang made a sudden appearance in the doorway. His face was red and he bit his lip in frustration.

"You're free to go," Lang said in a tone of utter disbelief. "You're free to go."

XVIII

It was almost midnight. Cass was ready.

Whatever questions that had raised concern in her mind from the encounter with Rodham at the orangery were now pushed aside. Whether Rodham was telling truth or she was working for the Russians were matters eclipsed by the .357 Magnum on the kitchen table and the five rounds of death contained within its cylinder.

Her three-five-seven gave her comfort but the snub-nosed revolver was unwieldy and difficult to conceal on her person. The recoil would be difficult to control, but she didn't care: only one shot was required. The chrome-brushed finish paired with the worn mahogany grips made the weapon of choice appear sinister and menacing, as if the revolver wanted to do the killing just as much as she did. The report from the shot would be loud, but if Cass had wanted to use her standard issue Sig Sauer, trying to find a silencer and sub-sonic 9 millimeter ammunition would have taken at least a week. She didn't have the time and she had already made her choice. It was going to be the Magnum.

While the questions in her mind had been discarded, fear continued to circulate. She had never killed anyone before, and while she had seen many dead bodies, there was a big difference between seeing a corpse and turning somebody into one. She wondered whether she had what it took to pull the trigger. Could Harkem even be killed? What gave her the right to be the one to put him in the ground, and after all, how many people before her had tried and failed?

She paced around to the ticking of the clock on the wall. Unlike her previous one in Mostar, this flat was stylish and modern. The building was so new that Cass could detect the biting scent of pigment from the painted walls. A few cardboard boxes that she had yet to unpack had her questioning why she had bothered to unpack anything at all; once she pulled the trigger she would not be coming back, no matter what happened.

The view from the single pane windows in the living room was impressive. In the distance one could see the neon skyline of Warsaw, the Palace of Culture taking center stage supported by a backdrop of modern skyscrapers. Past the center and across the river Wisla, construction cranes spanned the sky in constant motion, a sign of Poland's newfound economic prosperity despite the recession in the rest of Europe.

Earlier hours had passed without pleasure for Cass as the sunlight reflecting off from the windows within view of her apartment had protected the residents behind the glass from her eyes. But as it changes many things, night had ended that. Cass studied the binoculars resting on the windowsill. She walked over and picked them up.

She adjusted the focus knob and soft clicks sounded in her ears as the night came into view. Bright white and incandescent yellow mixed together as the panes filtered the light out from each kitchen, bathroom or bedroom. Her heartbeat increased and she put down the binoculars to check the clock. The Magnum was loaded. Her shoes were on and her jacket was by the door. She had time.

Cass focused on a man sitting at the dinner table reading the *Rzeszspospilita* newspaper. Two children played in the next apartment while their mother did the last of the day's cleaning. In another flat, she watched a young couple fight; fingers were pointed, doors were slammed and apologies waited in vain.

She panned across the horizon and settled on a new apartment building. Most of the lights were off, but on the top floor there was a flat with a bedroom light turned on. A young teenager with a Clash poster on the wall sang into his fist as if he were on stage. Interestingly, only when her binoculars crossed his window could she hear the sound coming from his stereo.

One by one, the lights were gradually turned off and darkness filled windows that only a moment before had held light. Cass thought in that moment that this was symbolic of life itself, for every one of those people had their own lives, hopes and dreams, yet one day their lights too would turn off forever. Cass wondered if what each person did before their light went out really mattered at all.

The fearsome certainty of death had weighed on Cass even as a child, and before the death of her neighbor. At times she fought it bravely, or found peace in it; for the other times when the lonely bottle of red wine failed to push it away, she would tell herself that she did not remember her birth and would therefore not remember death. What if Harkem was right? Or wasn't crazy? What if there really was life after death?

A bathroom light turned on in the distance. Cass picked up the binoculars. A young woman came into view.

The woman walked to the window and stared out into the night. Cass pulled back instinctively, as through the binoculars, it appeared as if the woman was staring directly at Cass with an accusative glare. Cass knew it would have been impossible for the woman to see her, but even after all of the years that Cass had been a voyeur, she always felt that in some instinctive way when she looked into her subject's eyes that they knew they were being watched.

It reminded Cass of one of her favorite novels - *Midnight*, by Dean Koontz. A character in the book, bound to a wheelchair, connected to the outside world only by spending his evenings looking through his telescope. Cass felt a connection to this character and the way he described that it always seemed through the lens that they were looking right at you. She also found that her sense of smell increased. She could smell the food cooking on the stove, the scent of the soap in a shower or the plants on the kitchen sill.

Cass watched the woman unbutton her shirt, and then unzip her skirt. Unlike the character in *Midnight*, Cass didn't turn away. The young woman, naked, turned to face the window, her hips visible above the sill, her breasts symmetrically balanced and her arms slender. All the lines of the human form were visible, highlighted by the sharpened shadows from the light inside her room.

For Cass, it was the fact that there was only herself and the woman, alone together. It was not always sexual or erotic; simply, in that moment Cass didn't feel lonely. She watched the long strands of hair fall down across the woman's spine after she released the clip that had held the locks in place. The woman walked out of view. The light turned out.

A siren called out in the night from some distant street as Cass focused the binoculars on the large face of the clock set atop the Palace of Culture. Clearly visible just above the roman number six was Warsaw's own Siren, the symbolic image of the defender of the city. She was set there, embossed in gold, forever vigilant with her shield against her breast and her sword held high. The clock chimed once, the siren continued and Cass knew it was time to go.

She hit the street. It was one of those special nights that softly whispers in your ear that morning will never come. Time itself seems content to sit and slowly watch the stars above. The air was warm and refreshing and the blood moon rose up proudly against the skyline, as if its only purpose was to serve as a splendid decoration in the night.

Cass was surprisingly calm, and by some miracle, her mind separated itself from what it was about to do. The Magnum rested in a shoulder holster, concealed behind a light blazer, which stylishly paired with her faded denim jeans and casual sneakers. Removing the tie from her wrist, she pulled her hair back into a ponytail, leaving only a strand or two to curl up around her ears. She wasn't an expert shot, and she wasted no time trying to lie to herself about it now. She rationalized that if wars were waged in Africa with nine-year-olds and Kalashnikovs, then there was no reason why she would not be able put a bullet in Harkem's skull from only a few feet away. She entered the metro station and waited for the train.

The largest station, Metro Centrum, was clean but dated. Besides a few billboards, it had no hint of style or design like other European tubes. She waited only a minute before the train arrived, and after the briefest moment of hesitation, she boarded. The carpets were worn. Plastic, faded seats barricaded Plexiglas windows carved by the razor blades of the local soccer hooligans. On the floor, a large decal stated *Zakochaj sie w Warszawie.*

"Fall in love with Warsaw," Cass said, translating the phrase and finding it ironic.

Three drunks leered at her. A few babushkas, a homeless man and a young child who appeared to be alone stared at her. Everyone stared at her. She hated it. It was as if the national pastime in the whole damned country was staring. She had tried to ignore it, then she decided to stare back, and once she resorted to waving. None of it worked. The whole city kept right on staring.

Having reached the end of the train farthest away from the drunks, Cass sat down. The man next to her was American; of this, she was certain. He seemed a bit younger than her, but he was striking. After some debate Cass decided she would even go so far as to call him dashing - not that she ever used the term - but she found that in this instance, it was appropriate. He was strong, masculine, and exuded sexuality. A slight scar above his left eye hinted at something wild, even dangerous. Now Cass was the one staring.

She was waiting for it to hit her: the fear, the doubt, and the full realization that she was about to take the life of another person. Maybe killing another person was something more than it had been made out to be. She had heard the contractors brag about how it was better than the first time they got blown or the first time they snorted cocaine. Cass didn't feel any of those emotions. In fact, she felt let down, but then again, Cass had never been blown and had never snorted cocaine. She expected it to hit her suddenly, but as the train stopped at the next metro station, she found herself still preoccupied with the American next to her.

A recorded voice came over the intercom to announce the arrival of the Holy Cross station. Cass stood up, smiled at the American, and then left the train. This station was even smaller and plainer than the last. The platform was flanked by two sets of stairs serving as exits. A large map detailing the surrounding streets above was placed in the middle of the station. Cass sat down on the bench behind it and her eyes sought the nearest clock.

It was a large digital timer with bright yellow numerals that counted down each second like a doomsday clock. Two minutes to midnight. Two minutes until the last metro arrived and until she found out if Rodham was telling the truth. If so, in mere moments, Cass would pull the trigger and Harkem would lie dead on the stairs of the one of the ugliest metro stations in Europe.

The digits counted down mechanically, without emotion or hesitation. For the first time Cass became aware that one of her feet was tapping nervously on the tiled floor. She unzipped her blazer just enough to reach inside and feel the steel pressing up against her breast.

"Don't look into his eyes," she said.

With ten seconds left, the platform began to shudder as the vibration on the tracks pulsed throughout the station, announcing the arrival of the train. The hollow tunnel drove the sound of the approaching train into Cass's ears. The whistle sounded out from somewhere behind the black wall of the tunnel's shadows and it sent a chill running down her spine. The cry of the train sounded to her in that moment like souls of the damned caught in purgatory. She shook her head to pass the thought off as foolish. She looked down: now both of her feet were tapping on the tile.

The light from the engine charged forward. The final whistle sounded and a blast of air followed the train, churning the atmosphere of the station into a tempest. Suddenly everything was calm. The metro stopped, its doors opened, and Harkem walked off the train.

The emptiness of the station held only Harkem and Cass. She swallowed.

"The eyes," Cass said, trying to be confident as she pulled the Magnum from its holster. "Not into the eyes."

Harkem was a mountain of a man with a stride that drove him forward like a locomotive. His shoulders spanned wider than any Cass had ever seen and his neck was thick. He was a force of nature, but she experienced a pang of disappointment as he moved towards the stairs.

She had expected a maniac, a monster, even the Devil himself. He was just a man in a black jacket and jeans, a briefcase hanging from his left hand. Despite his stature, he didn't even really look out of place. He didn't look like a killer, he didn't look crazy, he just looked like a man heading home.

Passing behind the map, Cass shielded her approach but soon found that she was out in the open with the revolver in her hand. There was no turning back. She was going to kill Harkem.

"Jesus," she said, struggling to keep up with Harkem's gait. "You're going to do this, you *can* do this!"

Harkem reached the stairs.

"If I shoot him in the back, does that make me a coward?" Cass asked herself as she closed the distance, both hands now firmly on the revolver.

As Harkem crested the stairs and turned the corner, Cass decided that honor and chivalry were subjects better left for men to argue. Why would it matter how she killed him? The only thing that mattered would be that he was dead. It was for the greater good, for humanity and for that promise Cass had made.

For the first time, she felt the weight of the revolver in her grip as her forearms twisted under her skin and adrenaline opened up a highway in her veins. She no longer felt calm or at ease. It took all of her strength just to cock the hammer of the gun. The trigger pull on the revolver was heavy. Her heart raced as she wondered if she had enough strength in her finger to fire the shot.

"Eyes," Cass spoke her mantra. "Not into the eyes."

The polished, linen-white tiles on the wall cast her reflection back into her peripheral. She could see her hair flowing behind her as she neared the corner. Cass could see the reflection of the revolver, and she could see fear in her own eyes.

Striding with all her power around the corner, she wrapped her finger around the trigger and took up the slack. As she passed the corner and raised the steel she stopped. Harkem was there, only a foot away - his back was turned and he was leaning forward. Details sharper than any Cass had ever sensed before flooded her core. Harkem's hand was outstretched to the ground, the one hundred zloty banknote in his fingers. A homeless beggar on the ground accepted his gift with tears.

Suddenly the light above her went out. Harkem turned and Cass hesitated.

It happened in a flash. In the moment of his compassionate act, Cass had lowered the revolver to where a shot now was impossible. She was frozen. She had made the one mistake she had primed herself against, she had looked into his eyes. Harkem was upon her in an instant. The revolver was no longer in her hands and she heard it scatter down the stairwell before the pain arrived.

Each heartbeat felt like the blast of an inferno, threatening her soul. Harkem's first strike had disarmed her; the second one followed instantly. His attack, an open backhand, lifted her from her feet and put her on the floor, sending her to the brink of consciousness. Cass's vision narrowed to a white tunnel.

She heard voices and footsteps as Bombay suddenly filled her fading vision. His pistol was drawn but it was not pointed at Harkem.

"Shoot!" Cass tried to scream. "Shoot him!"

Bombay lowered his pistol. Harkem walked away. Cass lost consciousness.

XIX

It was four in the morning, and the woman in the kitchen had already been at work for over ten hours. She boiled potatoes in a large stainless steel pot, stirred borscht, poured compote into jars, and on a flat range under a single light bulb, she cooked beef chops. Through a window behind her and across a deli counter was a large table surrounded by red metal folding chairs. These had been donated from a primary school across the street. A few drunks sat at one end of the table, while at the other, a young woman took her plate of food and sat down next to Josie.

The eatery was a remnant of communist times. Traditionally categorized as a Milk Bar, a government-funded cafeteria open at all hours to provide food for the homeless, it now stayed in business by catering to paying students and alcoholics.

The soup was bitter. The potatoes were hard and the small squared chop of beef was tough and suspicious in taste. The compote, on the other hand, was amazing. One of the drunks stirred, shot a look of malicious intent towards the girl, but soon leaned back in his chair and passed out. Josie understood that the girl had chosen her seat next to him wisely, using him as a shield of protection. There was something about her that tugged at his attention in the way that words hover at the tip of one's tongue.

As she ate, she would occasionally look directly at Josie as if she wanted to start a conversation. The eye contact would last only a second or two before she returned to eating and flipping through the pages of her student identification, which was next to her purse and cell phone on the table. Josie thought she was much too beautiful to be so bashful but also much too obvious to be a threat.

"Dzien Dobry." The young woman seemingly worked up the courage to speak.

"Morning," Josie replied casually.

"English!" Her eyes widened and a bright smile came across her face. Her shoulders dropped and she leaned forward, speaking in a quiet voice as if she had discovered some fantastic secret. "You're American, yes?"

"Irish."

"It is my favorite country!" She managed to squeal with excitement while maintaining a hushed tone.

"Ireland?"

"America!" The young woman entirely ignored Josie's reply.

He shrugged and took a drink of compote.

"My Aunt, she is living in your city of Chicago. I am here in Warsaw today to apply for a J1 Visa. You are so lucky! If only I could know what it feels like to be an American!"

Josie determined that a J1 Visa would allow her to find employment once she arrived in the United States, and that as soon as she found work, her employer would exploit her to the fullest. She would be overcharged for some shithole hotel room, worked like a slave, and if she raised any protest at all for the way they treated her, then they would threaten to call immigration. Josie also knew that whatever money she could save, she would surely blow it all on clothes, perfumes and handbags, and by the time she returned to Poland, she would be tired, overweight, and flat broke. She would get her wish to know what it feels like to truly be an American.

"Boston, New York City, Vegas!" She continued to finger her student identification while she rattled off the names of places she wanted to visit. "Golden Gate, South Beach!"

He swallowed the last bit of food, forcing down the hardened beef chop and chasing it with the final warm drop of compote. Looking for an opportunity to politely excuse himself and head out the door, he stood up from the table. A departing smile was halted on his countenance.

"Son of a bitch." His tone was colored more with disappointment than shock.

How had he missed it? Every student in Poland is issued a student identification booklet on the first day of university. Upon receiving it, one turns to the final page, where the signature of the university's President will be inked the day the degree is completed. A superstitious tradition dictates folding the final page evenly in half. The young woman held the booklet open before him now: the last page was unfolded. Unmarked. Pristine.

She had stopped talking and a melancholy, pleading look had replaced her youthful bashfulness and earlier enthusiasm. Innocence had flown. She was not a student. She was a professional.

"I'm sorry," she said, her voice suddenly mature and strong.

Josie dropped the napkin from his hand as he fled to the door.

Like a man who has spent the entire night sitting on a barstool and running up a tab, he knew as soon as he stood that he was rocked. Except Josie also knew he wasn't drunk. He was poisoned. As his head began to drive itself into confusion he wondered why did she bother to warn him? Why didn't she just let him die? Was she trying to save him? Maybe she just wanted to let him know before he died that he had made a mistake.

"Russians!" Josie croaked.

He remembered the question Tatianna had asked him during their drive to Hungary. It might not have been a rainy day in Moscow – instead, it was a humid morning in Warsaw - but more than ever what Josie needed at that moment was luck.

As he struggled down the street, he felt death flow into his veins, which seemed to tighten and bulge throughout his body. A tram stop loomed only fifty meters away at an intersection, but the first service of the morning wouldn't arrive for another two or three hours. Disorientated, he turned around once or twice, trying to focus. He watched his hand trace by his face as if time was fragmented and delayed. The colors of the city pounded into his eyes with such vibrancy that he had to squint to see anything at all.

The nearest hospital was north in the district of Zoliborz; the kilometer that separated it from him was too far to make it on foot. He would be dead before he could find the nearest bus station, let alone make it to the hospital. Pain surged through his hands and set into his shoulders, while his legs grew stiff and heavy so quickly that his knees locked, causing him to lose his balance and fall into the street.

A loud blast from a car horn twisted into his eardrum so painfully that Josie cried out. He closed his eyes to a bright pair of headlights and commanded his muscles to move. The driver of the car exited the vehicle, circled it rapidly and began to scream, delivering one swift kick to the fallen man's mid-section. Josie didn't feel the strike; the pain surging through his body was so great that nothing could challenge it. Disconnected, and no longer in control, he watched these events transpire from outside of himself, as if they passed by watching it on a television screen. On this screen he saw that the car that nearly killed him was a taxi. Here was the luck he had needed.

With all the strength he had left, Josie lunged forward, grabbed the cabbie's shirt and pleaded in Polish to be taken to the hospital. "Szpital! Poprosze!"

The cabbie surely would have protested, kicked Josie once more and spit on him before dragging him out of the street and continuing on his way, but he didn't. Clenched in one of Josie's hands was a thick roll of banknotes. The cabbie took the fare.

From the backseat of the taxi, Josie watched as each passing streetlight streaked by the window in long unbroken chains of light as if he had taken a blotter of LSD, yet if it was acid, it was not the right set, and certainly not the right setting. He could hear the engine accelerate, and the radio as well as the cabbie warned him not to vomit in his taxi.

As Josie's limbs locked tighter, his teeth clenched together and he could feel his jaw slowly pushing off to one side. The pain had reached such a climax that each moment seemed to last an eternity. He could see the cabbie's frightened eyes looking back to him from the rear view mirror. The fear dwelling there was not out of concern for Josie; the cabbie feared for his own life, as if Josie was some about to turn into a werewolf or some creature of the night.

Fighting hard to breath, Josie began to dry heave as he choked on his own spit. He could feel his heart kick into overdrive in a last ditch effort to circulate blood through the system. A black tunnel formed around his eyes, narrowing his vision to a focused point of blinding light.

Suddenly, a cold blast of air filled the backseat of the taxi as the door was opened. He was pulled from the cab and could dimly hear shouting and the sound of people running towards him. He heard a woman scream. The cabbie cursed and a doctor shouted orders as he felt himself being carried, the bitter taste of bile on his lips and the powerful scent of a Turkish cigarette curiously over-powering it all. Josie blacked out.

XX

The morning sun had yet to clear the horizon, but Gibbs was already awake. The dying embers from the fireplace cracked and spit their last bit of pulsing warmth near his feet. The cold air chilled his skin when he removed the wool blanket and he hurried to dress. He laced his boots, holstered his Glock and shouldered his pack.

While the comfort of the fire from the night before was pleasant and peaceful, Gibbs slept restlessly. Slumber came to him in short bursts, lasting only long enough to let him know that it had actually happened. Despite his twisted core and sore back from the leap into the Adriatic, Gibbs felt strong and ready.

He was surprised to find Niska standing directly behind him. Her face was without judgment or concern even though she had seen the pistol. The weight of sleeplessness was absent from her bright face and her clothes were refreshed except for last night's apron tied tightly around her waist.

Niska didn't seem curious about why Gibbs was awake at such an early hour, or that he had been about to leave without saying goodbye. He was troubled that Niska somehow knew the weight of Amir's death despite her calm, accepting countenance.

To offer her money or any other gesture would be an insult, but he felt that he had to give her something. His guilty eyes darted to a string of garlic above the fireplace and followed it to a nearby red pepper resting at the base of an olive oil jar. All of the money that he had left in his wallet now rested beneath the jar. A few hundred euros wouldn't begin to compensate for Amir, but it was all he could do.

Niska spoke to him in a soft, understanding tone at the door. Gibbs was crossing the threshold to the world outside when she suddenly grabbed his arm and held up a finger. She wanted him to wait.

She fetched two oranges and a bottle of spring water from her kitchen, and he instinctively raised his hands in protest. She pushed her gifts deeper into his palms and he looked at the floor in silence before turning again to the open door. Her parting touch was a prodding at his shoulders, as if to tell him that all was well and forgiven. He turned from her to the thick mist that dawn had yet to burn away. Somewhere a rooster called. A goat with a bell began to stir and bleat while the first bird of the morning began to call. The night was over. It was a changing of the guards: from dark to light, and from predator to prey, dawn stirred on the horizon.

A small stream alongside the dirt road led the way out of the village; it was the forest he sought and he walked into it at the earliest opportunity, which came when he reached a sharp bend in the road. Within a few meters, just as Amir had described during their conversation in Mostar, Gibbs encountered a natural stone path that led further up into the mountains soaring above. The path was a series of deep gouges where the soil had been washed away and the exposed limestone had been carved centuries before as the last of the glaciers made their retreat to the sea.

He climbed higher and higher and witnessed the Balkan sun crest the distant mountains and replace the crisp taste of morning with its caustic heat. The forest valleys below held the mist in the fingers of their branches but the rocks underfoot blasted the radiant sun back squarely under his chin and narrowed his visible surroundings to a painful mirage.

The peak was now in view and its summit would not yield without a fight. Each step forward on the terraced stone was dangerous; every rock was sharply angled and the scree, loose and slick, served as a constant reminder that gravity pulled no punches. One false step might result in only a scrape or bruise, or it could equally result in becoming a red mess on the rocks hundreds of meters below. The margin was slim. Watching his shadow and fighting heatstroke, Gibbs met the summit as a steady trickle of sweat fell from his nose and landed on rocks between his legs, evaporating instantly.

The salt of perspiration burned his eyes. It also dried on his clothes, forming a pattern of angled white lines contained within each wrinkle of fabric. He could see for what looked like a thousand miles, and somewhere down there in the interior and through the wild forests was what he was looking for.

The descent was long and tedious. He would often have to about face and circle back towards the peak to navigate around a series of sheer limestone cliffs that offered one way down, a way that he was inclined to describe as quite unpleasant. Within two hours, he was welcomed by the extending curtain of shade provided by the tree line at the base of the mountain. He drove his fingers into the rind of an orange and tasted the sweet twist of citrus in his mouth, a welcome refreshment of the heat.

Chewing the seeds from the fruit, Gibbs reviewed his mental map. Amir had mentioned a square field somewhere in this valley that served as the indicator of the cave's entrance. Beyond the green and black depths of the forest, Gibbs focused his eyes. It was there in the distance, unmistakable and within reach.

While spotting it had taken only moments, reaching the field took Gibbs nearly three hours. He picked landmarks on the horizon and walked in straight lines but it took him much longer than expected. He began to doubt his earlier view from his perch above the tree line. After doubling back on his trail, he noticed a break in the trees ahead and then, as if it had been just a step or two away all along, he entered the field.

Wild grass grew nearly to his shoulders. It was yellowed and dry but changed progressively to the color of green that borders on neon, the kind of virgin color that is held within each leaf of spring before the chlorophyll flushes through the system of the tree and darkens to a deeper hue. The ground grew moist, and with each step his feet sank deeper into the water that was lying beneath the surface.

He parted the last of the grass that rose in obstruction and found himself standing on the banks of a swiftly flowing stream. Fed from the mountains above, its water was so cold that the day's heat seemed a distant memory; in fact, his chilled toes began to long for the heat of the summit.

In the shade of a large willow, the second orange and bottle of spring water from Niska were consumed. Gibbs roused himself from his resting place and followed the stream through the small mountain range. Although covered in trees at this altitude, the mountains rose from the earth at such odd angles that there were exposed routes of stone visible. One of these originated out of the stream, and as Amir had said, a shadow was visible at the top of it.

Standing at the base of the cliff and looking up, he searched for a way to reach the cave's entrance. The cliff ran at a vertical angle and a massive crack split up the center of the face and stopped just below the shadows of the cave. The only obstacle to his path was a slab of limestone which pushed out into the void, forming a roof which would have to be climbed to reach the entrance.

"Nuts," Gibbs said, extending his hand towards the rock.

As he struck the palm of his hand on the face of the cliff, a fine dust sparked into the air. He looked at his palm. It was white and cleansed of sweat and orange pulp. Taking a deep breath, Gibbs studied the wall in front of him while going over the route one more time. He didn't want to give himself much time to think twice about keeping his two feet on the ground. He tightened his laces, raised one foot from the earth, and began to climb.

It had been over a decade since Gibbs had last rock climbed. With each step, however, he settled into a confident pace. The crack provided excellent holds; at times, he could insert his entire foot into it and rest or secure a firm grip with a finger or two and keep moving. Soon he was above the tree tops and arrived quickly at the termination of the crack. Here, a series of eroded holds made the rest of the climb up to the roof as easy as walking up the rungs of a ladder.

The view was amazing and the exposure was wild. As the cliff rose higher away from the mountains, the valleys drifted further below, giving Gibbs the sensation that he was thousands of feet in the air rather than a hundred or so. Without warning his body tightened as he felt gravity work its fingers into his shoulders and do its best to pry him free from the cliff. Resting his forehead against the face, he took a deep breath and did what he had always done when vertigo struck: he closed his eyes and began to whistle.

It was not helping this time.

The boots on his feet had thick soles and as he stood there on a small ledge separating him from death, he began to trust his feet less and less. He edged up closer to the base of the roof. If it had not been for the firm holds above his head for his fingers to grip, his shaking legs would have failed him.

Looking up now at the roof, Gibbs could see that it stretched out farther into space than he had expected. It seemed as if it were out of reach. Holding fast with his hands, he tried to position his feet higher so he could reach out and try to find a hold. His adrenaline rushed across his body like a howling wind and the earth below him seemed to drop into the void. Lactic acid burned in his shoulders and his feet slipped. His hands panicked and began to grasp at anything they could hold onto.

There was nowhere to run to. Gibbs had seconds until his body would yield to inevitable death.

His vision narrowed and a melancholy feeling of nostalgia swept across his brow. He remembered his father teaching him how to ride a bicycle, the smell of Christmas cookies his mother would make, his siblings and his dog. The day he became a Ranger played out in his mind. Then, Gibbs remembered Josie.

Josie believed in him. That was all that it took.

Gibbs opened his eyes with renewed determination and saw right there above him on the edge of the roof a sharp outcropping of limestone the size of a baseball. It was the perfect hold.

Both hands clung to the hold so securely that it seemed as if nothing could break his grip. His legs kicked free of the face. For a moment his lower body launched out into the empty space but his hands held firm, and with everything he had left, Gibbs pulled himself up and over the roof. On a slope no steeper than a manicured lawn, he dropped to his knees and shook uncontrollably. He let the tears of strain bond with the sweat of pain washing down his face. Gibbs looked up. The cave was right before him.

At the mouth of the cave the darkness drew a hard line. After a few steps inside, Gibbs could not even see his hands held up only inches from his face. He wondered how Amir had made the climb – and how he had ever made it back down – but more than that, Gibbs wondered what was inside the cave.

Five hundred lumens from the Surefire flashlight he retrieved from his cargo pocket screamed out, filling the cave with a searing white light. Its brilliance was so great that the walls of the cave washed out entirely and appeared as a continual white reflection. Blinking, he noticed a small arrangement of stones at his feet. It was a fire pit. It looked like it could have been from a thousand years ago, Gibbs was aware that it was only a decade old, dating from when Amir had first fled from the war.

Corroded and oxidized electrical wires ran the length of the walls, leading further into the darkness. Heavy machine marks were visible on the floor which revealed that the cave itself certainly was man-made and at the edge of the beam from his flashlight, he saw a door. Powerful governments had spent billions trying to find this door, and Gibbs marveled at the ease with which he approached it.

A thick gauge of steel formed the door into an intimidating obstruction, and its pair of massive, rusty hinges defied even the thought of dynamite. At his waist there was a stainless steel rotary wheel not unlike the kind used on bank vaults. Shrugging, Gibbs placed his hands upon the wheel, lowered his frame and readied his feet. The results were not what he expected: the door opened with little protest.

The damp scent of stagnant water and earth rushed across his nose, making a run to freedom from the chamber where it had been locked in for countless years. A concrete tunnel awaited Gibbs on the other side of the door. It was so tight that as he walked inside, he felt his elbows scrape alongside the walls. The frame of the door behind him was higher than the floor of the tunnel and it acted as a dam, keeping a bronzed pool of water held in place. The water rose to his knees.

While the light from his Surefire fought back the darkness, it again reflected so intensely on the close walls that it lost its reach and only illuminated a few meters of the passageway ahead. The eternal night of the tunnel was kept at bay like some wild beast, and Gibbs spun around in the water as he heard something splash from behind him.

He opened his jaw to pop his ears and tilted his head to listen. Besides his runaway heartbeat and the constant drops of water from the concrete overhead, everything was silent. Minutes passed until his ears tuned into a sound that had been present all along: the echo of breathing right in front of him.

The Glock ripped free of the holster as Gibbs clenched the Surefire. The tunnel was empty. The silence returned.

A stench rose up from the water and overpowered the smell of decay and mold, it was the smell of cigarettes. He froze and clicked the Surefire off. Holding his breath as the burning air passed beyond him and headed for the door, Gibbs felt the darkness laugh in his face. He was tempted to empty the magazine into the black tunnel. Had he imagined it all? Gibbs turned on the flashlight.

The tunnel exploded back into view, and it was empty.

"Fuck." Gibbs wanted out.

He shifted his weight and was about to turn around in retreat when he discerned a turn in the tunnel up ahead.

He edged up to it slowly and cleared the intersection with his Glock before blasting it with his flashlight. This tunnel was empty too. He couldn't take the chance to venture down this new passageway without a spool of string or other method of return. It would only take one turn to get off course and he would spend the rest of his life trying to find his way out. The batteries would not last that long. Gibbs moved past the intersection.

The humid grip of the tunnel eased and soon the drops of condensation ceased their assault on the water below. The taste of the air lost its bitterness and Gibbs relaxed his grip on the pistol as he began to draw deeper breaths.

A reflection sparked at the end of the Surefire's beam. It was not a reflection from a piece of machinery, a light, or even from a piece of broken glass. It was instead the worst kind of reflection, the kind that is bright and yellow, that follows you with every step: the eyes of a predator.

"Wolves," Gibbs whispered, leveling the pistol at the eyes ahead.

A terrible silhouette of muscle, power and instinct crouched in the shadows. Survival rested on how fast Gibbs could empty those fifteen rounds of nine millimeter from the Glock in his hand. He tightened his finger around the trigger. The wolf glared at Gibbs with those deadly and hypnotic eyes. Gibbs tried to break the trance.

He dropped his gaze to the water as a droplet of sweat cascaded down his nose and met the water around his ankles, causing ripples to disturb the rusty grime floating on the surface. The water began to move, forming small rolling waves that lapped up against the side of the tunnel and ran past his feet. Like a train pulling into the station, his thoughts arrived slowly as they formed into a conclusion: the scent of cigarette smoke was in fact the musk from the wolf's hide, and now as he watched the small waves form around his ankles, he realized that there had indeed been something behind him all along.

With a wild jerk he spun and emptied the magazine of the Glock into the tunnel behind him. A wolf soared past him unscathed by the hollow points, and in the light from the muzzle blast Gibbs could see those terrible yellow eyes and feel a brush of fur against his arm. He lined up the sights on the head of the escaping beast and pulled the trigger. The magazine was empty. He depressed the magazine release and slammed the second clip into the pistol. The wolves were gone.

He ran forward through the tunnel fueled by adrenaline and instinct, dimly aware of the obstacle at his feet. His foot caught on a mound of soil and he stumbled to an earthen floor, blinded by a cloudless blue sky overhead. As the unmistakable smell of pine blanketed his senses, he lay on his back. The mound of earth extended from where he was at a steep angle to the forest above. The tunnel had obviously collapsed years ago, and judging from the sets of prints, the wolves had claimed the passage as their own.

He rolled and propped himself up on his knees and, shined the light past the beams of sunshine and back into the crushed tunnel. There was a door at the end of the tunnel, crawling through the debris of earth, steel and roots, he reached it.

Within the frame of the door there was a laminated piece of paper folded in half. He pulled it free and the hinges cried in protest. Holding the laminate in one hand and reaching out for the handle with the other, Gibbs pushed the door open.

A massive chamber opened up before him. Gibbs swept the light left and then right. His mouth dropped open. He couldn't believe what he was seeing.

As his hands began to shake, the little laminated note announced itself. Inserting his finger between it and expanding the piece of paper, Gibbs looked down. Efficiently drawn, the image was so direct and powerful that it nearly caused Gibbs to pull his hand back in shock and drop the paper. The drawing was off a shark and a jackal.

"Son of a bitch, Josie!" Gibbs cried. "How did you ever...."

Looking up from the note to the miraculous chamber in front of him, he finally understood.

XXI

Josie opened his eyes.

The incandescent light over the hospital bed painfully greeted the return of his vision. There was a door just past the foot of his bed. It was open and Josie watched as people passed by in the hallway. At the threshold was a black cat. She was staring directly at Josie. He wondered whether the animal was real or a hallucination, and as he tried to focus his eyes, the definition of the room faded and everything began to spin. He clenched the rails of his hospital bed and squeezed his eyes shut with nausea. His back arched high and he blacked out again.

He woke hours later. He cautiously lifted his head from the pillow and opened his eyes: the cat was gone. An IV and a doctor were at his side, and curiously, a laminated wall chart across the room detailed the female reproduction system. Josie became aware that his legs were spread apart and elevated, held in place by stirrups rising from each corner of the bed.

"Either I am dreaming, or I have just delivered a baby!" Josie muttered out loud to the doctor.

"I can assure you that you did not give birth." The doctor spoke in a humorless tone. "I can also assure you that you are very much awake and this is certainly not a dream."

Josie felt the intravenous in the joint of his arm begin to throb as the painful bite of circulation began to spasm back into his veins. Starting slowly, he tried to move his fingers, then his hands and arms, and then continued on to check each muscle to make sure it was operational and under his control. Once this was complete, he issued his body the command to sit up, pull the IV and get the hell out of wherever he was. For a moment, his body tightened as if it were going to comply, but after a few seconds of tension, it relaxed. He eased back into the mattress of the bed; he knew he wasn't going anywhere.

He counted the drips from the intravenous bag above his head. There was already one empty bag on a stainless steel operating table by his shoulder, and he estimated that he had been lying in bed for at least six hours. He strained to read the printed label on the IV bag.

"Relanium," the doctor said, noting Josie's struggle.

He was a lean and slender man whose defining facial features were a set of high cheekbones and a narrow brow. While Josie did not find the doctor intimidating, these features combined with a slight grin and fixed expression made him seem foxlike. The doctor tapped the bag once to ensure circulation before pulling a green stool out from the corner and placing it directly next to Josie's bed.

"I would like to apologize about your current situation," he said, sitting in the chair and gesturing to the fixed stirrups that held Josie's legs. "Our emergency ward was full and this was the only room available."

Josie forced a pleasant understanding look on his own face while the gears of his mind turned quickly. Why had the doctor started the conversation with an apology? Was it meant to disarm? To befriend? For all Josie knew, the room he was in could have been in a prison back at the CIA black site in Kiejkuty.

"Mister....Mister Rojas, yes?" The doctor read a name from a white plastic insurance card in his hands. "Los Angeles, USA?"

"Culver City," Josie lied. "Please call me Andre."

The medical insurance card which the doctor held was one that Josie had lifted from an American tourist in Mostar. He had used it only once before in the Balkans. The card was long past its expiration date; if the hospital had tried to investigate, the process would take at least a few days to get word back from the States.

"How are you feeling?" The doctor flicked the card with his thumb as he held it in his fingers. He seemed disappointed, as if he knew that Josie was lying.

"I feel great," Josie said, his focus on getting his muscles working.

"I'm curious," the doctor said. "If you don't mind, could you describe what happened to you before you arrived at the hospital?"

Josie answered truthfully.

"Did you experience any gastrointestinal discomfort in the past few days?" The doctor stood and glanced out of the window behind Josie's headrest.

Giving a nod that could have meant either yes or no, Josie watched as the doctor moved to the foot of the bed.

"Metoclopramide," the doctor said, turning away from Josie and closing the room's door softly, then leaning on it as if to reinforce to his patient that there was no way out.

Josie attempted to repeat the phrase that the doctor had spoken, but the Relanium running through his veins limited his tongue.

"Metoclopramide," the doctor repeated. "It is a common gastrokinetic agent that is primarily used to treat severe cases of gastroparesis."

Josie listened.

"Diarrhea," the doctor said, putting it in layman's terms. "Was it prescribed to you here in this country?"

Josie took a gamble. "Yes."

"Where?"

"Mokotow." Josie named a district.

"How many milligrams was the dosage?" The doctor returned to the IV bag.

Josie feigned confusion.

"The typical dose is five milligrams. We won't truly know until we get the blood labs back in a day or two, but I would say from the reaction you had that surely you must have ingested well over a hundred times that amount."

He wondered why the doctor wasn't pushing him for answers. At every turn, he gave Josie an out from the questioning. The doctor was revealing too much and getting nothing in return; perhaps he wasn't working for the Agency after all.

"Mr. Rojas, you have suffered a toxic reaction to an overdose of Metoclopramide." The doctor's air retained that initial flavor of disappointment. "The dosage which you ingested induced a condition known as Neuroleptic Malignant Syndrome. You were a dead man walking; another five minutes, and you would have been covered with a white sheet rather than a blanket."

Josie felt his muscles start to spark to life as he inclined his head in gratitude. Lifting himself slightly higher on the pillow, he issued another command to his body to get on his feet. Nothing happened.

"At what time did you take the prescription?" the doctor inquired, setting up an easy opportunity for Josie.

"The depends. What time it is now?"

"It's a quarter to four."

Josie tightened up. Why had the doctor used the American format when answering the time? Was the doctor even Polish? Was Josie even in a hospital? A pleading command to rise again went unanswered by Josie's body.

"Neuroleptic Malignant Syndrome is quite rare," the doctor murmured shooting another quick glance out of the window. "It is so rare that even with your symptoms, it would have been nearly impossible to diagnose you in time. Mr. Rojas, the only reason why you are alive today is because nearly a decade ago, a young boy with the same symptoms died on my table. It was my fault. I lost him. When they pulled you in on the stretcher, I remembered that little boy. I took a chance."

"Thank you," Josie said.

The doctor made no acknowledgement of Josie's gratitude. Josie suddenly remembered the forty-five. It hit him in an instant: the doctor was buying time. He was waiting for the police to arrive. Josie struggled to get to his feet. He made it no farther than kicking the sheets free from his body before his muscles protested and he sunk back into the bed.

"Mr. Rojas," the doctor said, pushing his hand down firmly on Josie's chest.

"Andre," Josie said.

"If you are not going to use your actual name, I would prefer that we keep matters on a formal basis." The doctor said. "I have left enough Relanium in your system to limit any attempt of escape, but I'm sure you have already discovered that."

"Fair enough," Josie said, relaxing into the mattress and pulling the sheets up over his body again as if he were complying. He proceeded to begin to covertly remove the IV from his arm.

"There is a small city; it is just to the south of Warsaw. The city is called Lodz. I am sure that you have heard of it?" The doctor shifted his eyes to the door. "If you had died earlier today I could have taken your body to this city and sold your organs to the Ukrainians there for ten thousand euros."

Josie wondered why the doctor hadn't mentioned the pistol. Why had he stopped asking questions? Why didn't he let him die and sell his organs? Maybe ten thousand was not enough? Maybe he wanted the hundred thousand dollars the Agency was offering for Josie's head.

"I am just a simple doctor, Mr. Rojas. Last month I delivered nine babies, saved seventeen lives and lost only one. In that same month I made only twelve hundred zloty. In your country, that is less than four hundred dollars."

If all that the doctor had wanted was money then surely he would have let Josie die. Maybe his conscience had gotten in the way - his obligation as a doctor to save lives, or he had already cashed in on the Agency's reward and was getting some kind of sick pleasure from sharing company with his prisoner. Whatever it was, Josie had to at least try to offer a bribe. The amount had to be high, but not so high that it would seem to be an impossible amount or one that would alert the doctor to the value of the man lying in the bed.

"I can pay," Josie offered, his hand outstretched as if searching for his wallet. "Two thousand dollars. Please, I can pay you for your help, I promise!"

"Promises are not required." The doctor reached down and ripped the blanket free from Josie's body, catching him in the act of removing the intravenous. He twisted it free from Josie's vein. "I also do not require your money. You have already been paid for."

As the doctor lifted Josie up into a sitting position, a rush of blood crashed into Josie's brain and his heart shifted into a spasm of circulation as the last of the Relanium coursed its way through his body.

"Your withdrawal will be severe. In the next few minutes, you will feel quite recovered, but I would suggest getting some rest and staying off of your feet for a few days. At the very least I would suggest that you stay very close to a bathroom, as you will find that the control of certain muscles will be slow to return.

Motioning to a drawer in a small wooden desk placed underneath the anatomy chart, the doctor informed Josie that he would find all of his belongings there.

"She told me that you were strong, that you were going to make it." For a moment the look of disappointment pulled back from the doctor's face. He looked at Josie and gave him one final nod as he opened the door to the hallway. "Please, Mr. Rojas, do not ever come back here. If you do, then next time I will call the Ukrainians in Lodz."

"She?" Josie stuttered. The doctor left and Cass walked through the door.

"Cass!" Josie said, rising to his feet.

"Don't you 'Cass' me, you bastard!" She crossed her arms and glared at him as if she wished him dead.

"Your face?" Josie questioned, noting the bandages. "Cass, what happened to you?"

"I will tell you what happened. Last night as I was standing outside of this hospital trying to enjoy a cigarette, a taxi pulled up and you fell out of the back. That's right - you, my sweet Juka from Mostar." Cass backed up and bit her lower lip. "Your name isn't Juka, is it? Your name is Josie...Josie Bircher."

Raising a finger, Cass threatened. "There is a man waiting down the hall. He is dangerous and he wants you dead. He wants you dead so much that if he knew you were here, I wouldn't hesitate for a second to say that he would shoot you down right here in the middle of a hospital."

"Bombay." Josie shrugged.

"With each step down this hallway I intended to come in, call you a bastard, slap your face and walk back down to Bombay and turn you in." Cass's lower lip trembled and tears formed in her angry eyes. "But now, Juka...Josie...now, standing here in front of you, I can't."

Josie held her as she cried.

"You used me, Josie. You took my laptop, discovered that Harkem was being released and you knew that you had little time," Cass said plaintively, pushing back in his arms so she could look up at him. "It's my right as a woman to hate you, but I left Bosnia knowing I would never see my Juka again. I reasoned that it was part of the job and that you were a casualty of my career. I'm no different than you, Josie. I'm sorry."

Josie kissed her forehead.

"There is one thing I need to know," she said, taking a deep and nervous breath. "When we first met - if you remember - it was snowing and you offered to walk me back home to my apartment. You held my hand, kissed me and told me that you wished that that moment would never end. Was that the truth?"

"Yes," Josie said honestly.

Cass turned her head away and whispered softly in protest. "How can I believe you?"

"Because I knew that someday I would have to leave you and that someday you would find out who I really am. Someday that moment would have to turn into this one, and there would be no other way around it."

Cass clung to his shoulders.

"Bombay says you're a terrorist and a murderer, but I think he's wrong. Something happened to you in Gradiska. I know about the massacre there, Josie. I'm not saying that I understand what you went through or what you have had to live with. Maybe I don't really know anything at all about you but I know that whatever you intend to do means so much to you that it must be for the right reason.

Josie listened.

"The Ambassador is being evacuated from Warsaw. There is a train waiting for him at a rail yard next to the National Railroad Museum on Towarowa Street. He leaves in one hour."

"Thank you."

"You're not coming back, are you?" Cass's swollen eyes looked directly into Josie's. "You're never coming back?"

"No. I'm never coming back."

Cass shook her head in acceptance. She had known the answer, but in the small, unlikely event that she was wrong, she had had to ask.

"I don't know what I believe in anymore, Josie. Maybe everything I have ever known was a lie. Maybe none of it matters anyway. Suppose Harkem is right about life after death. Do you believe in it, Josie?"

Josie kissed her cheek and whispered in her ear. "I believe."

Cass turned her face to his and pressed up against him. They kissed. "In another life then, Josie?"

"In another life."

Cass removed herself from their embrace and held her purse tightly with both hands. "You told me once, Josie, that all a man can ask of a woman is that she believe in him."

Josie smiled, remembering the conversation from their first date.

"You told me that when a man climbs a mountain and loses heart, and wants to turn around, he is stopped by the image of his lover there behind him. That just before he throws in the towel, he turns and sees his woman there behind him." Cass wiped a tear from her eye and reached into her purse.

"She doesn't speak. She looks at him and points her finger to the top of the mountain. She is telling her man to pick up his balls, to find his courage and to do whatever it takes to succeed. In that moment he knows that she would rather be a widow and mourn his death every day for the rest of her life than to have him quit and give up on his dreams. Whatever it takes to do what he believes is right – well, he must do it. He has got to make it to the top of his mountain."

Cass removed Josie's forty-five from her purse and handed it to him. "Well, here I am. To the top, Josie. To the top."

XXII

The glass pane was dirty and rippled from the effects of time and gravity. The paint had long ago peeled free from the sash. The glazing cracked and fell to the floor as Swan pried the window open with the blade of his K-Bar.

Two stories below, a set of tracks ran off into the distance. To his left was the abandoned National Railroad Museum, and on his right, a line of factories and warehouses. Set in between the two lines of track was an empty platform where the Ambassador's train waited.

The platform was accessed through an underground tunnel which Swan had scouted earlier and he had posted a team of contractors at its entrance to wait for the Ambassador's arrival. Despite the line of rooftops on his right, Swan knew that they offered a potential sniper no safe nest as a thick bound line of industrial electrical wires effectively blocked any shot.

There was only one way to get to the Ambassador, and that was to come charging from a point of concealment somewhere along the tracks and up onto the platform. That is where Swan came in. He adjusted his seated position a few feet from the window and leaned forward in his chair. The M-14 rested on the table, steadied by a tripod and a stack of books. The safety was off and a round waited impatiently in the chamber.

Swan's position gave him the perfect view of both sets of tracks. If someone was foolish enough to make a charge, he would have plenty of time to draw a sight on their forehead and shoot them down. His perch in the abandoned school was a sniper's dream: the only issue was the setting sun. If the Ambassador didn't arrive soon, it would be bearing right down upon him, flaring in his scope. Swan would be forced to sacrifice minute-of-head accuracy for a shot in the dark.

Swan tried to get comfortable. The table was small, with a laminated top and a plastic chair attached to it with a single steel pipe. Its position low to the ground had offered the perfect rest for his rifle, providing a stable platform which afforded a great angle of fire from the window.

There were a dozen tables identical to his scattered around the room. Some were turned over, and others were stacked on top of one another. Dried pigments in glass jars by the chalk board and a few yellowed pages tacked to the wall with drawings of elephants, horses and other assorted animals (only the child who drew them knew what the hell they actually were) suggested to Swan that this room had once been used for art class. Some frames and easels were on a cabinet in the corner. Pencils and crayons peeked out from the rubble of textbooks and plaster that had fallen from the ceiling decades ago.

Swan thought it was a damned sad place to die, to have his body found amongst drawings by children rather than metallic fragments and body parts from an IED explosion. He had discerned that the Ambassador was leaving Warsaw permanently. Something had happened - what, he did not care – and as of twenty four hundred that night, his contract would be terminated and he would be out of a job. His loaded pistol sat on the floor next to him. A hollow point plus P plus rested in the chamber, and as soon as the last whistle on the Ambassador's train sounded its departure, Swan would bring the pistol to his temple, feel the sear release the hammer, and then feel no more.

Swan didn't think about it. Just like the Colonel in the novella by J.W. Joseph, *Patrizio*, it didn't really matter anymore: his mind was made up and he had already settled the little doubt he had concerning his ability to actually go through with it. The chance of Bircher learning of the Ambassador's evacuation was small, and the chance of him making it in time to give Swan one last fleeting chance for glory was nearly zero. Even the biting memory of Mosul no longer created a fire sufficient to alter his resolve. He was detached; it was a feeling he had felt often, usually right before a firefight. When the Ambassador's train would pull free from the platform and move towards the horizon, headed towards some distant station, it would signal the end of the line for Swan.

The Ambassador was already an hour late. Each minute the sun pushed further across the horizon and into his line of fire. Slowly, the orange light walked across the floor of the room before finally breaking into the pane of the window he looked out from. Securing the rifle to his shoulder, Swan took a final glance at the pistol.

The wood against his cheek was hard and familiar; his cheekbone could drive itself into the grains and fibers, securing the picture in his sights. The scent of linseed oil drifted from the stock. It reminded him of being a boy in his father's wood shop. The smell of the oil, sawdust and all of the other wonderful masculine scents that reminded him of his father washed through his nose. A tear rolled down the stock and onto the table. Swan looked down at it curiously, as if he didn't know where it had come from.

Through the telescopic sight, he saw one of the security contractors walk up from the underground tunnel and stand on the platform. Soon another man followed, anchoring himself nearby and holding his assault rifle at the ready. The Ambassador had arrived and was being escorted through the tunnel by his security detail.

The sun was now at the edge of the world, sinking down to meet the tracks in the distance. In the final moments before its blaze was pulled below the surface, Swan realized that it would be the last sunset he would ever see. He debated standing up to shoot himself, then decided that it didn't matter and remained seated. He put down his rifle and lifted the pistol to his head, put his finger on the trigger and took one last look out of the window.

Swan's eyes opened wide. At the end of the tracks, silhouetted by the sun, there was a man approaching the train. Swan put the pistol down just as all hell broke loose.

XXIII

A Mercedes signaled, changed lanes and pulled over next to the sidewalk. The car was dated, its stenciled letters on the driver's side door worn and faded, but the word Taxi could be discerned. The building that the cab had stopped in front of was the abandoned National Railroad Museum. The passenger side door opened. Josie staggered to the curb.

Standing caused a rush of blood to stream through Josie's head: he staggered and hunched over as if he were trying to conceal an erection from those passing by. The Relanium had left his system on the cab ride from the hospital, but a surging headache pounded in his right temple. Nearly all of his muscles were back in working order. As the doctor had warned, he had little control of his bowels. Racing to an alley next to the museum, he relieved himself.

To his right above a brick wall, he could see a large red and white striped smokestack paired with the façade of a large warehouse. The tremors of a passing train beneath his feet told him that the tracks were on the other side of the wall. Josie closed his eyes and leaned his head against the wall's bricks. The Ambassador's train was to have left an hour ago, but something inside urged him to keep moving.

Standing in the shadows of the alley, he could see a tram spark past and make a turn at the intersection of Towarowa and Kolejowa Street. A bus station was to his left and a liquor store to his right, and besides a young couple waiting for the next bus, there was no one in sight.

Clenching his fist and driving it into his chest, Josie choked back a series of violent dry heaves. Another passing train sounded like an alarm clock in his ears. *Keep moving.* He walked deeper into the alley hoping to find a way over the wall. The other walls were marked with graffiti, bottles littered the ground, cigarette butts rolled freely in the wind and a single shoe kept company with a used condom.

The brick wall turned at the alley's end and formed a barrier ten meters high with not a single hold for climbing. The rain gutter next to the wall was so rusted that with one slight pull, it came apart in Josie's hands. The museum walls also offered no purchase; in keeping with Soviet styling, they had no windows or sills that could be reached.

Retracing his path past the condom, the shoe and the bottles, he arrived on the street again. He braced his back against the frame of the museum's main door and casually brought his right leg up behind him for support. His only way down to the tracks was through the abandoned museum. He looked for the young couple at the bus stop and noted their departure. The street was empty. His elbow went through the glass door and he turned the handle.

He hoped over two ticket counters and a metal turntable that served as the barriers to the large entrance hall of the museum. Josie gripped one of the ticket counters for balance; the slight exertion had magnified his headache. The hall opened up above him with an arched ceiling four stories high. A small pack of square window panes below the ceiling revealed that the museum had once been a factory.

Picking an angle and moving quickly, Josie crossed the hall. Large paintings of locomotives hung like tapestries from the walls and small glass display cases were arranged around the museum's floors. Some of the displays were filled with bearings, others with screws or whistles; one case held various types of grease used to lubricate wheels.

At the hall's end, a large showpiece held various gauges of railroad track used around the world. Next to this display was a large directory, the ubiquitous *You Are Here* map.

The directory was divided into two levels, and listed the attractions and their locations within the museum. Josie stood on the second level and traced his finger along the map to locate access to the first floor via a set of stairs to his right. From the first floor, there was a courtyard; next to the courtyard was the illustration of railroad tracks. He headed for the stairs.

The windows high above cast long shadows from the waning sun as he approached the stairway, where a thick dust protested each step, releasing mold and decay like a breathing entity. A large industrial light that had fallen from the ceiling blocked a portion of the stairs, forcing Josie to jump over the railing and land in the stairwell.

Despite their condition, the stairs were impressive. A hand-carved maple baluster gently curved in upon itself, its delicate turned spindles holding it above a red velvet carpet. The Russian flavor of the museum oppressed the visitor, but the stairs were so pleasing and beautiful that Josie wondered if he was hallucinating. When he failed to see a black cat anywhere in the vicinity, he decided that he wasn't.

The last brilliant streaks of the sun's bands illuminating the hall failed to penetrate down to the base of the stairwell. With every step down each riser, his movements became more cautious as he allowed his eyes time to adjust.

A faint banner of light glowed far in the distance downstairs. Large bales of insulation from the ceiling had fallen in soaked piles in the center of the room, edging him away from the protection of the walls.

On a table in his path there were small toy models of villages, rising hills and a small glass lake painted with little white crests to give the illusion that waves were reaching the shore. Die cast cars and figurines were arranged around the towns and villages as a seemingly endless supply of track connected each of them together. The toy trains were sitting motionless on the track. The whole set felt as empty and desolate as the museum itself, like a miniature forgotten city. Josie pushed away from it and headed for the light at the door.

Reaching the door, Josie ran his fingers along its frame and found a set of bolts that held it locked in place. Releasing the bolts, he opened the door and a warm rush of orange light greeted his eyes and instantly warmed his face. The courtyard beyond resembled a prison; where gardens had once grown, thick brush and wild grass took root, and concrete benches and broken displays lay in ruin.

A steel fence and another brick wall separated the courtyard from the tracks beyond. A pile of bricks had crumbled long ago from the wall and as Josie cautiously approached, he observed that the vegetation offered perfect cover for his transition down to the tracks. Angling himself so that his vision would not be hindered by the sun, he backed his way to the opening in the wall and looked across the tracks. He leaned out and froze.

It was there, bathed in the tropical colors of the setting sun, and framed for Josie's eyes to see. Everything ceased to move, frozen in time as if the sun itself would never set, and as if all of the years that he had been searching had passed in only a blink of an eye. The Ambassador was on the platform.

The train was there, across a set of tracks next to the platform which the Ambassador was standing on. The armored locomotive was smooth and sleek, not bulky or square like trains commonly seen in Poland left over from the Great War. Four wagons were hitched behind the engine; each of them was clean and polished, riveted and streamlined. The train looked out of place against the backdrop of ruined factories and warehouses; it looked like it was something from the future.

Josie had seen two men flanking the Ambassador. He had also seen one man pacing restlessly at the front of the locomotive, and one more standing at the far end of the platform. Leaning forward again, he scanned the rooftops and the banded smokestack and then checked the museum behind him. There was no sniper in sight.

Two sets of rails were all that separated him from the Ambassador. They were the last obstacle that nearly a decade of training, hate and guilt had given him the power to overcome. The locomotive stirred to life, releasing a thick black breath of smoke as its batteries sparked and its engine fired. There was no time left for Josie: he released his forty-five from his waistband, held it firmly, and prepared to charge.

All hell broke loose. The sharp crack of a rifle sounded from above, sending a screaming piece of lead past him and he tumbled over the wall and down to the gravel next to the tracks that offered no cushion to his fall. He heard another shot whistle high overhead and snap off into the distance. The platform transformed into a warzone as automatic gunfire echoed in his ears.

On the third shot from the rifle, Josie realized that the bullet was not aimed at him but further down the tracks. Crawling forward, he looked down the rails and into the setting sun, and saw the silhouette of a man at the end of the platform where the shots were directed. Josie was certain that it was Harkem.

The sniper had missed his first three shots as the sun had burned into his sights and obscured his vision. On the fourth shot, Josie traced the sniper's perch to an open window on the second story of what appeared to be an abandoned school. On the fifth shot, above all the shouting, the shooting and swearing, was the unmistakable sound of the long stroke recoil from the charging handle of an M-14. It sounded like a cash register being opened. Josie listened again at the next shot, counting quickly he knew the sniper had only one more round before he would have to switch his magazine. The rifle snapped again, Harkem reached the platform and Josie charged the train.

The loose gravel scattered in all directions as Josie struggled to find his footing. Like sand beneath his feet, the ground churned and slowed his sprint. As he cleared the first track, he stumbled and nearly fell before regaining his stride and moving towards the train. A series of three round bursts sounded from an automatic rifle on the platform before a single shotgun blast roared above them all. Josie heard someone scream.

In the one instant of silence after the scream stopped, Josie clearly heard a voice.

"Shitbird!" The Marine from the train shouted from high above and Josie felt the sights of the M-14 now upon him. With the platform in reach, the first round zipped by inches from his head and exploded into the concrete wall in front of him.

Clearing the platform with superhuman effort, he pulled himself up beside the train as a security contractor ran past him, heading down the stairs leading into the tunnel. Josie heard the sound of the contractor's rifle and then the single concussion from a shotgun: this time there was no scream.

Two more shots were loosed from the rifle in the school, but neither found their target as Josie turned from the tunnel and charged up the stairs leading into the train.

Just as he cleared the metal steps, a blurred figure passed in front of him and into the next wagon. With his inertia driving him forward, Josie braced himself as he shouldered into the wall of the train before catching his fall and spinning on his heels. Turning around he focused his eyes, and turning, came face to face with the Ambassador.

"I heard you were a dead man, Bircher," the Ambassador said. He stood casually, as if greeting an old friend. "First, at the prison in Poland. Second, in the airstrike in Yemen, and thirdly, the rumor is that the Russians tried to poison you!"

Josie said nothing. He leveled the forty-five at the Ambassador's head.

Standing in the hallway of the wagon, the Ambassador took little notice of the pistol. "Jesus Christ, Josie, you made it. You were a free man. Why couldn't you just let it go?"

"I was never free, you know that." The front sights hovered between the eyes of the Ambassador.

"I got a call from that babbling fool, Gibbs. He told me that you said you were coming for me, that you had spent the last ten years of your life training for this very moment." The Ambassador leaned against a window and put his hands in his pockets. "Is this it? Is it everything you imagined? Everything you fantasized about, Josie?"

"Daddy!" A voice sounded from behind Josie in the next wagon. It was the Ambassador's daughter; she had been the figure that had rushed by Josie as he had charged into the train. She was crying.

"Do you think it will change anything? Do you think it will change what happened?" The Ambassador extended a hand to signal the girl to stay where she was. "Don't tell me it's about making things right. There isn't such a thing as closure, Josie, trust me. It's all a bunch of bullshit."

"Please, Daddy!" The girl sobbed as she reached her hands out.

"Christ, Bircher, you were a Ranger! You were the best of the best. Don't let a little blood on your hands get the better of you!" The Ambassador's face contorted with disgust. "Have some dignity. We don't pin that yellow tab on your shoulder for nothing!"

Josie tightened his finger around the trigger.

The Ambassador cautioned. "You know, it won't change what you've done. You do realize that? It won't change who you are inside. Deep down, Josie, you know you're no better than me! I chose to move on, but you chose to live with a bunch of goat herders just because a few innocent people got killed."

The girl stepped forward as if she was going to run, but Josie stood between her and the Ambassador. She pulled her foot back and held her hands up to her eyes, wiping the tears away as quickly as they arrived.

"Putting a bullet in me won't change a damn thing! It won't bring them back, not a single one of them. No, Josie. You're no hero, you're just a fool. Don't forget that you were there too, Josie. You killed as many people as I did. You killed for the mission, for your country. You did what you had to do. Now let it go!"

Josie clenched his teeth. It was the truth.

"So what? We killed all of them, every single last one of those villagers."

"Not everyone," Josie shook his head sharply, motioning to the girl. "Not her."

The Ambassador looked past Josie to the girl. "Not even you were a cold enough bastard to kill a baby girl, Josie, so don't expect me to have done it, either. I've given her a better life. If not for me, she would have ended up as a whore in Germany, or even worse, some old maid in that shithole of a village in Bosnia. Besides, Josie, you're the one who killed her parents, not me!"

The girl stopped crying. Her eyes were glazed over, and her bottom lip began to tremble.

The Ambassador stepped forward, an inch away from the barrel of the pistol. "Damn you, coward, pull the trigger! Go ahead, Josie, see if you still have it! Do you know who I am? Do it! See if you have what it takes to kill an Ambassador!"

"It isn't about killing," Josie said. "I didn't spend the last ten years of my life training to kill you, but to come and save a life, the life of the last survivor of the village. I'm here to save the girl."

"From me?" The Ambassador laughed.

"From Harkem," Josie said, fighting with himself as he tightened his finger on the trigger as the pistol began to shake. "The list, you know about it. You know he won't stop - he won't stop until everyone is dead, until she is dead. She is not your blood. She doesn't have to die!"

"Well then, Josie, looks like you've got a choice. Are you going to take a life or save one?"

"I made that choice a long time ago." Josie dropped the magazine of his pistol, racked the slide back and released the forty-five from his fingers, letting it fall to the floor of the train.

He was no longer looking at the Ambassador but into the cabin behind him. The Ambassador noticed. It was too late.

"You're a son of a bitch, Bircher." Fear hardened the eyes of the Ambassador and his voice cracked.

Harkem was standing directly behind the Ambassador, the ten bore in his hands. Both barrels rested a few inches from the Ambassador. Josie swooped for the girl, holding her tight with both arms and tucking her head into his shoulder as he dove for the other wagon. He bolted the door shut. He scrambled to his feet as the Ambassador screamed and the report from both barrels of the shotgun fired.

Josie sprinted through the hallway of the wagon with the girl. It was well armored: the windows were thick, the walls were bulletproof, and the door that Josie had locked was heavy and secure. He spoke clearly and without emotion to the girl in his arms. "You need to listen to me. It's very important."

He reached the other end of the wagon as the door in front of him opened with such force that it seemed as if the entire train shook. Instead of Harkem with his double bore, Josie was confronted with Swan and his M-14. He was trapped. In that moment, the girl understood that Josie was there to protect her, and while she didn't know who he was, she knew today was a matter of life and death. She wrapped her arms around his neck and pulled herself in tighter to his body.

"Coward!" Swan screamed. He hesitated to fire off a shot with his rifle for fear that he would hit the girl.

With a sweeping movement, Josie lowered the girl to the floor with one arm as he charged forward and knocked the weapon out of Swan's hands with the other. The M-14 discharged, jumping off the ground and landing between the two men. Throwing an uppercut, Josie missed, but followed with an elbow that found its target. Swan took the hit, then charged forward and brought Josie to the ground.

Pulling guard, Josie wrapped Swan in close, limiting the power of the Marine's attack. From his back, he unleashed a rising elbow, catching Swan low in the jaw, and with one swift push of his legs, rolled Swan up and over top of him, landing hard against the floor. In trading strikes both bloodied men had regained their footing, but suddenly both stopped the battle and looked to the door.

Harkem.

They could hear him kick the door, take two steps back, and then the sound of the shotgun being closed. A faint click of the safety being switched off. Suddenly, a blistering shot ripped into the wagon where the two men and the girl stood.

The hinges to the armored door screamed in all directions, while the bolt itself simply dropped to the floor. As Harkem kicked the door open, a powerful force of air rushed past Josie and Swan. Looking down to his rifle laying in the middle of the wagon where it had landed when Josie disarmed him, Swan froze. He looked at Josie. Josie looked at him. Time stood still, the two men no longer enemies, each man knowing what had to be done. Swan nodded once then charged for the rifle.

The ejectors of the double shotgun in Harkem's hand slapped the empty shells free. A ring of smoke trailed from their hulls as they bounced off of the carpeted floor at his feet. Swan was halfway to his rifle. Harkem now held two fresh rounds between his massive fingers and dropped both of them into the chamber. Swan reached his rifle. It was in his hands and he was about to fire. Harkem snapped the barrels forward and pulled both triggers.

While Warsaw was quite a distance away from Mosul, and while Swan was not with his beloved company of Marines, as he fell to the floor, the final electrical pulses from his brain sent a smile across his face. After all of those years and thoughts that had haunted him and all of those problems that he couldn't drink away, he was finally free. He had died for something. He had his glory.

Josie held the girl at the end of the wagon. His hands were over her eyes and his lips to her ears as he spoke the words of truth that would save her life. "Remember, please, only you can save yourself. Please remember what to say!"

The girl tried to be brave. She looked up to Josie and nodded.

"Please." Josie held her hand. He kissed her cheek.

Harkem released the top snap, the barrels dropped, and the ejectors kicked out the two spent shells.

Josie stood up from his position by the girl, straightened his shoulders and turned to face Harkem.

The smell of gunpowder burned in the air as smoke poured freely from the open barrels of the shotgun. Two polished brass hulls appeared in Harkem's hand and made a hollow sound as they dropped into the chambers. With the slightest flick of his wrist, the barrels snapped forward again and locked into the receiver. The hammers were cocked and Harkem's fingers were on the triggers. Josie took a step forward.

The warm barrels rested up against Josie's chest, burning circular rings into his shirt. Harkem's eyes tore into Josie's and while they were certainly black, they were not empty, as so many before had described them. They were distant and weary, almost as if they wished to escape the chains that their master bound them to and all of the destruction that they had witnessed. Silence filled the wagon.

Josie closed his eyes and inhaled. It was a very long and peaceful breath, the kind that one does before sleep. The bite of the gunpowder no longer was sour in his nose; instead, the air he breathed was clean and pure. It held the smell of flowers, honey, mountains, and streams. It was the smell of Bosnia, the one place where Josie felt he truly belonged. Home.

He opened his eyes. Harkem was there, his emotionless eyes waiting as if almost wanting Josie to step aside. They were telling him it didn't have to end this way. Josie smiled as if to answer their question, shook his head from side to side, then shrugged. With his smile widening, Josie lifted his arms slightly, gave one final nod and stared right back into those black eyes. He had given his answer.

Harkem pulled the trigger.

XXIV

The rain arrived after midnight. Lights from the Palace of Culture were obscured in the downpour, but had enough voltage to illuminate the base of the storm clouds overhead. Just past a bus stop, next to a row of newspaper racks, there was a phone booth. Cass was standing inside of it.

She could feel the dampness from the rain wash up from the concrete and find its way into the booth, penetrating her to the core. Her whole body was shaking, but not from the cold. Her fingers tapped on the top of the black receiver mounted to the booth's wall. She lifted the receiver, and then returned it to where it rested, burrowing her hands deep into her coat pockets.

Gibbs was dead. Guilt filled the phone booth as she waited for the taxi she had called to bring her to the airport to catch her flight back to Washington. She remembered how she had always judged him; she had laughed behind his back and never stood up for him when she should have. He was a good man and she wanted to tell him this. Even though he was dead, calling his phone was the only resolution that she could think of. Maybe some Albanian had already stolen the phone from his body or maybe a bullet had ripped through it as he had held it up to his ear. Cass couldn't be certain, but she had to try.

She picked up the receiver and dialed. The phone rang.

Ten long tones sounded out before the final one was cut short and a recorded message began to play. It was Gibbs's voice, sounding so alive that surely it seemed he would receive the voicemail. She listened and thought how lonely the world had become with technology, and how strange that long after a person had died, there were so many electronic traces of their life in existence. A tear came to her eye. She hung up.

After she had left Josie in the hospital, she was dropped off at her apartment by Bombay. She had walked inside, slid the latch closed, dropped to her knees and wept. Josie was on his way to death, Gibbs was dead, Harkem was on the loose and she felt responsible for it all. Hours passed as a train of tears washed into the carpet at her knees. When she finally found the power to rise again, she called for a taxi and went to the National Railroad Museum. She arrived long after the shooting had ended and the blood had dried, but it was plain to see what had unfolded: a massacre.

Bombay was there. He told her that he knew she had been turned by Rodham, that she had told Josie where to find the Ambassador, and that Agent White would be coming for her. He called her a bitch and an idiot, and then he called her worthless. Cass shrugged, maybe he was right.

Leaning her head up against the receiver in the phone booth, she thought about everything that had happened. Beads of water formed together and raced along the glass in front of her face, she didn't care about anything anymore - not her position, her career, the Ambassador or even about killing Harkem. She just wanted to tell Gibbs he was a good man.

Cass picked up the receiver and hit redial.

As the phone rang, she readied herself for the message she would leave this time. What would she say? How do you leave a message for a dead man?

The final tones sounded and she inhaled, ready to speak, but the voicemail didn't pick up.

"Hello?"

"Gibbs?" Cass asked, gripping the phone tightly. She felt foolish. Of course it wasn't Gibbs.

"Hello," Cass tried again as tears ran down across her cheek. "This...this number, it belonged to a man named Gibbs. He was my friend."

"Cass?" the voice on the other end asked, distant with the poor connection.

Cass felt her legs melt. Her head began to spin; the booth closed in and she pulled the phone as close to her head as possible.

"Gibbs!"

"Cass?" the voice repeated. The quality was much better and she could hear clearly that it was indeed Gibbs.

"No, it can't be," Cass said. "You're dead, they said you're dead...Bombay..."

"Bombay is a son of a bitch," Gibbs said, interrupting her.

Cass opened her eyes and blinked, dropping the last of her tears free from her lashes. She released a long breath of tension. "I can't believe it!"

"It's true. He is a son of a bitch."

Cass laughed and shook her head. "I know, I know."

The line crackled as if it had been disconnected. She bit her lip and leaned forward as if her position would somehow reconnect the call.

"Where are you?" Gibbs inquired, the sound quality poor again.

"Warsaw."

"Cass, are you okay?"

"No," Cass said, still shocked to be talking with a dead man. "No. Yes. Yes, I'm okay."

"Do you know that Bombay and White sent me into Monte Negro to die?"

Cass nodded as if he could see her. Gibbs continued.

"Cass, listen to me. I'm in Bosnia...I..."

The line cracked with static.

"Gibbs!" She gripped the phone with both hands.

"The Ambassador? What happened?"

Cass shook her head in the booth. "Dead."

"Harkem?"

"Yes," Cass said. "Harkem killed him."

The connection had momentarily stabilized but silence returned on the other end of the line. Gibbs was there, and she believed he was holding back from asking the next question.

"Josie," Gibbs forced. "What about Bircher?"

Cass didn't reply.

"Shit." Gibbs understood her silence. "He was right all along, Cass. Jesus, I tried to..."

Cass stopped the confessional. The time for her to say what she needed was now. "Gibbs, you're a good man. Do you hear me? You're a good man!"

Gibbs heard her.

"Harkem killed everyone, didn't he?"

"Everyone." Cass felt the weight of guilt release from her shoulders. "He killed them all - the Ambassador, his security detail, and he killed Josie too. Everyone, everyone except for a girl."

"A girl?"

"She was the Ambassador's daughter."

"The Ambassador's daughter?"

"She was the only one left alive. I found her on the train next to Josie. She told me that he saved her."

Street lamps behind the phone booth began to burn out. Lights flickered on a passing tram and half of the windows in the Palace of Culture blacked out, a man's silhouette visible against the clock's illuminated face.

"It's all over, it's done."

Gibbs continued to speak. Once again, the connection waned and his voice trailed off, undercut by interference. She heard him speak in broken phrases. She could hear the words *mountain*, *found*, and *truth*. Finally the static vanished and Gibbs's voice was clear and direct.

"I've found it," he said. "Cass, I've found The Site."

A siren howled nearby. A cold chill bit its way up Cass's spine as she suddenly realized that she was being watched.

"Can I trust you, Cass?" Gibbs asked directly. "Can I trust you?"

Cass shook her head up and down, but didn't reply.

"Cass?"

"Yes," she answered. "Gibbs, yes! You can trust me!"

Cass felt the oppressive weight of those peering eyes bearing down as she clung to the black receiver. Instinctively, she looked up and saw the backlit figure atop the Palace tower. The siren rounded a corner and closed in on the plaza as a spotlight blasted up from the police car identifying the man above.

It was Harkem.

He moved to the edge, his toes overhanging the streets far below and his hands at his sides. From the proximity of the phone booth, she could actually see his face. He locked his gaze with her for just a moment, and then he took a final step into the night's abyss.

Cass's eyes were fixed on the clock and the Siren just above the six, her shield back and her sword raised. She was ready for war.